ROLLING *with the* TIDE

ROLLING *with the* TIDE

BY JEFF CALL

BONNEVILLE BOOKS™

Springville, Utah

ISBN: 1-55517-719-0
e.1

Published by Bonneville Books
Imprint of Cedar Fort Inc.
www.cedarfort.com

Distributed by:

Cover design by Nicole Cunningham
Cover design © 2003 by Lyle Mortimer

Printed in the United States of America
10 9 8 7 6 5 4 3 2 1

Printed on acid-free paper

Library of Congress Cataloging-in-Publication Data

Call, Jeff, 1968-
  Rolling with the tide / by Jeff Call.
      p. cm.
   ISBN 1-55517-719-0 (pbk. : alk. paper)
1. Alabama Crimson Tide (Football team)--Fiction. 2.   Quarterbacks
(Football)--Fiction. 3.   Football players--Fiction. 4.
Alabama--Fiction. 5.   Mormons--Fiction. I. Title.

  PS3603.A44R65 2003
  813'.6--dc22

                      2003016769

DEDICATION

**To my wife CherRon,
and my sons Ryan, Brayden, Landon,
Austin and Carson.**

CHAPTER ONE

Chances are you already know about Gunnar Hanshaw, also known as "The Mormon Gunslinger." At one time, there were a million stories, most of them true, floating around about him in the great state of Alabama. Not just in Tuscaloosa, but in places like Bayou LaBatre and Wetumpka, too.

Folks in Alabama love their football, so when a captivating gridiron tale comes along, especially when it involves one of its Crimson Tide boys, folks lap it up like a bowl of Dreamland barbecue sauce. Gunnar Hanshaw became a bonafide star in those parts. You would have thought he was the second coming of Joe Willie Namath or Kenny "The Snake" Stabler. Even Bear Bryant from his seat somewhere in the Spirit World must have been proud.

After a while, the rest of the country also began talking about Gunnar Hanshaw. He became a national phenomenon. You probably saw his amazing string of miraculous come-from-behind victories. Then there was the Alabama sports information department's massive, not to mention exorbitant, Heisman Trophy campaign on his behalf. Some called Gunnar Hanshaw an enigma. He rose to greatness at Alabama, although his career didn't last long. At the height of his popularity and fame, he quietly disappeared into the sunset.

That only added to his legendary status.

Some people made him bigger than life. I think that's because he made just about everyone he met feel like *they* were an All-America player. Everyone who knew him felt like Gunnar was his best friend or a part of his family.

Gunnar didn't exactly enjoy the attention heaped upon him, but he took it in stride. He understood that surrendering his anonymity was the price he had to pay for success on the field. And since he had already experienced the wrong side of success, he wasn't going to complain too much. Besides, he realized it was all great publicity for his Church. How many guys can say they've been on the cover of

The Church News and *Sports Illustrated*—in the same week?

It was ironic, really. The guy who played the highest-profile position at one of the nation's highest-profile football programs—a place where college football ranks just below God in terms of importance and a place populated predominantly by Baptists (bless their hearts)—was a member of The Church of Jesus Christ of Latter-day Saints.

When he was on campus, he was like a rock star, only he was well-mannered, clean-cut, sober, and tattoo-free. Okay, so he wasn't like a rock star, but, boy, could he attract crowds of adoring fans. He never wore his letterman's jacket, but that didn't stop people from bothering him in public. He couldn't walk more than ten feet without a guy asking him for a minute to talk football or a girl asking him on a date. Then they'd detain him for a half-hour, congratulating him on beating Notre Dame one minute, then grilling him on how he planned on beating Auburn the next. He was always gracious, too nice to disappoint them by explaining that his European history class had started fifteen minutes ago.

A couple of times he was mobbed while eating at a restaurant. Someone asked for an autograph, and before he knew it, a long line had wrapped all the way back to the restrooms. He had to start signing left-handed because his right hand got so sore. I know of at least a couple of coeds who stalked him. They found out his class schedule from the Registrar's Office and they would follow him as he strolled from class to class. To me, it was pretty funny how he attained this celebrity status thousands of miles from his home. Just a few years earlier, he was as anonymous as they came. Not a soul knew who he was. He was preaching the gospel of Jesus Christ in South America, and the only thing he was trying to beat was dysentery.

For the most part, the press got the story right. I compiled newspaper clippings about him and the majority of the articles I've read have truth in them, mingled with some half-truths because they never fully understood him. Gunnar was popular with the media because he was a pretty good quote and, from what I observed, he charmed just about all the reporters he met. Still, he held back a lot of information.

Not that he had anything to hide; he was just too modest to go on and on about himself. Every chance he could, he gave credit to his teammates and coaches and equipment managers and trainers.

Reporters from the *Los Angeles Times*, the *Dallas Morning News*, and the *Atlanta Journal-Constitution*—to name a few—scurried around trying to find out the scoop on him. The media and the fans turned him into a folk hero of sorts. I guess people like an underdog, and he certainly was that. After all, he wasn't even really recruited after he finished high school. Heck, he didn't even play football his senior year. He emerged on the scene in Tuscaloosa after spending a couple of years at an obscure junior college in Utah. Some called him an "overnight sensation."

But I knew better.

In fact, I know the whole story because long before he became The Mormon Gunslinger, he was Elder Hanshaw, my missionary companion. After only a few days together on our missions, he and I almost instantly became best friends—as inseparable as Siamese twins.

The first misconception I want to dispel is that Gunnar was an overnight sensation. Far from it. Most overnight sensations, I've found, take years to develop. But I do believe Gunnar was destined to play football for the Crimson Tide. There was a time when kids all over Alabama wanted to be like Gunnar. Because of him, they thought *leche con platano* and avocado sandwiches were the *real* breakfast of champions.

When I first met Gunnar, while we were serving missions in Chile, I figured out right away that he was a humble, down-to-earth guy (it was almost hard to believe he was from southern California). At that time I never would have guessed he would one day become a star quarterback. He was, though, a natural leader, a trait that served him well in the mission field and on the football field. Aside from the fact he possesses a howitzer for a right arm, uncanny quickness, and a brilliant football mind, he's pretty normal.

While he was the unassuming type, he was supremely confident in his abilities and in the Source of those abilities. Emotionally, he was stronger than month-old laundry. He had to be, with all the adversity that was thrown at him. Maybe throwing a football was one of his ways of dealing with it.

So, I'd like to set the record straight. Despite what some naysayers think, Gunnar didn't spend two years in South America perfecting his passes and working on his abs. People who believe that missions are an unfair advantage need a reality check and a no-expenses-paid, month-long tour of the mission field. Football was the furthest thing from his mind.

Funny, when Gunnar finally attained his goal of playing college football on the Division I level, much of the attention wasn't just on what he accomplished on the field. It was fixed on his age (he was 25 during his senior year at Alabama) and his religious affiliation.

Personally, I don't know how he did it. He had to juggle being a football player, a husband, a role model, a solid student and a symbol of the Mormon Church in the Deep South. That's quite a burden to carry, but he did it in wondrous fashion. In sports, the knock on many returned missionaries —especially quarterbacks—is they never fulfill their potential after serving a mission. In his own way, Gunnar debunked that theory. Some said that Gunnar succeeded in spite of his two-year missionary experience. In my humble opinion, he succeeded *because* of his two-year missionary experience. Some would agree, but for the wrong reasons. They said it was because he was a couple of years older and wiser than the rest of the players, like a man among boys. They said it was an unfair advantage. Hogwash. If it were such an unfair advantage, don't you think every college coach in America would ship their players to the nethermost reaches of the globe for two years to learn a foreign language? To spend countless hours on their knees in prayer? To be chased by rabid dogs? To be yelled at by rabid ministers from other faiths? I don't think so.

Gunnar Hanshaw. Isn't that a great name for a quarterback? It was a publicist's dream, which explains the Mormon Gunslinger label. By the way, Gunnar wasn't crazy about that nickname at first. He was a little embarrassed by it. He used to joke that it made him sound like a serial killer. I thought it sounded like the title of a Clint Eastwood movie.

Gunnar's mom, who is of Scandinavian descent, explained to me once that his given name is Scandinavian. Roughly translated, Gunnar means "the King's most trusted soldier" or "guard at the castle gate." That, to me, describes Gunnar perfectly.

There are plenty of things that people should know about him but don't. I, on the other hand, could have told people plenty of interesting stuff, but nobody ever bothered to ask me. Maybe that's why I felt compelled to write all this stuff down (I'm glad I wrote faithfully in my journal all those years). Some of the best anecdotes about him have nothing to do with football.

You know the Old Testament story about Joseph, the boy who was cast into a pit and sold into slavery by his brothers; then he worked his way up to become Potiphar's top servant until Potiphar's wife accused him of wrongdoing. Later, he eventually interpreted some dreams and ended up running Egypt. Well, Gunnar was kind of like that. He was Mr. Buoyancy. You could put him in the most abysmal situation and you could always count on him rising to the top.

Sure, everyone knows Gunnar Hanshaw as a football hero, but to me he was a hero, period. Alabama fans consider him a legend. I do, too, but not because of his ability to hurl a pigskin 75 yards. Without him, I don't know where I'd be today.

He was always more concerned about scoring points in heaven than scoring points on Earth. So, here's my humble account of how Gunnar Hanshaw, The Mormon Gunslinger, carved out a place for himself in Crimson Tide lore, not to mention a place in modern-day Church history.

As Paul Harvey (he's kind of a non-Mormon version of a General Authority emeritus) would say: Now for the rest of the story.

CHAPTER TWO

This book isn't about me, of course, but it only makes sense that since I'm writing it you should know something about me.

My name is Preston Brady and I grew up in Salt Lake City, Utah. I've always been a huge sports fan—crazy about baseball, basketball and football (not in that particular order—it depended on the season). My parents tell me that when I was four, I would stand in front of the television during the World Series and imitate the hitters' batting stances and swings. By the time I was eight, I could recite from memory the everyday lineup and pitching rotation of every Major League Baseball team, as well as all of the players' numbers, home-towns, and ages. I also knew the nicknames of every professional franchise in alphabetical order and I had memorized the nickname of nearly every college team. I guess you could say I had an elephantine memory when it came to sports. Without even trying I could remember stats and trivial information.

School work was a different matter. I had the attention span of a gnat in the classroom. The closest I ever came to the honor roll was sitting next to Cynthia "Brainiac" Plympton in science class. If grades were given out for daydreaming and sports trivia, I would have been my high school's valedictorian, hands down. My mind always wandered, and I would imagine myself at places like Wrigley Field or Yankee Stadium. I didn't take academics very seriously. I was something of a math whiz, though. When I played little league baseball, I sat in the dugout and told my teammates their updated, season-to-date batting averages that I figured out in my head. I had plenty of time to do it, too, since I spent most of my time on the bench.

My friends and family thought it was morbid, but one of my favorite pastimes growing up was reading teams' injury reports. I enjoyed learning the medical terminology—fractured tibias, sprained abductor muscles, torn anterior cruciate ligaments. It all started at recess one day when I was in grade school. As I threw a pass downfield, I stepped into a large sinkhole and broke my ankle. The pain was excruciating, though it was tempered by the fact we scored a touchdown on the play. That same week, as I walked around in a cast, one of my favorite NFL quarterbacks suffered a similar injury to the same ankle as mine. So I began studying injury reports. For some reason, athletes' injuries fascinated me. In other words, I was not well. Medically speaking, I think that condition is referred to as an advanced stage of psychosis.

My parents wished I had spent as much time reading American literature as I did reading the sports page. When I'd hear the newspaper hit the front porch every afternoon, I'd race out the door, pull out the sports section and spread it out in my living room floor. I'd lie down on my stomach and study that section. I'd pore over every story, every boxscore, every transaction. By the time I'd get up about an hour later, my Mom would tell me to wash up for dinner and my hands were black from the newsprint.

My dad, who was a seminary teacher for thirty-one years, was glad I had discovered sports as a hobby to immerse myself in, but he also warned me that such trivial knowledge wouldn't help me when it came to the Afterlife. "The Lord," he'd say, "probably isn't going to ask you at the Final Judgment which team won the Super Bowl in 1985."

"But if He did ask me," I'd reply in a smart-alecky way, "I could proudly tell Him that it was the San Francisco 49ers."

Dad was not amused.

I think he had a hard time with me. His other three sons—I was the youngest—followed in his footsteps and became seminary teachers. I have nothing against seminary teaching, but it wasn't what I wanted to do. In a way, I suppose I was considered the black sheep of the family.

My dream was to be a college athlete, then go on to the pros. But because I wear my parents' genes—I'm five-foot-eight-inches in gym shoes and I run the 40-yard dash in roughly 4.4 minutes—you know, the Mormon answer to "Rudy"—I figured out at a relatively young age that my dream wasn't going to pan out. When that realization dawned on me, just after I was cut from the eighth-grade basketball team, I was devastated. After that, I had no clue what I would do with my life.

My grandfather always told me that if I wanted to be happy, I should find something I loved to do, then pursue it as a career. "Chase your passion," he'd say, "not your pension." Grandpa was the wisest man I ever knew. He used to take me on drives around his farm and randomly dispense unsolicited advice. "The Lord sent us here to Earth with a bag of talents in one hand and a bag of trials in the other," he'd say, overlooking his vast cornfields. "The key to life is learning to see the trials as blessings and keeping the talents from turning into trials."

Until I met Gunnar Hanshaw, I don't think I really understood what Grandpa meant by that.

In high school I never really fit in. I wasn't cool enough to hang out with the jocks. I wasn't smart enough to hang out with the nerds. Not that I was an outcast. I had friends, but no close friends.

Much to my dismay, sports were no longer an option once I got to high school. Not that I fretted very long about that. I took some comfort in knowing that for me, life ended at age 19. That's when I would leave home to serve a two-year mission to some far-flung part of the world. At the time, two years might as well have been an eternity. I knew if I could survive that, I could survive anything. I would worry about my life's work after my mission.

I remember so vividly that spring day I received my mission call. With trembling fingers I opened the letter signed by a prophet of God and read, "Elder Brady, you have hereby been called to labor in the Chile Viña del Mar Mission." It went on to say that I was to learn Spanish. I admit I was a little disappointed at the time. I didn't know how to react, mainly because I couldn't have located Chile on a map. I always dreamed of being sent to somewhere exotic, like Italy or Japan or Australia or Hawaii. I wasn't counting on being sent to South America, much less a country that sounded like something I ate on Boy Scout camps. The only Spanish phrase I knew was "Taco Bell." Back then, I wondered if the Church's missionary department simply drew names of missions out of a hat and matched them with prospective missionaries by the luck of the draw.

I don't think that way now. Not anymore. I've come to learn that the word "coincidence" is not in the Lord's vocabulary.

They say that the place where you're called to serve a mission is exactly where the Lord needs you, but where nobody wants you. They also say that by the time you leave, it's a place where you're not needed anymore but still wanted. There's a lot of truth to that.

I didn't know it at the tender age of 19, but Chile is the greatest place in the world to serve a mission—no offense to any of you who have served a mission elsewhere. Viña del Mar means "Vineyard by the Sea," and as missionaries, we were working in the Lord's vineyard, gathering his elect. I'll spare you from that syrupy, hackneyed fluff about my mission being "the best two years of my life." It wasn't. My mission was the best two years *for* my life. There were difficult times, but there were glorious times. It was there in Chile that I grew up, strengthened my testimony, and figured out what life was all about. At least, I thought I had figured life out.

Anyway, enough about me.

It was because I served a mission to Chile and met Elder Gunnar Hanshaw that I wound up at one of the cradles of college football— at the University of Alabama. That's where I realized many of my own dreams, most of which had absolutely nothing to do with sports.

Who would have guessed that?

CHAPTER THREE

The amazing thing is, I didn't even become acquainted with Elder Hanshaw until the latter part of my mission. I was vaguely familiar with him before we became companions. We had never served in the same zone before, so to me he was simply a face in the crowd, a name on a list. All I knew was he was from California, and in our mission, the elders from Utah and missionaries from California didn't fraternize very much.

I had about six months remaining on my mission and things were going well. I was even thinking and dreaming in Spanish. Teaching the gospel became second-nature to me. I was especially proud of my flea collection. Most American missionaries when they arrive in Chile are eaten alive by fleas. I was no different. I had never even seen a flea before, then one morning I was covered with bites and my white sheets were covered with splotches of blood. Those fleas (Chileans call them *pulgas*) must enjoy imported blood because they never seemed to bother the Chileans. Early in my mission, I caught fleas with a piece of Scotch tape, then I stuck them in my journal. If you squeezed the fleas just right, blood would ooze out onto the page. I figured that if I ever had kids, maybe they'd think it was cool.

Anyway, before I became Elder Hanshaw's companion, I was serving with Elder Soriano in the town of Quillota in central Chile. One morning, the young boy in the family we lived with burst into our bedroom and shouted, "Elders! The phone's for you!"

We were in Chile, remember, so it wasn't like we could go in the living room and answer it. The phone was actually six doors down the street, sitting on a grocery store counter. Elder Soriano and I were in the middle of companionship study, so we looked at it as a nice break—we almost collided trying to get out the door. One of the zone leaders was on the other line, informing us of the stunning and devastating news—Elder Luis Ledesma had died the night before.

Elder Ledesma and Elder Hanshaw were companions in the city

of Valparaiso. They were returning home from their last discussion of the night when Elder Ledesma suddenly collapsed on a dirt road. Elder Hanshaw immediately attended to his companion, called for help and gave him a priesthood blessing. Within 20 minutes Elder Ledesma was gone. The ambulance didn't show up until it was too late. The autopsy never produced a cause of death. His heart simply stopped beating for reasons nobody but the Lord knows.

Elder Ledesma was the oldest of seven children. Back at his home in northern Chile, his mom had scrimped and saved in order to be able to send him on a mission. Yeah, it was a sacrifice, but she knew that was what the Lord wanted.

My companion and I lugged our scriptures and heavy hearts to the corner and caught the next bus for Viña del Mar. Our mission president, F. Gerald McPherson, had called a special mission conference that afternoon. It was about the longest bus ride I'd ever taken.

When we arrived at the chapel in Viña, the mood was obviously somber. Everyone loved Elder Ledesma and his cheery disposition. When he asked you, *"Como esta, Elder?"* you knew it wasn't just an empty catch phrase for him. He meant it.

I remember seeing Elder Hanshaw there in the chapel, sitting alone on a pew, hunched over, his head down. Nobody dared say anything to him. We could only imagine what he was going through. In the mission field, you're taught never to leave your companion. No one prepares you for when your companion leaves you—and this life—simultaneously.

President McPherson was a tall, imposing man with a surround-sound stereo voice. He took on a more paternal role than ever with us missionaries that day. He shared personal stories about Elder Ledesma, then he read powerful scriptures about missionary service and the reward the Lord promises those who lose their lives in His service. "Elder Ledesma has completed his mission," the president said, his voice cracking, "and I know that the Lord greeted him beyond the veil and said, 'Well done, thou good and faithful servant.'"

I don't know about anybody else, but I couldn't see through my tears. I had goose bumps from head to toe.

After the meeting, we missionaries remained pretty quiet, reading our mail from home and preparing to return to our various areas. Then Elder Tompkins, the assistant to the president, tapped me on the shoulder.

"Elder Brady," he said, "the President wants to see you at his house. *Al tiro.*" *Al tiro*, loosely translated, means *right now, if not sooner.*

I knew there would be some impromptu shuffling in the mission due to Elder Ledesma's death, but I didn't think it would mean a move for me. After all, I had been in Quillota for just a month or so.

A few minutes later, my companion and I were standing on the doorstep of the president's home. Sister McPherson welcomed us in and I couldn't help staring at the carpeted floor. I hadn't seen carpet since the day I arrived in the mission field. After 18 months of seeing mostly dirt floors, the carpet caught my attention. I looked around the home, which was modest by American standards, but I felt as though I was inside Buckingham Palace.

Sister McPherson offered us a drink of root beer. Her daughter-in-law back home sent cases of the stuff to her on a regular basis since they didn't sell root beer in Chile. The Chilean missionaries who tried it said they didn't like it. To them, it tasted like cough medicine. Elder Soriano and I politely declined a drink. Then President McPherson appeared. He smiled, shook my hand, and ushered me into his office.

"Come in, Elder Brady," he said. "Please sit down."

President McPherson wasted little time getting to the point. "Elder, we're re-opening up an area called La Chispa, a couple of hours down south, and I'm assigning you and Elder Hanshaw to serve there together as co-equal companions."

My gut twisted violently. Here I was getting a companion in Elder Hanshaw, whom I figured was probably an emotional basket case after what had happened to Elder Ledesma. Not only that, but I had been on my mission for 18 months and I had never received a leadership position above that of district leader. Heck, I had been a senior companion for only a few months of my mission. I supposed that I just wasn't leadership material. I constantly wondered if something was wrong with me.

The biggest problem, though, was that La Chispa was a baptismal wasteland. According to mission rumors, it was a place where successful missionaries had failed and, I had heard, never recovered. It was the Hotel California of the mission—you could check in, but you could never leave. It had been closed to missionary work for a few years and I thought about asking the president why he wanted to ruin the last part of my mission. The work was going gangbusters in Quillota and suddenly he was telling me I had to leave for La Chispa.

Maybe because of the look on my face, the President felt he owed me an explanation.

"Early this morning I knelt here at my desk and asked Heavenly Father about what I should do with Elder Hanshaw," he said. "Almost immediately, your name came into my mind. I don't know exactly why, except that I know you two are supposed to be together. I have full confidence in both of you and I have no doubt you'll be successful. President Ramos is the branch president and you'll stay with him and his family for the time being. He is a good man and he'll rely heavily on both of you. I feel you and Elder Hanshaw will do an outstanding job there."

"How is Elder Hanshaw doing?" I asked.

"It's been tough for him," the President said. "He's taking this awfully hard. I hope he doesn't blame himself for what happened, as irrational as that sounds. You will help him get through this. He needs a fresh start in a new area. He needs to immerse himself in the Lord's work again. I've been contemplating opening La Chispa again for a while and this is as good a time as any. May the Lord bless both of you."

With that, he left the room and returned shortly thereafter with the Elder Hanshaw.

"Hi, Elder," he said, extending his hand.

"Hi, Elder," I replied, extending my hand.

Elder Hanshaw wasn't a really big guy (he was a few inches taller than me—then again, that's not saying much) but he did have a finger-crippling handshake. We agreed to meet the following day at the mission office in Viña del Mar and make our way to La Chispa together from there.

That night, Elder Soriano and I returned to Quillota, taught some discussions, then I packed up my belongings. We awoke early the next morning and Elder Soriano walked with me to the bus station.

"*Buena suerte*, Elder," he said as I stepped aboard the bus bound for Viña del Mar.

I thanked him, but I knew all the luck in the world wouldn't help Elder Hanshaw and me. Only the Lord could.

CHAPTER FOUR

As planned, Elder Hanshaw and I hooked up in Viña del Mar at a famous clock made of flowers that faces the ocean. We didn't have much to say to each other during the 90-minute bus ride south to La Chispa. Part of it was because the bus was standing-room-only and, being polite missionaries, we gave up our seats to an elderly couple carrying live chickens in a cage (don't ask me why). We were standing up, hanging on to the handrail above us for our dear lives every time the driver took a corner at 50 miles an hour on the narrow two-lane highway. One of those chickens kept pecking my kneecap. We were like a couple of Weebles—we wobbled, but we didn't fall down. The sign at the front of the bus said *"Capacity: 45."* Not that the bus driver paid attention to such minor details. There had to be at least 70 people on board.

I was sure Elder Hanshaw was thinking about Elder Ledesma. I know I was. In fact, I thought a lot about my own mortality during that bus ride. My biggest fear before leaving for my mission was that I would die somewhere in Chile and be shipped home in a pine box. At the very least, I did not want to contract some dreaded disease or have a tapeworm wrap itself inside my intestinal tract, hatch eggs, and live there comfortably the rest of my life. That's why I was very careful not to drink the water. The only time I drank unboiled water was when I partook of the sacrament. I figured that it had been blessed, so it must be safe. Grandpa had warned me not to ever eat dairy products or pastries from the street vendors and I heeded that advice, though a lot of the other missionaries thought I was paranoid. But, other than a couple of head colds and a slight case of walking pneumonia, I never did get sick on my mission. When I did feel a little under the weather, the Chileans suggested I place a round piece of a raw potato on my forehead. So I did, and it worked like a charm! I was up and proselytizing again in no time.

All Elder Hanshaw and I knew about La Chispa was that it was a popular resort town and the joke around the mission was that it was the Chilean equivalent of Rio de Janiero, on a much smaller scale. In the summer it filled up with people vacationing from Santiago and Argentina. In the off-season it was more or less a sleepy village, bordering on a ghost town. It was November when we arrived—south of the equator, the seasons are reversed from the ones in the United States—so we were a few weeks away from the busy summer season. After about March, it really calmed down.

As we entered La Chispa's city limits, Elder Hanshaw and I were struck by the town's picturesque setting. It was nothing like the desert climate where I had come from further north. Waves off the emerald Pacific Ocean lapped onto the golden beaches. Palm trees swayed in the breeze. The scene was straight off a postcard. This didn't look like a place to serve a mission. It looked like a place for Spring Break.

"This probably reminds you of home," I said to Elder Hanshaw as we peered out the bus windows. "Too bad we're missionaries. I wouldn't mind a little beach time."

"I won't tell if you won't," Elder Hanshaw joked.

By the time the bus rolled to a stop, we looked out the window and saw a man standing there, grinning at us. Had to be President Ramos.

"*Bienvenidos, Elderes!*" he shouted at us as we stepped off the bus. Then he buried his head into our chests. It was the most enthusiastic hug I had ever received in my life. President Ramos was stocky and barely five feet tall (for the only time in my life, I often felt like a giant while serving in South America), but I could tell immediately he had a heart the size of the ocean. He had graciously offered a room in his home for us to live with his family. He helped us with our bags and whistled for a taxi, which whisked us away. La Chispa was not a large town during the off-season, population-wise, but it was very spread out.

"Where do you meet for church?" Elder Hanshaw asked.

President Ramos smiled. "The closest church is about 35 minutes away. Before I was called to be the branch president, we used to attend there. A few years ago we were granted permission to hold our meetings here in town. I will show it to you in a few minutes."

Since President Ramos lived off the beaten path and we didn't have any mode of transportation other than our feet, I decided right then I was going to lobby the mission office for bikes.

President Ramos welcomed us to his humble home. Pictures of his family dressed in white and standing outside the Santiago Temple were proudly displayed on the walls. We got the obligatory *"mi casa es su casa"* speech. Then, he added, "My family and I are deeply honored and feel very blessed to have servants of the Lord staying with us."

Then he stretched out his stubby arms. "This is where we hold our sacrament meeting," he said of his living room. "The Relief Society sisters meet in the kitchen afterward and we have Primary out back."

Then we heard the sound of stampeding feet. Suddenly, there appeared three of the cutest kids I'd ever seen. Before introducing themselves, they gave Elder Hanshaw and me hugs. Elder Hanshaw did a couple of tie tricks and told a couple of jokes. After that, they clung to him like he was a long-lost uncle.

Hermana (Sister) Ramos greeted us with a plate of cheese empanadas to eat. "Our angels have come!" she said, brushing tears from her eyes.

Talk about having a lot to live up to.

The Ramos family couldn't have been more kind. Marisol Ramos was ten, Claudio was eight, and little Eddie was five. I thought Eddie was a strange name for a Chilean kid until I learned later that the name of the missionary that had baptized the family was named Elder Edwards.

President Ramos led us to a room where we would be staying. It had a standard, mission-issued bunk bed, which had been sent down from the mission office the day before. Compared to some places I lived on my mission, this was Shangrila.

La Chispa, on the other hand, was no Shangrila. While we ate dinner, President Ramos told us the story behind the Church's struggles in La Chispa. The most powerful religious group in the town wasn't the Catholic Church, like it was in most places in Chile. Rather, it was something called, loosely translated,

"The Light in the Wilderness Church," an offshoot of the Pentecostal Church we were told. Its leader, a man named Cesar Sepulveda, frequently distributed anti-Mormon literature to members of his congregation and often spoke out against the Mormons during his sermons. His protestations against the Mormons were so strong that even those who didn't belong to his congregation had formed preconceived, negative notions about the LDS Church. He warned the people that we missionaries were really CIA operatives and that our goal was to brainwash the men and take young women to the United States, marry them, and force them to live in an oppressive polygamist community.

Cesar obviously had quite an active imagination. Elder Hanshaw and I would later jokingly refer to him under the code name of Korihor.

President Ramos said that a few years earlier, Cesar lured two missionaries into one of his church services. The plan, ostensibly, was for the missionaries to teach a discussion to the assembled group. Cesar acted so sincere, so eager to learn about the Mormons from the missionaries. Little did they know, however, they were walking into Cesar's trap. The missionaries were not very experienced—one of the elders had been in the mission field about five months and he was training a missionary from Chillán, located in the southern part of Chile.

During that meeting, after a "miraculous healing" of a man's broken leg, they had the entire congregation shouting in unison at the missionaries: "*Diablos! Diablos! Diablos!*" (Devils! Devils! Devils!)

It wasn't exactly an ideal way for that new elder fresh from the Missionary Training Center to start his mission.

Both missionaries got out of there and returned to their living quarters. The new missionary was spooked and his trainer was pretty shaken up, too. The senior companion figured they would just go to bed, chalk it up as a learning experience, and start fresh the next day as far away from that church as possible. However, when he awoke the next morning, his companion was gone. Lying on the new missionary's unmade bed was a handwritten note: "Elder, I'm very sorry, but I cannot continue with my mission. I am going home."

Sure enough, he had packed up, sneaked out by dawn's early light and taken the first bus out of town.

The mission president at the time asked the other missionary to return to Viña del Mar with all of his belongings. Then he shut the area down indefinitely. When word about the missionary's departure spread in La Chispa, it generated all sorts of rumors. As far as Cesar and his congregation were concerned, they had exorcised the "demons" from their midst. "Cesar thought it was a sign from God," President Ramos said.

Little did Cesar know that because he had driven the Mormons out of La Chispa, he clinched himself a spot in the Lilburn W. Boggs Hall of Shame.

During the three years after that banishment of the missionaries, the La Chispa Branch survived, barely. President Ramos kept his tiny congregation together somehow.

After hearing that little pep talk, Elder Hanshaw and I turned in for the night, ready to re-open La Chispa for missionary work early the next morning.

Unfortunately, Sister Ramos forgot to put mints on our pillows.

CHAPTER FIVE

In Spanish, the word "chispa" has several meanings—spark, wit, and drunkenness among them. Elder Hanshaw and I chose the definition of "La Chispa" as "The Spark," a place where the Church would eventually turn into a raging fire of spiritual strength. But first, we'd have to get a spark. At first, that task was about as frustrating as rubbing two sticks together.

On our first full day in La Chispa, we awoke, took cold showers, read our scriptures, had companionship study, prayed, ate breakfast (bread and hot chocolate), loaded our backpacks with copies of the Book of Mormon, and headed out the door. Since we were located quite a ways from the more heavily populated residential areas, we knew we were going to have to walk a lot. That reminded me to write to the mission office about getting a hold of some bikes.

We decided to get our bearings of the town. We weren't more than five minutes into our journey down the dirt road when we heard a familiar catcall in broken English.

"Yankees, go home!"

"I've never been so offended in all of my life," Elder Hanshaw said to me in mock disgust. "*Yankees? Yankees?* How dare they say that to a *Dodger* fan."

I stopped in my tracks. "I'm a Dodger fan, too."

So we spent the next 20 minutes talking about our favorite Dodger players such as Ron Cey, Davey Lopes, Dusty Baker, Don Sutton, Burt Hooton, Mickey Hatcher, Steve Yeager, Fernando Valenzuela, and Mike Scioscia. We quoted statistics and recalled memorable plays. I imitated Vin Scully's description of an Orel Hershiser curveball. Elder Hanshaw mimicked Kirk Gibson's famous home run at the end of Game One of the 1988 World Series. We really got some strange looks when he started limping around in a circle and pumping his fist. I quoted Jack Buck's call of that famous at-bat: "I don't believe . . . what I just saw!"

Elder Hanshaw was laughing, probably for the first time in a while.

A couple of kids kicking a soccer ball in the street stared at us. We said hello to them and they scattered like roaches. Meanwhile, Elder Hanshaw and I became blood brothers: two strangers in a foreign country. We were both servants of the Lord who bled Dodger Blue.

"What's your favorite college football team?" I asked.

"UCLA," he said. "I used to go to their games all the time."

"How can you cheer for a school that wears powder blue?" I asked.

"It's just a lighter shade of Dodger Blue," he answered.

I was never one to carry a tune, but out of the blue I started humming the UCLA fight song. Elder Hanshaw started humming, too. We got some strange looks. Not only because we probably sounded like a couple of cows in labor, but because I think people were stunned to see the Americans—the Mormons—back in town. I noticed mothers hurriedly ushering their children in their houses and shutting the doors behind them, as if we were small pox incarnate.

President Ramos had given us a list of all the active members in the branch (there were eight, and four of them were in his family) and a list of all the baptized members in the town (there were 250). The branch's hometeaching program needed some serious help.

As we walked around La Chispa that day, between being rejected, we'd play little games to pass the time. It was as if we had been separated at birth. He loved sports as much as I did, so we'd test each other. He'd start by naming a school and I would have to supply the team's nickname.

"Central Michigan," he'd say.

"Chippewas," I'd reply.

"Akron."

"Zips."

"Arkansas."

"Razorbacks."

"Cal-State Santa Cruz."

"Banana Slugs."

"Georgia Tech."

"Yellow Jackets. Or Ramblin' Wreck."

"Saint Louis University."

"Billikens."

"Alabama."

"Crimson Tide."

Then he'd name a year, a player and a team and I'd have to supply the player's number. Or he'd name a player's number and a team and I'd have to supply the name of the player. Not once did he stump me. "Elder Brady," Elder Hanshaw said, shaking his head, "that's quite a gift you have."

It was the first time someone referred to that as a gift. My parents thought it was an abnormality.

Come to think of it, I will always be grateful to be sent to South America on my mission. Had I been sent stateside, I would have been way too distracted by sports. I would have known when there were games going on, I would have been tempted to read the newspapers and set up dinner appointments with members of the Church during those games so I could watch them on TV. There were no such temptations in Chile. The Chileans seemed to declare national holidays about three times a month for real important soccer games. It was amusing, but never distracting for me.

For some reason, La Chispa was drastically different from every other place I had served in Chile. When we tracted door-to-door, I had never had so little success in my previous 18 months in Chile. It was as if an unseen, evil power had a grip on the town. Most Chileans I found to be gracious toward missionaries, even if they had no desire of listening to our message. They were interested in meeting an American, so they'd talk to us for a while about movie stars and politicians and athletes from the U.S. But these people wouldn't even invite us inside the gates around their homes. They wanted nothing to do with us.

In fact, the only ones who were nice to us were the *caballeros*, the elderly gentlemen dressed in suit jackets who would wander the streets in 90-degree weather. They greeted us by bowing low to the ground to the point where I thought they were going to break their backs. When we tried to invite them to listen to our message they simply said, "No tengo tiempo" ("We don't have time") and would continue wandering.

The fact nobody wanted to talk to us gave Elder Hanshaw and me plenty of time to talk to each other. When we weren't talking about the gospel or sports, we often discussed other serious topics. Since we were alone together a lot, praying with each other, and working together and feeling the entire world had conspired against us, our friendship grew quickly. After a week it seemed like a month, but in a good way. Soon, he really opened up to me.

Only a few weeks before Elder Ledesma died, Elder Hanshaw had received a "Dear John" letter from his longtime girlfriend. She was supposedly waiting for him and had written every day for the first three months, then it started tapering off gradually. Soon, she had stopped writing altogether with no explanation. That is, until he received the bad news—or good news, depending on your perspective—along with a wedding invitation and the engagement ring he had bought for her before his mission. The guy in the picture with her happened to be a returned missionary from his stake.

Hearing Elder Hanshaw talk about it made me grateful I didn't have a girlfriend before I left on my mission. At the MTC I was a little jealous of those missionaries who would receive daily packages from their girlfriends. But when I saw what it was like to have your heart broken into a million pieces when that girlfriend moved on with her life, I realized it wasn't worth it. Besides, before my mission, I thought girls were the primary carrier of cooties.

When I asked Elder Hanshaw about his family, he told me he was the middle child, with an older sister and a younger sister. I asked about his parents and he said, in a matter-of-fact way, that a couple of weeks into his two-month stay at the MTC, the MTC president approached him one morning in the cafeteria and asked to meet with him privately. Then Elder Hanshaw received the devastating news: his dad had died in an automobile accident. The president gave him a few hours in his office to talk, to cry, to be alone, to pray. Then it was time to move on. By that afternoon he was back in class, conjugating

Spanish verbs. When you're on the Lord's errand, nothing can stand in your way. Not even your father's funeral.

That explained the 12-page letters he wrote faithfully every week to his mom. Before he told me, I had no idea his dad had died and, in fact, very few of those in the mission knew. If that wasn't enough, Elder Hanshaw told me that a couple of weeks after his father's death, he broke a bone in his left foot while playing basketball in the MTC. That almost kept him from being able to go to Chile. Doctors placed the foot in a cast and recommended that he be sent instead to the Spanish-speaking mission in Houston, Texas. When he heard that, he prayed to Heavenly Father and begged the MTC president to allow him to serve where he was originally called. He said he knew he was supposed to go to Chile. He had to spend a couple of extra weeks in the MTC, but he eventually arrived in Chile. Then he had a companion die on him.

Compared to all that, I had nothing to complain about. Compared to all that, the constant rejection in La Chispa was no big deal for Elder Hanshaw.

After he told me that personal stuff, I didn't know what to say. The death of a father and a missionary companion; a serious basketball injury in the MTC; and a girlfriend's wedding back home. It sounded like the plot of one of those melodramatic Chilean soap operas. That was a lot to take for one mission.

CHAPTER SIX

During those first days in La Chispa, we must have walked every square inch of that town. We found a lot of boarded-up houses and empty streets. One afternoon we had to cross a swift-moving river, so we found a relatively shallow part with large rocks we could use as stepping stones. We removed our shoes and socks, rolled up our pants and began fording across.

Well, Elder Hanshaw made it to the other side with ease. He looked over at me and I had gone only one-third of the way. While trying to leap to another rock, I slipped and fell into the frigid water. I never did have a very good balance. My clothes, including the shoes and socks I was carrying, were soaked. Elder Hanshaw couldn't help but laugh. Then I noticed my black scripture case, which held my Spanish triple combination and the Spanish Bible, being carried down the river, bobbing up and down.

To me, those scriptures were my most valuable possession. They were a part of me. I had spent countless hours underlining passages and writing important notes in the margins. I thought they were gone with the water. I looked over to Gunnar and he placed his own scriptures on the ground and sprinted like a 100-meter champion down the river bank, barefoot, in pursuit of my precious scriptures.

I lifted myself onto a rock and stood there, helplessly watching him. I had one eye on him and the other eye on my scriptures.

He dashed into the water and scooped them out. When he returned them to me, the case was still dripping wet. I wondered if they were ruined. But I was just glad to have them back.

"Thanks," I said. "Did you run track in high school or something?"

"No," he said breathlessly, "though now I know how it feels to do the steeplechase."

My name, which was engraved on the front of the case, was a little worn off. I unzipped the case and there were a few pages that had sustained some water damage. But, all in all, my scriptures were intact, thanks to Elder Hanshaw.

"When we returned to the Ramos' house to change our clothes, Hermana Ramos saw us and said excitedly, "Elders, you've had some baptisms already!"

Those few active members in La Chispa were so excited to have missionaries in their midst again. Elder Hanshaw, President Ramos, and I were the only priesthood holders.

During our first sacrament meeting there, Elder Hanshaw blessed the sacrament and I passed it. President Ramos gave us various callings in the branch. Sister Ramos had me teach Relief Society to the branch's three active sisters, for which Elder Hanshaw teased me unmercifully. Elder Hanshaw handled the junior Primary, but that wasn't too tough—there was only two kids, Claudio and Eddie. Afterward, we visited the homes of several members, encouraging them to return to church activity. We received a lukewarm response.

Needless to say, missionary work in La Chispa was slower than the first day in the MTC.

It got even slower after we visited a very poor family one afternoon. It was hot outside so they offered us a drink of juice. There was no way I was going to drink it, knowing they made it with unclean water.

"*Me cae mal,*" I said apologetically. That means, literally, "it falls badly on me." It sounds a lot better than saying, "I'm not drinking that fetid, germ-infested cup of juice."

Elder Hanshaw felt he had to drink the juice so we wouldn't completely offend the family. He not only drank the cup, the family filled it up again and he drank that, too. Within an hour or so he regretted that. He came down with a case of dysentery that took him days to get over. Despite feeling weak and sick, his body ravaged by microorganisms, he still worked hard. Walking down the streets, it was tough to keep up with him. The bikes, the mission office promised us, would arrive soon.

District meetings were an exercise in patience. The other missionaries couldn't help but snicker goodnaturedly at our report of weekly results, or lack thereof. The other companionships were teaching dozens of discussions and baptizing three people every week. Us? We were lucky to have three discussions a week. But we certainly led the district in the "doors-slammed-in-the-face" category.

That experience definitely made me change my view of mission statistics. Before my mission, I loved studying stats like assist-to-turnover ratios and passing efficiency ratings. I could recite the final score of every BYU football game, in order, over a 15-year span. In fact, I could have told you off the top of my head what BYU's all-time record was when it played on the road on an even day in October.

During the first part of my mission, I saw statistics as a way to compare my performance to other missionaries. I knew that there was a much larger, more important purpose than that, but until I arrived in La Chispa, I don't think I fully grasped the concept of the worth of a soul.

Elder Hanshaw and I knew that the Lord had not sent us to La Chispa to fail. We only had five months left on our missions, so we wanted to make the most of what we had left. There were times when I got frustrated, and I wondered if this was how I was going to end my mission. I wondered if I'd have any more baptisms. Heck, the way things were going, I wondered if I'd ever get past the first discussion again.

After district meetings on Monday mornings, the other missionaries would invite us to go to Viña del Mar for preparation day activities like going to lunch or bowling. Instead, we'd go back to La Chispa and talk about how we could improve. I think the other missionaries thought we were either crazy or acting holier-than-thou.

Unlike a lot of missions, we didn't have to spend our P-days ironing and washing and grocery shopping. My whole life, my Mom always told me I needed to learn those valuable skills so I could survive on my mission. Well, we had that taken care of for us by people like Hermana Ramos. That left us more time to focus on other, more important things. (Sorry, Mom.)

Of course, we paid the Ramos' for their services, but they went beyond simply feeding us. At night, after a long hard day of rejection, Hermana Ramos would make us whatever we wanted. Turned out, we both had the same favorite Chilean food—*leche con platano* and avocado sandwiches. *Leche con platano* means "milk with banana." It consisted of a quart of milk, a couple of bananas, and a little bit of sugar blended together. It's a refreshing, frosty beverage with a little froth on top. It was the perfect thing to wash down avocado sandwiches.

Before I arrived in Chile, I hated avocados. They seemed so squishy and slimy. I didn't care for that green color inside, either. But I soon learned that if you take a fork and smash the avocado real good, sprinkle salt on it, then spread it on a piece of bread like jam, there's nothing better. I'll admit, it's an acquired taste. Elder Hanshaw and I must have drunk *leche con platano* and eaten avocado sandwiches every night. We never tired of that snack.

One P-day, we decided to hike up a hill a few blocks from the Ramos' house. From that vantage point, we could see the entire town and the vast Pacific Ocean. La Chispa was beginning to fill up with visitors for the summer.

Being from California, Elder Hanshaw knew a lot about the ocean. In fact, he taught me about all I know about it. He showed me the point break, where the waves form and break around a point of land. He showed me the type of wave that breaks from top to bottom, causing a hollow tube. Gazing into that sea of blue-green, he said, "You know, Elder Brady, missionary work is a lot like surfing."

"Surfing?" I was beginning to think he had been out in the sun too long.

"Yeah. I used to surf all the time back home."

"Really?"

"You should have seen my hair when I was a sophomore in high school. It was pretty gnarly." I tried to imagine him hanging ten.

"Look," he continued, "when you go surfing, you look for the biggest challenge," he explained. "You wait for high tide. You take your board and swim out to it. Then you wait for the biggest, baddest wave, then let it carry you. When you get knocked down, you paddle out and try again. And when you catch that perfect wave, you're stoked. There's no greater feeling. I really believe that's how it's going to be here in La Chispa. We're paddling like crazy with no discernible results, but one of these days we're going to catch that wave and ride it all the way to shore. We just have to keep working and being patient."

While on top of that hill, we prayed together, then individually. We prayed for the Lord to soften the hearts of the people of La Chispa. We studied what the great Book of Mormon missionaries, like Ammon, did. He boldly went among the Lamanites and befriended them, offered to serve them. We decided to try to do the same.

An opportunity presented itself one Monday night, when we passed by a soccer field. Two teenagers were kicking the ball around.

"Mormones!" they catcalled, taunting us. Instead of ignoring them, as usual, we decided to make conversation. You know, like Ammon would have.

"Buenas noches, amigos," we said.

"We're not your amigos," one of them sneered.

"You guys are pretty good soccer players," I said, trying to be nice.

"How would you know? You're *gringos*." Then they both cackled. "Leave us alone."

"Mind if I kick one?" Elder Hanshaw asked.

The teens were taken aback by the request, but, surprisingly, they relented. Elder Hanshaw set the ball down, about 10 yards from the goal, and booted it way wide right. In fact, it rolled about a block down the road. Those kids doubled over with laughter as Elder Hanshaw chased down the ball, his tie flapping in the wind.

"You *gringos* are horrible at *fubol!*" one said.

"Why are you here, anyway?" the other asked, full of attitude.

"Because the Lord wants us here," I replied.

"How do you know that?"

"If you'll give us a few minutes of your time, we'd be happy to tell you," I said.

"We have no interest in your religion." one of them said.

By that time, Elder Hanshaw returned with the ball. "Would you be interested in a little game?" he asked, after catching his breath.

"You guys want to play *us?*"

"Why not?" Elder Hanshaw said. "First team to score five goals wins. Tell you what. You guys win, we'll leave you alone."

"And if you guys win?" one said.

"You've got to listen to our message," Elder Hanshaw said.

The two teens huddled and conferred about our challenge.

"We'll agree under one condition," they told us. One came over and started studying our watches. "If we win, we get your watches."

Elder Hanshaw agreed, even though my Mom gave me my watch as a high school graduation gift.

"Are you sure about this?" I asked him in English.

"Trust me," he said.

Elder Hanshaw and I put down our bags full of copies of the Book of Mormon, our scriptures, and our planners on the sidelines. We shed our ties. I can't remember many details, but we whipped them pretty good. Elder Hanshaw, our opponents soon figured out, was sandbagging when he missed that shot at the goal earlier. It was obvious that he was an excellent athlete. He scored all five of our goals. The two teens were dumfounded. Come to think of it, so was I.

"You're pretty good," one said to my companion, "for a *gringo*."

You got that right, Pablo.

"Now," Elder Hanshaw said, picking up his planner, "what day works best for you guys?"

They hemmed and hawed for a minute. "Meet us here tomorrow. Same time," they said.

Later, I asked Elder Hanshaw how many years he played soccer. "Until I came to Chile," he said, "I had never played soccer. Like I told you, I was into surfing."

"You're joking," I said.

"All you do is kick a little ball with your feet. What's so hard about that?" Well, he sure made it look easy.

We must have waited 30 minutes for those kids to show up that next day. They never did.

Things kind of went like that for the next week or so. Nothing seemed to go right, but Elder Hanshaw always remained positive. He always said that everyone on Earth had already accepted the gospel once, in the premortal world. It was our duty to remind them of that through the gospel and the Spirit. He was certain if people sincerely listened to our message, they would remember it and accept it again.

Maybe he was inspired by the ocean, but he kept telling me his surfing analogies. He used to go to the beach every morning after attending early morning seminary. "You just gotta keep getting up every time you're knocked down," he'd say.

In addition to working hard, we continued praying, fasting, exercising faith, and patiently bearing our afflictions. We believed in miracles and we needed a few. We knew the Lord would bless us eventually. And He did—in ways we never would have imagined.

CHAPTER SEVEN

Frequently, we would hold a special fast in hopes of receiving guidance and blessings. In fact, we were fasting so often in La Chispa (about once a week), Hermana Ramos asked us if we wanted a refund on our meal money.

One day, during the first 30 minutes we were out we had three people swear at us. One man sicced his dog on us. I started doubting again. We were fasting and praying for *this*? Those wonderful feelings I had felt the previous day seemed to be fleeing fast. I was trying hard to cast out all negative thoughts.

Luckily, Gunnar refused to be dismayed. He tried a baseball analogy on me.

"Look, Elder, the best hitters fail seven out of 10 times at bat," he said.

"At this rate, we must be due for a grand slam," I answered.

We were walking down the street when we saw a young boy sitting by himself, playing in the dirt.

"*Hola, compadrito,*" Elder Hanshaw said to him.

The boy raised his head but did not respond. So Elder Hanshaw crouched down to his level and pretended to pull a peso out of his ear. The boy smiled with wonderment. Then Elder Hanshaw did a trick with his tie. The boy laughed. Elder Hanshaw held out his hand and the boy stuck out his. Elder Hanshaw clasped his little hand, then snapped his fingers.

"Do it again!" the boy squealed.

Suddenly, an old woman with a leathery face and long, gray hair opened the door of her shanty. We were sure she was about to grab the boy and take him inside. Instead, she asked who we were. We introduced ourselves and she eagerly invited us into her home, much to our surprise and delight.

Inside, pictures of Jesus adorned the walls. Her Bible was prominently displayed on a table. On one side of the living room she had a 24-inch television. Against the other wall was the box the TV had come in, with a baby granddaughter sleeping inside it.

"Do you bring a message for me from God?" Hermana Raquel asked.

"Yes we do," I said.

"I've been expecting you." She then explained why. "Several months ago, my six-year-old grandson died of an illness. It was very hard for me," she said quietly, dabbing her eyes with her sleeve of her sweater. "I prayed many times for comfort but it never came. Then one night I had a dream I will never forget. My grandson appeared to me, gave me a hug, then walked down a corridor. I followed him. I didn't want to let him out of my sight. He hugged me again and said goodbye. A door opened and he walked through it. The door closed. I tried opening it and it wouldn't budge. There were two other doors and I opened them. In both, I saw countless people milling around, confused, alone, scared. Then I woke up. I had that same dream for three straight nights. For weeks, I wondered what it meant. I asked my pastor to interpret it, but his answer didn't satisfy me.

"A couple of weeks later, I had another dream. God sent two special messengers to me. Two North American boys dressed in white shirts and ties who could interpret my dream. In this second dream, I saw two young men walking down the street. I ran after them, but they kept moving farther and farther away from me. So today I open the door and see you two standing there, just like in my dream. That's why I invited you in. I know you are sent from the Lord. Could you please interpret my first dream please?"

Elder Hanshaw and I looked at each other for a moment. We told Hermana Raquel we would do our best to accommodate her.

"But before we interpret your dream, there are many things we would like to teach you," Elder Hanshaw said. "It will help you to interpret your dream for yourself."

The woman scooted her chair closer to us.

We began with the first discussion and midway through it, the woman's eyes welled up with tears and she said, "I know you're teaching the truth."

Talk about a golden investigator. Hermana Raquel was 24-carat.

33

All of her questions led to the next part of the discussion. We could tell it was all making sense to her, especially when we taught her about the Plan of Salvation and the three degrees of glory. As we went on, she figured out what her dream meant. Though her grandson wasn't baptized, because he died without that opportunity, he was to live with Heavenly Father forever. The door her grandson entered, that she could not, was opened by receiving baptism by a servant of the Lord, we explained. She asked what she needed to do to get baptized. She had no problem with giving up coffee and tea. She was fine with reading the Book of Mormon and praying about it. She told us she already knew it was true because we told her it was. But when we said she needed to attend church, she seemed concerned.

"Does that mean I have to join your Church?" she asked.

Elder Hanshaw and I looked at each other in exasperation.

"Hermana," Elder Hanshaw said, "when you're baptized, you become a member of The Church of Jesus Christ of Latter-day Saints. The Lord's church. You will be a great example for your family and friends."

Hermana Raquel still looked worried. "My pastor won't like that," she said.

"Who's your pastor?" I asked.

"His name is Cesar," she said.

"Cesar Sepulveda?" Elder Hanshaw asked.

"Do you know him?"

"No," Elder Hanshaw said, "but I feel like I do."

Hearing that name again gave me a sick feeling.

"If he knew I was talking to you, he would be very upset," she said.

"Yes, but we are servants of the Lord, just as you said," Elder Hanshaw said. "What do you think the Lord would want you to do?"

"Before I attend your church," she said, "I must talk to him."

"Hermana," I said, "you need to talk to Heavenly Father and ask Him what you should do."

"Yes, I will," she said. "But Cesar has done so much for me and my family. He is also a servant of the Lord . . ."

Despite her worries, we set a return appointment for the following day.

When we came back, she was confused and frightened. She had us come inside quickly. "I don't want Cesar to know you're here," she said. We felt like spies or something.

"Cesar told me all kinds of horrible things about your Church," she said. "He warned me not to let you into my home again. I insisted that you were sent by the Lord. Then he said that I should invite you to our church services this week."

Once again, Cesar had set the trap. Unlike our predecessors, though, we were prepared to step into it.

"Okay, we'll come," I said.

Hermana Raquel seemed relieved. "Thank you, Elders," she said.

During our lunch break, we prepared for the meeting by devising a plan of our own. We told President Ramos about what was happening.

"Are you sure you should go?" he said.

"We feel we should," Elder Hanshaw answered.

President Ramos said he would like to accompany us, but couldn't because of his work schedule.

"Please be careful, Elders," he said. "Cesar is a very cunning man. He's crafty. You remember what happened last time."

We did, which was one of the reasons we felt strongly about going.

We dropped by Hermana Raquel's home and together we went to The Light in the Wilderness Church. The congregation met in an enormous chapel filled with ornate pews and stained-glass windows. Everyone stared at us as we walked in.

A man in his mid-30s, dressed in a gray suit and wearing a mustache, approached us. "You must be Hermana Raquel's friends," he said, sounding as phony as a used car salesman. "I'm Cesar Sepulveda, the pastor. Welcome."

We saw right through his act. He escorted us to a pew near the front, just a few rows away from the pulpit.

I'd had a cold that week, so I was feeling a little ill and my head felt warm. I asked Cesar if I could use a bathroom and he obliged.

When I returned, Elder Hanshaw whispered to me, "While you were gone, Cesar came up to me and said that you had a fever and that your sins were being burned out of you. He said it was a sign."

I knew we were in for an interesting evening.

"So what did you say to that?" I asked.

"I said, 'Let him who is without sin cast the first stone,'" he said. "It's the only thing I could think of off the top of my head."

Cesar began the meeting by snidely welcoming us, the visitors. Then a rotund man in a black suit emerged from the back of the chapel and took a seat on the stand. Men started playing guitars and tambourines, leading the congregation in a song that had people clapping and gyrating and shouting. Some fell onto the ground and began shaking violently as if they were having seizures. This went on for about 15 minutes. Even Hermana Raquel was doing a little of it. Elder Hanshaw and I sat there patiently, marveling at the scene.

Then came the part we were waiting for: Cesar stood up in front of the congregation and began his speech. He was obviously very well-versed in LDS doctrine, for he quoted various scriptures straight out of the Bible, preaching about those who say there are scriptures in addition to the Bible. He warned about false prophets. He had rebutted the first discussion as a pre-emptive strike. This guy knew what he was doing.

Then he introduced a "visiting preacher" from Santiago who just "happened" to be in town for the occasion. This visiting preacher began "speaking in tongues." Cesar provided the "translation."

Well, things turned nasty. The man began speaking jibberish, carrying on like an infant. He spoke loudly, pointed at Elder Hanshaw and me, and began sweating profusely. Worse, spittle from his mouth rained down on us from time to time. They called us all sorts of things—anti-Christs, emissaries of evil, spies, liars, polygamists, American imperialists. They pretty much covered everything.

When they finished, the people who had been clapping and spinning and dancing and generally carrying on, sat down again. Then Cesar said he was going to give the visitors a few moments to speak. The chapel went silent and I stood and started by giving an abbreviated description of our beliefs. I told them about Joseph Smith and how I knew he was a prophet of God. Elder Hanshaw spoke of The Book of Mormon and the restoration of the Church. We urged everyone to listen to more of our message and we bore our testimonies of the truthfulness of the gospel. There was a peaceful feeling in the building for the first time that night.

Cesar just stood to the side, his nose in the Bible.

Elder Hanshaw then recited Galatians 5:22-23. "But the fruit of the Spirit is love, joy, peace, longsuffering, gentleness, goodness, faith, meekness, temperance ..."

I don't think the people got the point of it, though. Except maybe Hermana Raquel, who made her way to the front of the chapel and told the congregation about those dreams she had. "These young men are servants of the Lord," she concluded. "We need to listen to them."

At that point, Cesar realized Hermana Raquel and the Mormons had momentarily won over the crowd. He was not pleased.

We thanked everyone for their time and we decided not to allow Cesar a chance for another rebuttal—at least while we were there. The other missionaries who had that experience made a fatal mistake by sticking around for more abuse. We figured that we should leave right away and take the Spirit with us.

When Cesar saw us heading for the exit, he began refuting our testimonies. As we went out the door, we could still hear him bashing us, calling us cowards. That pulsating music started up again. Unfortunately, Hermana Raquel stayed behind.

As we walked down the street, Cesar chased us down. "What are you afraid of?"

"Really big dogs with rabies," Elder Hanshaw replied.

"Why are you leaving so soon?" Cesar said.

"Thanks for having us to your church," I said, "but we're late for another appointment."

"If you are truly servants of God, like you say, then why don't you speak in tongues? Can you speak in tongues?"

"Of course," Elder Hanshaw said. "We believe in the gift of tongues. Why, my companion and I grew up in the United States, yet we speak in Spanish. What do you think of that?"

You could see all the blood flowing to Cesar's head. He was

about to boil over. "That's not speaking in tongues!" he shouted. "You two are imposters! I don't know what kind of devilish tricks you used to confuse Hermana Raquel, but you had better stay away from her."

"Why?" Elder Hanshaw said. "What are you afraid of? Someday, *hermano*, you'll come to know that what we teach is true. I don't know when and I don't know how, but you will know."

That shut Cesar up. We walked away and didn't look back for fear we'd turn into a pillar of salt or something.

CHAPTER EIGHT

Our goal was clear—we had to pry Hermana Raquel loose from Cesar's clutches and baptize her. Even if we did nothing else right in La Chispa, we knew we had to do this.

However, Cesar must have said something that scared Hermana Raquel. Even though she believed we were the Lord's servants, she refused to meet with us. When we visited her, she'd open her door just a crack and say, "Hermanos, I'm very busy. I can't entertain you today. Come back another day."

Why would the Lord give her those dreams, send her the missionaries, then not help us baptize her?

Frustrated, Elder Hanshaw and I decided to turn our attention to the list of less-active members in the branch given to us by President Ramos. Our goal was to visit every one of them.

It made me feel sad knowing there were so many baptized members of the Church who were not attending their meetings. Elder Hanshaw pulled out his Bible, turned to the Book of Matthew, and read those verses about the one hundred sheep and the one that went astray. In this case, it seemed ninety-and-nine had gone astray. We needed to find them.

We started that day to seek out those people. It would have been nice to have bikes. Instead, we continued walking everywhere.

A few people we found told us they had joined another church. Others were ashamed that they hadn't been to church in so long and they asked where we met and what time the meetings started. They promised us they would start going. We weren't holding our breath. Some were adept at making excuses. One woman told us she couldn't attend meetings because they were too late in the day for her. We informed her that church started at 10 a.m. "Oh," she said with a straight face, "that's too early."

At one particular home, a young mother was holding a baby. She smiled when she saw us.

"Are you Hermana Diaz?" we asked.

"Yes," she said.

We introduced ourselves and asked her how long she had been a member of the Church.

"Since I was 12," she said. "Elder Vargas and Elder Smith taught me the lessons. Elder Smith baptized me."

She told us to wait, then came back out with her copy of the Book of Mormon. Tucked inside was a picture of her with the missionaries on her baptism day.

"Why haven't we seen you at Church?" we asked.

Tears filled her eyes. "I want so badly to go," she said. "But it's my husband. He's very controlling. He won't let me go. I want my son to be blessed in the Mormon Church. But my husband wants him to be baptized in the Catholic Church. We've been arguing about this for two weeks."

"Has your husband ever heard the discussions?" I asked.

"No," she said. "And you must not try to teach him. He doesn't want anything to do with the Mormons. Before we married, he said he had no problem with me being a Mormon. But after we were married, his friends at work started saying all sorts of bad things about the Mormons. Then he said I couldn't go anymore. I would invite you in, but I can't. If he saw me talking to you right now, he would be angry. He sees those members of that Light in the Wilderness Church and he thinks the Mormons are the same. I've tried to tell him about our Church, but he won't listen."

"Do you think he'd listen to us?" Elder Hanshaw asked.

"No, no, no," Hermana Diaz said. "He's a very kind man, but when it comes to religion, he has his own ideas. He says his parents were Catholic, his grandparents were Catholic, his great-grandparents were Catholic. He was born a Catholic and he will die a Catholic. Family is very, very important to him and he says that if he were to convert to another religion, it would be like turning his back on all of his ancestors' beliefs. He says it would be like spitting on their graves. I tell him I was Catholic, too, until I learned the truth. When I say things like that, he becomes angry and goes drinking with his friends. So I try to avoid talking about religion. But I feel our son needs to be blessed. My husband says he needs to be baptized the way the Catholics do it."

Elder Hanshaw noticed some paintings of the ocean on the walls of the home.

"Where did you get those beautiful pictures?" Elder Hanshaw asked.

"They're my husband's," Hermana Diaz said. "He likes to paint after work."

"Those are great," he said. "Does he sell them? I'd like to send one or two home to my mom."

"He sells them on weekends. You'd really buy some?"

"Yes, I would."

"What's your husband's name?" I asked.

"Eduardo."

"When can we usually find him at home?"

"In the evenings, but I really don't think he'll want to talk to you. He'll tell you he already has his religion. But if you dropped by to buy his paintings, then I'm sure he'd make some time for you."

When we came back a couple of days later, Hermana Diaz said that Eduardo would allow us to come for a business transaction only. That's all we needed. We met him and at first he was predictably standoffish, but then we complimented him on his paintings as Elder Hanshaw looked through his collection and picked out two to buy.

After money exchanged hands, he said we could have a seat, which surprised us. Then he disappeared into the kitchen.

"Elders, since it's been such a long time since I've been to Church," she whispered. "Could you teach me the discussions?"

We could hear Eduardo making a racket in the kitchen, but we got the feeling he was listening to what we were telling his wife. We picked the fourth discussion, which talks about the concept of temples and eternal families. Elder Hanshaw and I spoke somewhat loudly to ensure Eduardo could hear us. Then we talked about the way Jesus was baptized and how babies don't need baptism, but rather a blessing.

When we finished, Hermana Diaz thanked us for our visit. "That was so beautiful," she said.

We said goodbye and wondered if we'd ever see her again. The next day she tracked us down and said her husband told her it would be okay if we came by again. Over the next week or so, we retaught her all of the discussions. Not once did Eduardo show himself, but we knew he was eavesdropping in his kitchen.

It got to the point that Eduardo softened enough to let his wife come to church on Sundays. We had five less-actives coming to sacrament meeting, bumping up the attendance total to 13. We considered it no small victory. President Ramos gave them all callings, meaning I was relieved from my Relief Society teaching duties. Besides President Ramos, Elder Hanshaw and me, there still were no priesthood holders.

After we had contacted every less-active member on the list, we set aside time each day visiting those families again. If nothing else, we were the best hometeachers in the history of La Chispa.

CHAPTER NINE

The next P-day, we decided that maybe we should take a little break from the work, so we joined the other missionaries in Viña del Mar. The other missionaries were surprised to see us.

We met at a park there and one of the missionaries brought an American football. We decided to play a friendly game. No more of this *futbol* stuff. We were tired of soccer. We divided up into teams and even a few Chilean missionaries said they wanted to play, though I don't think they had any idea what they were doing. Most of the time we had to yell at them because they were lining up offsides and they kept trying to catch the ball with their feet.

"Using your hands is not only allowed, it's encouraged in this game," I kept reminding them.

I was on Elder Hanshaw's team. A couple of elders tried playing quarterback, including me, with less-than-successful results. Then I suggested that Elder Hanshaw give it a try. He did so, though reluctantly.

On the first play, I snapped the ball to him then turned around to wait for a pass. I was wide open but not once did he look my way. I was somewhat amazed at Hanshaw's ability to effortlessly elude the missionaries who were chasing him. Granted, most of them were not great athletes. After dancing around in the pocket for a moment, he stepped up and launched a 60-yard pass downfield. It was a perfect strike into Elder Patterson's chest. The force of the throw knocked him down flat but somehow he hung on to the ball. Touchdown.

Well, all of us missionaries just kind of stopped and stared at Elder Hanshaw for a moment. Our jaws were hanging down past our chests.

"Awesome pass," I said.

"Thanks," is all Elder Hanshaw said.

"I think I broke a rib," Elder Patterson gasped. Turns out, he didn't. It was just severely bruised.

On our next offensive series, Elder Hanshaw noticed that the opposing team was double-covering the receivers and rushing only one player. So, he simply tucked the ball under his arm and ran. Nobody could even touch him as he sprinted some 40 yards. Another touchdown.

Unfortunately, Elder Monroe, who stood about 6-foot-3 and 245 pounds, went down to the turf while trying to chase Elder Hanshaw. Elder Hanshaw and I helped him off the field. I suggested he take off his shoe. It was an ankle sprain.

President McPherson heard about our game and the injuries and the following day placed a moratorium on football games.

When Elder Hanshaw and I got on the bus to head back to La Chispa, I couldn't stop talking about his performance.

"Awwww," he said, "that was just a little game between a bunch of out-of-shape missionaries."

"But you look like you've played a little before. High school?"

He was quiet for a moment. "Yeah," he said softly.

"Quarterback?"

"Yeah," he said, even softer. I could tell he didn't want to talk about it, but I couldn't figure out why.

"Did you get any scholarship offers?"

"I really don't want to talk about it."

Naturally, I had to pester him until he did.

"If I tell you, will you stop asking me?" he asked.

"I promise."

He took a deep breath. "During my junior year of high school I talked to a lot of college coaches who said they were very interested in me," Elder Hanshaw said. "But then in the state championship game, I got hit while throwing a pass and two defensive players landed on my shoulder. I got hurt pretty bad."

"Subluxation?"

"Yeah," he said. "How did you know?"

"Lucky guess," I said.

"That turned out to be the last pass of my career," he said. "I had surgery and endured a year-long rehab. I missed my entire senior year of football. I didn't even dress for games—it was too hard to be part of the team, yet not be part of the team. College coaches stopped calling, and the letters stopped coming. It was like I disappeared. But it's just as well."

"You're a natural athlete, the way you can run and jump. Your shoulder sure looked good to me."

"Thanks," he said. "My shoulder feels even stronger than it did before my injury." Then he got a distant look in his eyes. He started talking as if I wasn't even there. "When I was a kid, I dreamed of being a college quarterback. After school, I'd run home, grab my helmet and my ball and throw for hours at the wood fence in the back yard. I got to where I could knock a soup can off a table from 25 yards away. My dad was a minor league baseball player in the Dodgers' organization before he started selling insurance. He wanted his only son to play sports and I wanted to play, too. When he got home from work, we spent countless hours playing together. He instilled a love of sports in me. He drove hundreds of miles shuttling me from base-ball practice to basketball practice to football practice." He paused, then said, "I miss him."

I just kept listening.

"Then came my shoulder injury," Elder Hanshaw continued. "That year away from the game forced me to rethink my life's goals. I prayed a lot and knew that I needed to go on a mission. I promised Heavenly Father that I would put the Church first in my life instead of football. When I did that, I felt at peace. I knew it was right. So, I honestly haven't given football any thought since."

I couldn't believe that after being with this guy every second of every day for more than a month that I never knew this about him.

"You can still live your dream," I blurted out.

"What are you talking about?"

"Your dream of being a quarterback," I said. "You can still do it."

My companion laughed. "I know we believe in miracles," he said, "but let's not push it."

"Just because you rearranged your priorities doesn't mean foot-ball can't fit in somewhere. Now, I'm no coach or scout, but I've watched enough football in my life to recognize talent when I see it."

"Even if I wanted to play again, nobody knows who I am. It's been almost four years since I played in a real game."

"You could walk-on somewhere," I said. "All you need is a chance to prove yourself. Once coaches see what you can do, they'll know who you are."

"Elder Brady, you're really nice to say all those things about me. But the reality is, it's tough to make it onto a college team, let alone play. What if I'm not good enough? What if I get hurt again? I couldn't go through rehab again. The doctors told me I should probably give up the game so I won't have future problems just doing normal things. Besides, I don't think about football anymore."

"You don't know what could happen," I said. "I'll help you."

"How are you going to help me?"

"We'll work out. We'll get a football and throw it around. We can do that before companionship study in the mornings."

I must have been convincing because the next time we were in Viña del Mar, we went to a sporting goods store and asked the manager for "un fubol Americano." It wasn't leather, but it was brown and oblong. It served our purposes.

"I suppose we could do this, just for fun," he said. "It's a good way to exercise."

We'd get up at six in the morning and go to the soccer field. I'd run all sorts of patterns on the rock-hard dirt and catch passes from Elder Hanshaw. His release was gorgeous, almost effortless. He threw hard, too. I'd come back to the Ramos' house with my hands red and stinging, but I loved every minute of it. I was so sure that Elder Hanshaw had a bright future in football. There wasn't a pass he couldn't throw—fade routes, fly patterns and darts over the middle. The ball was usually a tight spiral, right on the money.

"So," I said one morning as we jogged back to the Ramos' house, "you should be starting for BYU in about 18 months."

"You're crazy," he said.

"I'm serious."

"Awww, c'mon. You know that I'm just doing this to get some exercise."

While jogging to the soccer field in the mornings, Gunnar told me when he was thirteen, he got a paper route delivering the

Los Angeles Times. Have you seen the size of that paper? No wonder he had such great arm and wrist strength. His dad would pay him an extra dime for every paper he landed on the porch from the sidewalk.

I noticed a gleam in his eye. Then reality hit him again. "There was a time when I dreamed of playing college football, but I haven't played in years. I had my chance, but now it's gone."

"Don't you believe in second chances?" I asked.

"Of course, but quarterbacks are different. The doctor who performed the surgery said there was a good chance I'd never be able to throw the ball like I did before. He said many baseball pitchers who undergo that type of surgery never play again."

"But your mission is almost over. Why not at least try when you get back? If I had half of your talent, I would want to do everything I could to see where it could take me."

Once again he got a faraway look in his eyes. "You know, I miss running out onto the field and hear cheering and the band playing, to smell the fresh-cut grass, to throw a perfect spiral into the blue sky . . ."

Then he dropped the subject like a sack of manure, but the next morning he woke up at 5:30 and started doing pushups and situps. Then we went for a jog down to the beach and back. I was always about 50 yards behind him.

We returned home to find President Ramos standing in the kitchen, beaming.

"Elders!" he said. "I have some very good news!" He told us that the Church had approved the purchase of a small home a few blocks away where the branch could hold Sunday meetings. We spent our P-day sweeping, mopping, and washing windows. We moved the manuals, chairs, sacrament trays and hymn books to the new place. The members were so excited to have a place of their own. Hermana Diaz created a homemade sign that read, "The Church of Jesus Christ of Latter-day Saints. Meetings begin at 10 a.m. on Sundays. Visitors welcome." She taped it to the door. Everyone in the tiny branch—we were up to about 20 members—was so proud.

Elder Hanshaw and I prayed for the day when a chapel could be built in La Chispa. We prayed for the day that there would be a La

Chispa ward. In fact, we envisioned a day when the whole town would be filled with Mormons. Then there might even be a La Chispa Stake, as improbable as it seemed.

Yeah, we believed in miracles.

A couple of weeks after meeting in the new church for the first time, we walked past there one morning and our hearts sank. The first thing we noticed was the graffiti. Spray-painted messages said disparaging things about Mormons. Windows were broken. The front door had been forcibly entered. Chairs were tipped over, and there were holes in the walls. President Ramos' office was ransacked. We could barely bring ourselves to tell President Ramos that someone had vandalized the church.

We couldn't believe people could do that. Neither could President Ramos. He called some Church leaders in Viña del Mar, and some people were hired to repair the damage. No one was ever caught. If anything good came out of it, it brought our tiny branch even closer together. Very little seemed to be going right. It made us angry that someone would vandalize our little church. The Hermana Raquel situation was not progressing. She'd attend Cesar's church, then visit ours. She was very non-committal when it came to baptism. We spent a lot of time fasting and praying for her and trying to help her overcome her fears. On top of that, the mission office still hadn't delivered our bikes.

CHAPTER TEN

As I mentioned, for nine months out of the year La Chispa is nearly desolate. Many sections of the sprawling resort town lay dormant, roads go unused and houses are boarded up for the winter.

By mid-December, however, those houses come alive as their wealthy owners return for the summer. We witnessed quiet La Chispa transform into a noisy city, full of car horns blaring and buses packed like sardines roaring through the main street.

La Chispa's economy depended upon those three months to survive. Many residents earned most of their money for the year by renting out their homes for the summer to rich tourists while they took their families and camped in a tent in the yard. President Ramos usually did this in the summer, but he assured us that all the pesos in Chile couldn't compare to having the missionaries living with his family.

Anyway, Elder Hanshaw and I had been in La Chispa a month-and-a-half with no baptisms. We decided that it didn't make much sense to try teaching the gospel to people who were on vacation. Besides, we didn't want to subject ourselves to the temptations—girls in bikinis, guys on surf boards.

For a change of pace, we hiked several miles away from the hustle and bustle of La Chispa and the beach, fording a couple of streams in the process, to a little community called La Gloria. There wasn't anything glorious about the place, except for the fact we received return appointments for the next day at nearly every door we knocked.

We thought we had finally turned the corner. But when we returned the following day after an exhausting trip to teach discussions, everyone had an excuse not to listen to us. A mangy dog attacked us, biting at our ankles before Elder Hanshaw smacked it over the head with his 20-pound bag of copies of the Book of Mormon.

Indeed, it was as if we had a hex against us. In reality, a flyer distributed to the homes in the area was to blame. As we walked down the street we found a piece of paper warning people to beware of the Mormons and not to let us in their homes. Apparently somebody had been as busy as we had been. That somebody, we figured, was Cesar Sepulveda. We decided to leave La Gloria alone. Elder Hanshaw and I joked that Ammon never had it this bad.

The next P-day, back in La Chispa, we climbed up that secluded hill again, this time singing "High On A Mountain Top." We reached the summit and as we looked out over the ocean and the hundreds of people frolicking on the beach, Gunnar just started grinning.

"What are you so happy about?" I asked.

"There's got to be a reason for it all," Gunnar replied. "I just can't figure out what that is. It's not a coincidence that we're companions in this place, in this time. Right?"

"Right," I said, less-than-convincingly.

"Heavenly Father must have big plans for this place, or else this wouldn't be so difficult. My dad used to tell me that we need to learn how to see things the way Heavenly Father sees them. It's hard to see things that way, though. That's the essence of faith."

I had never thought of it that way before.

"Maybe he has big plans for us, too," he continued. "I really believe something special is going to happen in this place. We just have to have the faith."

I wished I had his brand of faith.

Then we pulled out our scriptures and read Alma 26 together as President McPherson had instructed us. I had read verse 22 hundreds of times before, but for some reason, that passage finally sunk in that day: "Yea, he that repenteth and exerciseth faith, and bringeth forth good works, and prayeth continually without ceasing—unto such it is given to know the mysteries of God; yea, unto such it shall be given to reveal things which never have been revealed; yea, and it shall be given unto such to bring thousands of souls to repentance, even as it has been given unto us to bring these our brethren to repentance."

There was the answer, the key to success in the mission field and in life—right there, in black in white. That same verse hit Gunnar between the eyes, too. After reading that verse, Gunnar asked, "Can you imagine bringing thousands of souls to repentance?"

"Not without an awfully large baptismal font," I said.

Gunnar looked out to the ocean. "We've got the world's biggest baptismal font right out there. And look at all of the potential investigators out there!"

When we were done reading, we offered a prayer together, then we prayed individually. I can't say I had many spiritual experiences in my life up to that point, but that one was the most powerful. It's hard to describe, but I felt that "burning in the bosom" I had read about in the scriptures. For that moment, my doubts and fears disappeared. It was as if the Lord was telling me that everything was going to be okay, both for the rest of my mission and for the rest of my life—as long as I was faithful.

Together, we decided to teach everyone, regardless of whether or not they lived in La Chispa. Suddenly, we were surrounded by thousands of potential investigators. To say we stood out would be an understatement. Most people wore swimming suits. We wore crisp white shirts, conservative ties, pressed pants, and black shoes. Many of the people we talked to were out-of-towners who were a lot more interested in getting to the beach than getting to heaven.

"If I ever want to hear about your Church," some would say, "then I'll just look you up at home in Santiago. We see you there all the time."

Still, the Lord blessed us immensely with dozens of humble, receptive souls who listened and believed our message. They eagerly accepted a copy of the Book of Mormon. Many desired baptism, but the length of their stay was usually brief. We could only urge them to continue reading the Book of Mormon and to look up the Mormon missionaries near their homes.

We soon realized that we were planting seeds that, we earnestly prayed, would blossom someday. The Lord had commissioned us to teach all people, not just La Chispa residents. However, we knew there had to be people there who were prepared for baptism. We longed to see the fruits of our labors.

CHAPTER ELEVEN

On the Sunday night after we had read Alma 26, we were about to write our weekly letters to the president. Then Elder Hanshaw said to me, "Elder Brady, we're doing everything we can. So let's test the Lord and see if He will produce a miracle for us."

President McPherson wanted to know what our goal for baptisms were for the week. Every week, we put down one without even thinking. After a lot of prayer, Elder Hanshaw and I boldly set a goal to baptize two souls the following Sunday. At the time we didn't know who these two souls were, since everyone we had taught the previous week had left town and new people had arrived.

The next morning, after companionship study and breakfast, we left at about 9 a.m. to find our two candidates for baptism.

Well, the Lord tested us that week. We knocked doors, we approached families in the streets as they headed for the beach, we talked to people on buses. We didn't know where we'd find two souls for baptism, so we searched everywhere. We fasted on Tuesday and there were times when I felt almost too weak to walk. It wasn't easy watching people indulge themselves on ice cream and barbecue beef sandwiches all around us. When we woke up Wednesday morning, we had no prospects whatsoever.

After breakfast and companionship study, Elder Hanshaw and I must have prayed for half an hour, begging the Lord for help. "There must be two souls ready for baptism," we pleaded. "Please, guide us to them."

For close to four hours we made our way through the neighborhood with not a single return appointment. We could smell someone barbecuing meat and our stomachs were growling.

"Let's finish this street," Elder Hanshaw said, "then I say we go back and end our fast."

"I won't argue with you," I said.

Despite my deep desire to reach our goal that week, I have to admit I was relieved that no one was home in the next three houses. I couldn't wait to eat some of Hermana Ramos' food. Then we came to the final house on the street. I secretly hoped no one would answer the door.

It was quiet for a moment, then we saw someone lift up a drape in the window and put it down just as quickly. Then the door flung open.

"Elders!" a girl in her early twenties said excitedly and bounded toward us.

We got a little excited, too, because there was actually someone who was happy to see us. She informed us she was a member of the Church from Santiago and introduced herself as Maria. "Please," she said, "come back tonight when all of my relatives are home. None of them are members of the Church and I'd like them to hear the discussions."

We agreed to return at seven o'clock that night.

After lunch we continued tracting with little success. By seven, we arrived at our appointment. We were eager to sit down and rest, if nothing else. We waited about five minutes before Maria invited us inside.

"I'm having a little trouble convincing them to listen to you," she whispered. "Please wait here and take a seat. I'll see what I can do."

Over the next few minutes, a steady stream of people quickly sneaked out the door without even acknowledging us, as if there were a fire in the house. Elder Hanshaw and I figured this was just a waste of time.

"Sorry for keeping you waiting," Maria said. "My relatives have all left, but I have a couple of friends who say they'd like to listen to you. They'll be here in a minute."

Maria, who expressed her desire to serve a mission someday, ushered us into a cramped bedroom with two lumpy beds. We sat down across from her when two of the oddest-looking guys I had ever seen sauntered into the room. Their hair was long, unruly, and outdated by at least a decade, as was their polyester, florescent, flower-patterned attire. They were flower children, Chilean-style. Their names were Sixto and Maximo and they were a few years older than us. They were caught in some sort of 1970s time warp, straight from *Hawaii Five-O* reruns. Later, Elder Hanshaw said they looked like a couple of surfers he knew back home.

I wondered where Maria had gone to dig these guys up. We really were that desperate for people to teach, but I immediately knew this would be a complete waste of time.

Sixto and Maximo were natives of La Chispa, but they were only going to be around for a few days before they had to leave that weekend for work in the mines in the northern part of Chile, some 500 miles away. They did not seem like the type who would be interested in the gospel.

We talked to Sixto and Maximo for a few minutes, trying to get to know them, and I figured they would begin preaching to us, extolling the virtues of "peace," "love" and "feelin' groovy." I wondered what the Spanish word for groovy was. I figured they would inform us that our beliefs were too constraining and that we should loosen up, grow out our hair, and wear beads around our necks like they did.

I was a little encouraged when Maria offered a sincere, heartfelt prayer, thanking the Lord for her friends, Sixto and Maximo, and the two missionaries that had come to teach them.

As we breezed through the first discussion, I noticed they had bloodshot eyes. *They're probably on drugs,* I thought. Still, they seemed interested and listened to every word. After teaching Sixto and Maximo about prophets, Joseph Smith, and the Book of Mormon, we told them about baptism. We pulled out a picture of Jesus being baptized by John the Baptist and they were mesmerized by it.

"It's too bad you guys are leaving so soon," I said off-handedly, "because to be baptized, you have to listen to the other discussions and that generally takes a couple of weeks. Maybe when you get back from your jobs again, you can listen to more from us or other missionaries—"

Much to my surprise, Sixto cut me off.

"Well, if you guys say we're supposed to be baptized," he said, almost in a scolding tone, "then we'll quit our jobs. We want to be baptized. That's more important than our jobs."

"Same goes for me," Maximo said.

Elder Hanshaw and I were stunned beyond belief. We were speechless. It took us a moment to realize what they had said.

"Like my companion said, it may take a little while to get yourselves ready for baptism," Elder Hanshaw said.

"Whatever we need to do, we'll do it," Sixto said.

The Spirit filled the small room. Maria brushed the tears from her eyes.

So we taught the second, third and fourth discussions that night. We didn't know what kind of guys these were, so we boldly taught them the commandments. Elder Hanshaw came up with a great surfing analogy, at least one I had never heard him use before. He told the story about how he surfed back home in California and that the smart surfers would go elsewhere when there was a low surf advisory. "It's very dangerous to ignore the warnings," he said. "The commandments are like those warnings." Sixto and Maximo seemed to understand perfectly.

At one point during the discussion dealing with the Word of Wisdom, we asked if they smoked. Maximo said he did. We explained that smoking was prohibited for anyone wanting to be baptized and be a member of the Church.

"Then I just quit!" Maximo said triumphantly.

We were amazed by their childlike faith. They believed everything we taught them. Sure, they had questions and some pretty bizarre views of the world, but we painstakingly attempted to answer every question by using the scriptures and the Spirit, then we would share our testimonies. Then they'd nod in agreement.

"If you guys say so, it must be so," they'd say.

Before we left, we gave them copies of the Book of Mormon and they acted like we had just given them the keys to a Mercedes-Benz. Then they asked, "When can we get baptized?"

"It depends on you," Elder Hanshaw said. "Read those chapters we assigned you and we'll come back tomorrow."

As we walked home, we wondered what we should do. Could two guys like that change their lives in just a few days?

We weren't sure. We decided we had better seek President McPherson's counsel.

Elder Hanshaw called first thing that morning. He explained the situation and the concerns we had. These two young men wanted to get baptized, but they were leaving in five days. Was it enough time for them to join the Church? Then he added that these two were even willing to quit their jobs to get baptized.

"Well," President McPherson said after listening to everything, "what do you think should be done? What is the Spirit telling you?"

That wasn't the answer we were hoping for.

"We feel they should be baptized," Elder Hanshaw said.

"Then follow the Spirit," the President said. "If they receive all the discussions, commit to live the gospel, pass a baptismal interview and attend church on Sunday, I don't see why they can't be baptized. They don't need to quit their jobs, though I'm sure the Lord is very pleased with the desires of their hearts."

We told Sixto and Maximo the good news and they were thrilled.

"If you do everything we ask, you can be baptized on Sunday," I said. "But there's a lot of work to do. Are you willing to prepare for your baptism?"

"Absolutely," they said.

We spent the next few days preparing them for baptism. We taught them all of the discussions twice. We had them read the first 50 pages of the Book of Mormon. They read another 50 pages on their own. Maria helped them and answered more of their questions when we weren't there.

The zone leader came to La Chispa on Saturday for their baptismal interviews. He felt good about them getting baptized, too. It was hard to believe that we were finally going to have some success, after three months of struggles in La Chispa. Finally we were going to baptize two men, yet they would be leaving right after their baptisms.

We told Sixto and Maximo they needed to attend sacrament meeting Sunday morning before their baptisms. We explained there was a baptismal font the next town over and we could take the bus there in about 35 minutes.

They looked a little disappointed. "We were hoping to be baptized outside, you know, like Jesus was," Sixto said.

"Where do you have in mind?" I asked.

"The ocean."

"Yeah," Sixto said, beaming. "In the ocean."

Elder Hanshaw and I looked at each other. "That can be arranged," we said simultaneously.

The bus that would take them to the North was scheduled to leave early in the afternoon. There would be just enough time to baptize them and confirm them members of the Church before they would have to go back to their jobs.

Sunday morning was resplendent, not a cloud in the sky. Sixto and Maximo showed up at our little church with several relatives and friends, including Maria. We broke a branch attendance record that day. The relatives were skeptical, but they said that they would support Sixto and Maximo.

Even Hermana Raquel showed up that day, on her own.

Elder Hanshaw and I bore our testimonies during sacrament meeting about the truthfulness of the gospel. President Ramos announced at the close of the meeting that we would witness two baptisms in the ocean, located a few hundred yards from the church.

Elder Hanshaw suggested that I perform the baptisms and I wasn't going to turn down that opportunity. It had been a few months since I had performed a baptism. Sixto, Maximo and I took turns going into the bathroom and changing into our white clothes. Then the group of us—about 35 in all—made our way to the beach. You can imagine what the beach looked like in a resort town, on a sunny Sunday in the middle of summer. You can imagine the looks we got, particularly myself, Sixto and Maximo dressed in white shirts and white pants, walking on the beach toward the water. There were people barbecuing, playing volleyball. There were people scantily clad, sunbathing, listening to loud music. Yet they all seemed to stop what they were doing. I certainly felt the weight of all the stares on me with two long-haired Chileans marching toward the beach, not to mention a few dozen people dressed in church clothes trailing behind.

"Look at those three men dressed in white!" I kept hearing as we passed. "What are they doing?"

Initially, I was worried. After all, baptism is a sacred ordinance and I didn't want this to turn into a public spectacle or some circus sideshow. So I said a silent prayer in hopes of receiving some divine help.

There was a pool of water formed naturally by some large rocks. Elder Hanshaw and I had scouted it out the night before and it looked like it was a perfect makeshift baptismal font. However, on that day it was filled with kids playing. Well, I marched over there and said, as humbly and kindly as I could, "Excuse me, kids, would you mind getting out for a couple of minutes? We have two baptisms to take care of. It won't take long, I promise. Thank you."

In an instant, the kids got out of the water. Never in my life had anyone taken orders from me like that. All eyes were fixed on me.

I entered the water—it was comfortably warm—and motioned for Sixto. He followed me in and held onto my arm as I raised my arm to the square. Maybe it was just me, but I swear the whole beach went silent. I couldn't hear a thing. As far as I was concerned, it was just me and Sixto.

After uttering the baptismal prayer, I baptized him and when he emerged from the water, he embraced me. There were a few claps from some onlookers. Then I baptized Maximo. There was another smattering of applause. A handful of people came up to Elder Hanshaw and me and asked what we were doing.

"If we stay," Elder Hanshaw joked, "maybe we'd baptize one hundred people today."

We hurried back to the church where Sixto, Maximo, and I changed back into our clothes. Elder Hanshaw performed the confirmations. Using powerful language, he blessed them that they would be faithful members of the Church. We spoke with the group of relatives who had accompanied Sixto and Maximo, and I think they were impressed by what they had witnessed. Maria couldn't have been happier.

"Remember to read the Book of Mormon every day," we

counseled them. "And when you get a chance to get to a town with a church, be sure and go."

"We will," they said.

We said our goodbyes and we watched Sixto and Maximo, each with a copy of the Book of Mormon in hand, go to the bus stop with their families.

Elder Hanshaw and I knew we'd never see them again. Despite the marvelous experience we had baptizing them, I started to doubt a little. Just a week earlier, these two non-conformists had no idea what Mormonism was. Now, they were official members of the Church. They were going up to the mines with hardened men who cursed, drank, and chased women. They would have many temptations and trials ahead of them as they tried to live the gospel of Jesus Christ. Did they have a chance? We prayed that they would.

When we returned home, we went straight to our room and offered up a prayer of gratitude. It was He who had effected that miracle. It was He who had helped us reach our goal of two baptisms.

That night, while we were writing our weekly letters to President McPherson and trying to set another goal for baptisms, there was a knock on the Ramos' door. It was Hermana Raquel. We welcomed her inside.

"When you did those baptisms today, I realized that I should be baptized, too," she said. "The Lord sent you to me. I have read the entire Book of Mormon. I told Cesar that I'm not going to his church again. I was wondering if I could get baptized."

"Yes," I said. "How about next weekend?"

"I would like that very much," she said. "By the way, my family wants to listen to your message. Would that be possible?"

"I think we can squeeze that into our schedule," I said.

Hermana Raquel was the beloved, respected matriarch of a large family, which turned out to be a nice fringe benefit.

She also requested that she be baptized in the ocean. The next weekend, we held another baptismal service, although we did it in the early evening in order to avoid most of the beachcombers. Still, we had another big crowd of onlookers—almost all were Hermana Raquel's relatives. They all told us they wanted to be baptized, too.

Our problem was trying to figure out how to meet with all of them at once—there were 24 in all. So we divided it up into shifts, teaching groups of about four at a time. Hermana Raquel was so thrilled to be a member of the Church, she stayed all day long with us and she ended every discussion by bearing her testimony. Her relatives, in turn, invited their friends to listen to us, too.

For the most part, our days of knocking doors in La Chispa were over. Instead of going to the people, the people came to us. Plus, we were able to save time, too, since our bikes still hadn't arrived. We enjoyed teaching this way, since over the previous three months, we had knocked on every door in La Chispa twice. We were sure that Ammon would have been proud.

We noticed a few people from Cesar's church who listened to the discussions and they, too, were baptized. The more bad things Cesar said about us, the more people, it seemed, came to listen to our message.

We kept extremely busy teaching, all without leaving the confines of the little church. Sister Ramos would bring us lunch every day, including *leche con platano* and avocado sandwiches.

After a couple of months suffering through a drought, the Lord's blessings poured down on us like a torrential rainstorm.

Without warning one Sunday, Hermana Diaz's husband, Eduardo, showed up at church with her. He was a little more cordial than he was during our first meeting. But we could tell he was still leery. "I just want to see what my wife is getting herself involved in," he told us. "If I don't like it, she doesn't come back."

Hermano Diaz sat with his wife and son on the back row, and I could tell he felt uncomfortable. "There's a future bishop," Elder Hanshaw joked with me.

"What are the odds that Hermano Diaz will get baptized?" I asked.

"I don't know," Elder Hanshaw said. "About the same odds that I'll win the Heisman Trophy. But you've gotta have faith."

A couple of days later, while Elder Hanshaw and I were playing catch, one of his passes drilled my extended left thumb. As soon as it hit, I knew it was broken. I didn't say anything for a while, though, because we had just started.

"Hey," Gunnar finally called out to me, "why are you catching passes one-handed? Trying to show off?"

Then he walked closer and discovered that my thumb had swollen up to the size of a dill pickle.

"Did I do that?" he said. "Elder, I'm sorry. We've got to get you to a doctor."

Yeah, it was broken. When word of that reached President McPherson, he banned playing with footballs altogether. We gave our ball to President Ramos' kids to play with.

"What's wrong with this ball?" little Eddie asked. "It's shaped funny. It looks like an elephant sat on it."

That night, after we had written our letters to the president, I lay in my bunk, staring at the ceiling. "You're going to play when you get home, right?" I asked Elder Hanshaw.

"No way," he said. "It's been so long since I've played. I'm ready to move on with my life. I can survive without football."

"I know you can survive without football. But don't you miss the game?"

"Not enough to play again. The doctors told me I'm susceptible to another shoulder injury. I don't want to live the rest of my life as a cripple. It's not worth it. All I want to think about these last couple of months is the Lord's work."

The Lord continued to bless us. We saw many souls enter the waters of baptism, though I don't want to say how many because I don't want it to sound like I'm boasting or anything. It was the Lord who blessed us and He deserves all the credit. He listened to, and answered, our many prayers. He led the pure of heart to us. Suddenly, around the mission, everyone wanted to be transferred to La Chispa. Everyone who just weeks earlier thought that it was a baptismal wasteland suddenly believed it was a baptismal wonderland.

President Ramos was happy, but this sudden growth concerned him, too. I couldn't blame him. He was responsible for all of these people, and he was having trouble just learning their names. Our average Sacrament Meeting attendance was upwards of 50. It was standing room only in a cramped, broiling hot room. We needed another upgrade.

President Ramos told his stake leaders about this plight and they told him to keep the house for a place to have weekly activities. For sacrament meetings, they said we could meet at the nearest church, about a 30-minute bus ride away. Members of the branch collected money every week and rented a bus that carried us there. Everyone prayed that someday La Chispa would have its own chapel.

One family we baptized was extremely poor. The mother worked at nights and her six children fended for themselves most of the time. The father was gone for months at a time—he worked in the coal mines up north—so maybe they looked up to Elder Hanshaw and me. The kids—ranging in age from 15 to four—were a joy to be around. They listened to our messages while chickens roamed around on the dirt floor in the one-room home. They asked us a million questions about our families and about the United States. They asked when our birthdays were. When we gave them something as simple as a pamphlet, they would hold on to it tightly like it was a Christmas present and keep it under their pillows.

One night when the kids were asleep we asked the mother about her husband. She said he would send part of his paycheck to her in order to buy essentials for the children. Many times, the kids went hungry. Once they were baptized we felt bad we couldn't spend as much time with them.

We stopped by one day to check up on them and one of the girls told us we needed to return the next Sunday because their grand-mother wanted to hear the discussions. "You have to come," the girl insisted. "It's very important."

We committed to be there.

Well, every day after that she reminded us, telling us how her grandmother had to listen to the discussions. At church on Sunday, she asked again, "You are coming to our house this afternoon, aren't you?"

"We are," we said. The children seemed so excited that we would be coming over. Their grandmother, we thought, must really want to hear the discussions.

After eating lunch, we headed over to the family's house and knocked on their door.

"Come in!" all the kids yelled in unison.

We opened the door and saw their humble little shack festooned with balloons and streamers. The kids and the mom wore festive hats. The table, which usually had scraps of bread on it, was filled with a cake and a variety of pastries and treats.

"Happy birthday, Elder Hanshaw!" they yelled. He was turning 21 that day. I hadn't even remembered it was his birthday.

Elder Hanshaw smiled, but at the same time, his heart sank. This family was so poor. Elder Hanshaw didn't feel worthy of such a sacrifice. He could barely speak. They must have spent two weeks' worth of food money on him.

"We surprised you, didn't we?" one of the young boys said, grinning.

"Yes, you did," Elder Hanshaw said. "I don't know how to thank you. You shouldn't have done all of this."

"You're far away from your family on your birthday," replied the eldest daughter. "You're like a member of our family."

Elder Hanshaw sheepishly blew out the candles on his cake and felt guilty about all the expense and trouble the family had gone through. Still, to see the smiles on those kids faces, to see it make them so happy to make Elder Hanshaw happy on his birthday made it a special moment. That day, that impoverished family taught us a lesson about love that was more powerful than anything we had ever taught them.

While eating cake, Elder Hanshaw said, "So, where is your grandmother?"

All the kids laughed. "She lives in Puenta Arenas," one of them said. "We tricked you!"

Elder Hanshaw got down on all fours and allowed the younger children to ride around on his back. "The kids have never been so happy," the mother told me.

We were there for a couple of hours, then told the family we had to leave because we had other appointments.

"Please don't go," they pleaded. "Please stay."

"We're sorry," Elder Hanshaw said, "but we have other people we must visit."

All of the younger kids jumped on Elder Hanshaw's legs and arms and shoulders. The youngest one clung tightly to his shoes.

"Leave the Elder alone," the mother said. "They need to go now."

A few of them started to cry. We promised them we would come back in a few days.

We had a seven o'clock appointment with a recently baptized family, but we had no idea what time it was. The band on my watch had broken, so I didn't have it with me. One of the kids had borrowed Elder Hanshaw's watch and he never did get it back. We saw a man walking down the other side of the street. "Excuse me," I said. "Could you tell me the time?"

He looked frazzled and in a hurry. But he stopped and stared at his watch. Then he started tapping it with his finger.

"This was just working a minute ago," he said in frustration. "I don't know what's wrong with it."

Then he looked up at us. "I've seen you guys around. Are you the Mormons?"

"Yes, we are," I said.

"I've heard a lot about you. You're the ones who teach that alcohol is bad for you, right?"

"Yeah, among other things," I said. "Would you like to hear more?"

"I'm in a hurry."

"Can we set up an appointment with you?"

"No," he said. "It's now or never. I'll listen for a few minutes."

The three of us sat down on the street corner.

The man's name was Carlos, and he had some of his own ideas about deity. He had read the Bible a couple of times. We gave him his own copy of the Book of Mormon. When we finished that first discussion with a prayer, he looked down at his watch. "That's funny," he said, "my watch is working again."

For the second discussion we met on the same street corner. He had read the Book of Mormon all the way through Mosiah. He had a million questions and we tried to answer them all. When we taught him about the Word of Wisdom, he started spouting scientific research about the health benefits of wine and scriptures in the Bible about Jesus drinking wine. We explained again that the Prophet Joseph Smith had received a revelation concerning the Lord's code of health.

At that point, he stood up and walked away from us.

It took us two weeks to track Carlos down. Acting on a tip, we found him at a local tavern, drinking a cheap Chilean beer. We were worried about avoiding the appearance of evil—believe me, word of the Mormons going to a bar spread around La Chispa—but we figured we had a soul to save.

Carlos was inebriated and he became quite angry when he saw us. When he passed out on the floor, we carried him to our makeshift church. We asked President Ramos if he could stay there until he sobered up. President Ramos trusted us implicitly. When Carlos was back to normal, he apologized and begged us for help. "The day I met you two," he said, "I was on my way to the tavern. After I heard your beautiful message, I vowed not to touch a drop of alcohol again. But I realized that would be impossible. I want to be baptized with all my heart, but I know I can't unless I quit drinking. I can't do it. I thought, why resist? I can't quit."

"Yes, you can," Elder Hanshaw said. "The Lord will help you. So will we."

Now, Elder Hanshaw and I didn't know anything about Alcoholics Anonymous or the 12 steps to quitting or anything like that. We did, however, know something about faith and the Lord's power and His ability to work miracles.

"How badly do you want to quit?" Elder Hanshaw asked.

"I'll do anything," Carlos replied.

"I have an idea. Elder Brady, you and I are going to fast for 48 hours and ask the Lord to take away the desire to drink from you. Are you willing to do that?"

"You mean I can't eat or drink *anything* for two whole days?" Carlos asked.

"It's only 48 hours," Gunnar said with a smile.

"You two would do this for me?"

"Absolutely," Gunnar and I chorused.

He agreed to do it.

When we closed our fast, we each knelt down in the church. We were so weak we were shaking. Each of us prayed, beginning with Elder Hanshaw and me. We poured out our souls for several minutes each. When it was Carlos' turn, he closed his eyes and was quiet for a long time. "Heavenly Father," he said humbly, "Thank you for sending these two disciples to me..."

Just after ending his prayer, he stood up and announced, "Elders, I have no desire to drink again."

During a span of a few weeks, Carlos made a remarkable change, particularly as a husband and father. He didn't have any money for a suit, so since he was roughly my size, I gave him one of mine. He wore it to church proudly. We met his wife, Carmen, and their two young children. Carmen readily accepted the gospel when we taught her. When they got baptized, he hadn't touched a drop in weeks. Whenever he felt the urge to drink, he would find us and hang out with us. His enthusiasm for the gospel was infectious, and he wanted to share his joy with everyone he saw. He often accompanied us during our discussions and while riding buses, he'd stand up and start telling the Joseph Smith story and quoting Book of Mormon passages. He found a job he loved at a wood shop as a carpenter. President Ramos also put him to work. Carlos served as a home-teacher, visiting all of the members of the ward, sharing gospel messages. Several less-active members who wouldn't listen to us listened to him. He made the entire branch stronger. Soon he received the priesthood and President Ramos called him as a counselor. Finally, the La Chispa Branch had another strong priesthood holder. How could we ever doubt the Lord's ability to work miracles?

CHAPTER TWELVE

By the first part of March, there seemed to be a mass exodus out of La Chispa. Stores closed down and houses were boarded up again for the winter. It once again became a quiet town.

It was hard to believe, but Elder Hanshaw and I had been together five months. We were both scheduled to go home in a month. When that news got around the branch, people said they were saddened. Some said they were heartbroken. Imagine that. Five months earlier, nobody wanted to give us the time of day.

Of course, not everybody was going to be sad to see us leave. Cesar Supulveda, for one. We were walking past his church one day and saw him standing out front. We greeted him, and he greeted us back. "Someday," he said smugly, "you will discover the errors of your ways. I will pray for your souls."

Fat chance, I thought.

Anyway, we kept too busy to be "trunky." But every once in a while, usually while we lay in our beds, Elder Hanshaw and I talked about what it would be like to go home. We were looking forward to returning to the United States where we could watch a ballgame and order a pizza. On the other hand, we knew we would be returning to a much different life. For the first time, Elder Hanshaw would have to deal with his dad not being around.

That final month together was bittersweet. I knew once we returned home, we'd have to move on with our lives and we wouldn't be together anymore. He was the best friend I had ever had.

We attended our last mission conference in Viña del Mar and during President McPherson's talk, he told a story about two young men who were attending a ward in the northern part of the mission. He was there to interview them to receive the Melchizedek Priesthood.

"They were fine young men with strong testimonies," President McPherson said. "I asked them when and how they joined the Church and they told me they were in the town of La Chispa during the summer before they returned to working in the mines in northern Chile. They said they believed the words of the missionaries and were baptized in the ocean. They left right after their baptism on a bus with only their copies of The Book of Mormon. They spent a week there before quitting and finding jobs in La Serena, where they went out of their way to serve the Lord and His Church. Their names are Sixto and Maximo, and they were taught and baptized by Elders Brady and Hanshaw."

At that moment, I finally understood what Ammon must have felt when he said his heart was brim with joy.

After the meeting, the missionaries who were serving in that ward in La Serena presented Elder Hanshaw and me with pictures of Sixto and Maximo. I didn't even recognize them. They had short hair. They were wearing white shirts and ties. Their whole countenances shone with the light of Christ. As if I didn't realize it before, I was convinced at that moment that this wasn't my work or President McPherson's work. It was the Lord's work. It was another miracle.

Heading into our final week in La Chispa, we received a delivery from the mission office. Wouldn't you know it? They finally sent us bikes. At that point, all we could do was laugh. We knew the missionaries who would be replacing us would enjoy them.

We figured we had better visit the poor family that had thrown a party for Elder Hanshaw. We must have knocked on the door for five minutes before it creaked open slightly. The mother asked what we wanted. We were surprised by her cold reception. It took us a while, but we persuaded her to let us in. When she did, we noticed her face was bruised and cut.

"Hermana!" Elder Hanshaw said. "What happened?"

"My husband returned last night," she said solemnly. "He had been drinking and he was angry."

"About what?"

"Everything," she said. "I'm just glad he didn't hurt the children."

Elder Hanshaw and I were experiencing some very un-Christ-like feelings. We wanted to tear the guy apart. He had already gone back to work and we were going to leave soon, for good. There was nothing we could do, except pray and hope that Heavenly Father would protect that sweet family.

Before we knew it, our last Sunday in Chile arrived. We were scheduled to fly out on Tuesday night and everybody in the branch reminded us of that fact. Everyone was acting so sad, as if we were going to die or something. I guess to them, we were. We gave them our home addresses and told them if they wrote us, we'd write back.

While we were getting ready that morning, Hermana Diaz showed up at the Ramos' house. "Elders," she said breathlessly, "my husband wants to talk to you as soon as possible."

"What's going on?" I asked.

"He found out you two are going home in a few days and I think he wants you to bless our son."

I guess all those times we visited the Diaz's home, while he listened from the kitchen, those messages sank in. More than that, though, I think Hermana Diaz taught him the gospel through her example.

During the bus ride to the church, all of the members sang church hymns and cried. "We're going to miss you, Elders," they kept saying.

Prior to the sacrament, Elder Hanshaw blessed the Diaz's child. The sacrament meeting program featured two speakers: Elder Hanshaw and me. When it was our turn to speak, we bore our testimonies and encouraged the members of the branch to continue working hard to build up the Lord's kingdom in La Chispa. There were plenty of tears shed in that meeting. As I scanned the congregation, every person felt like a brother or sister to me. Indeed, in the eternal scheme of things, I knew they were. Knowing I'd probably never see them again in this life was painful. The closing hymn was "God Be With You 'Til We Meet Again." We sang all the verses and halfway through Elder Hanshaw and I were bawling. After the meeting, the members lined up to shake our hands and give us hugs.

Those last couple of days were a whirlwind of activity. We continued to teach discussions, we packed up, and we gave the missionaries who had arrived to replace us a little orientation. We felt sorry for them. Not to brag, but we were pretty popular in La Chispa.

Elder Hanshaw and I learned that the branch had planned a surprise farewell party for us at the church. So many people showed up that we actually had to have the party outside. People brought plates of food and they performed skits. They presented us with small gifts to remember them by. A part of me didn't want to leave them. But the biggest surprise of all came when Hermano Diaz asked to talk to us privately.

"Elders," he said, "I was wrong about you and your Church. The blessing you gave my son on Sunday touched me deeply. It made me want to be the best man, and father, I can be. I've never felt that way before. I would very much like to be baptized."

We called the other missionaries to come over for the baptismal interview and at sunset the entire branch stood on the beach. Dressed in white, Elder Hanshaw and Hermano Diaz stepped into the water. Hermana Diaz held her baby in her right arm and gripped my arm with her left hand. I couldn't have envisioned a better way to spend our final hours in La Chispa. After Hermano Diaz was confirmed a member of the Church, he thanked Elder Hanshaw and me and promised he would dedicate his life to serving the Lord. Then he presented Elder Hanshaw with a painting he had done of him being baptized in the ocean by Elder Hanshaw.

At 10 p.m. we announced that we needed to pack and get ready to leave. We formed a large circle around a campfire on the beach and we sang hymns. Then, it was more hugs and goodbyes. That was tougher in many ways than saying goodbye to my family before my mission because I knew we'd never see these people again. Hermana Raquel told us she would pray for both of us every day.

The Ramos family got up early the next morning and ate breakfast with us. We caught a cab, filled the trunk with our suitcases, and we left La Chispa. President Ramos thanked us for our months of faithful service. I had an empty feeling inside—a feeling I never thought I would have when I arrived there six months earlier. I never dreamed that I could love the Chilean people as much as I did.

Right after Elder Hanshaw and I boarded the bus and found our seats, we looked out the window.

"It's Carlos," I said. He was standing there, tears streaming down his cheeks. We got up and asked the driver to wait a *momentito.* "I will never forget you," he said. "I hope you will never forget me."

Then he presented us each with wooden rolling pins, mounted on small oak stands. He inscribed messages to us. It must have taken him hours and hours to create them. To me he wrote, "Elder Brady, Thank you dear friend for teaching us this beautiful gospel. Thank you for making us participants of the many blessings and joy that my family and I have received by being members of the Church. I will always pray to Our Heavenly Father that your life will be filled with blessings and happiness. With love, Carlos and family."

After thanking him and exchanging hugs, we boarded the bus again. As we drove away, Carlos remained there, watching us go. I remember feeling at that moment that if the only reason for my mission was to meet and teach Carlos, it would have been worth it. I thought of the scripture in Alma 29:10: *"And behold, when I see many of my brethren truly penitent, and coming to the Lord their God, then is my soul filled with joy; then do I remember what the Lord has done for me, yea, even that he hath heard my prayer; yea, then do I remember his merciful arm which he extended towards me."*

I remembered something he had told me after I baptized him. "I know we have been friends forever," he said. "I feel a special bond with you. From the first time I met you, you seemed familiar to me. That's why I decided to listen to your message. I bet that before we came to Earth I made you promise you would find me and teach me the gospel. You have done that, and I'm so grateful."

I imagined our next reunion taking place in the Celestial Kingdom.

We arrived at the mission home and had our exit interviews with President McPherson. "Elders," he said to Elder Hanshaw and me, "what you have done in La Chispa is truly remarkable. With the help of the Lord, you have performed miracles in that place and you will both be blessed the rest of your days because of your dedicated service."

Later on, Elder Hanshaw and I boarded our long flight to Atlanta. We sat next to each other, but we were both so tired from lack of sleep the previous week, we didn't talk much.

As we made our descent into Atlanta, we realized this was it. He would be getting on a connecting flight to Los Angeles and I would be heading to Salt Lake City.

Elder Hanshaw was planning to find a job for the summer. His mom had enrolled him at El Camino College in Southern California for fall semester. My mom had enrolled me at Snow Junior College in Ephraim, Utah. We wished we could go to school together, but we realized it wasn't possible.

"You've got to promise to stay in touch," Elder Hanshaw said as we hugged each other in the terminal in Atlanta.

"Yeah," I said, "and you'll have to keep me updated on your football career."

"I know a couple of the coaches at El Camino. I'll give them a call when I get back and see what happens."

"You'd better," I said. "And I'm coming to the first game you play in."

CHAPTER THIRTEEN

For the first time since arriving at the MTC, I was alone, without a companion. And though I was 21 years old and had just spent two years living in a foreign country, I was as scared as a five-year-old on his first day of kindergarten. I missed everyone in La Chispa. I couldn't stop thinking about the image of Carlos standing at that bus stop, crying.

Never in my life had I felt so nervous. I couldn't even eat the meal on the flight from Atlanta to Salt Lake City. There was a sense of satisfaction, that I had worked hard during those two years. Simultaneously, there was a sense of panic. I tried to conjure up those powerful, comforting feelings I had experienced on that little hill in La Chispa.

The man sitting on the next aisle was reading *Baseball Weekly* magazine and I had never heard of the player who graced the cover. It was surreal. In one way, I was so glad to be back on United States soil. In another, I was terrified. My whole life I had planned to serve a mission—no questions asked. I knew a mission was what the Lord expected of me. Now what?

Before my mission, I decided to put all of my energies after high school graduation to working and earning money. I didn't want to be bothered with things like going to college and dating or thinking about post-mission life. I never could have imagined myself as a returned missionary. At that moment, sitting on that plane, I couldn't comprehend what lay before me—college, responsibilities, dating—eternal marriage. I was excited to see my friends and family again, but I knew that they wouldn't be the same.

No wonder I was on the brink of hyperventilating. My stomach was doing summersaults.

"Are you okay?" the woman sitting next to me asked. "I notice you're not eating your meal."

"I'm not real hungry," I said.

"Mind if I have your meatloaf?"

"Go right ahead."

She scraped it off my plate and onto hers.

"You seem nervous," she said as she shoveled mashed potatoes into her mouth.

"Do I?" I said, feeling self-conscious. "I guess it's because I've been out of the country for two years."

"That's a long time," she said, scarfing down my meatloaf. "Where have you been?"

"Chile."

"Chile?" she said excitedly. "I'm from Santiago. I moved to Canada about 10 years ago. I'm returning after visiting my family."

"I was in the Viña del Mar area."

"That's a beautiful place. So where's your family?"

"They're at home in Salt Lake City."

"You mean, you were by yourself, in Chile, for two years?"

"That's right."

"Your parents let you go? You look so young."

"I'm sure I'll grow out of it, ma'am."

"What were you doing? Study abroad? Peace corps?"

"A mission—for The Church of Jesus Christ of Latter-day Saints."

"Never heard of that church. I'm a Catholic."

"You probably know us as 'Mormons.'"

"Oh, yes, Mormons," the woman said. "You're the ones who have those pretty churches and talk about family values. Why do they call you Mormons, anyway?"

I pulled out a spare copy of the Book of Mormon and started telling her all about it while she ate my airline meal. If nothing else, it took my mind off of my uncertain future. I wrote a dedication inside the book, encouraging her to read it and to test Moroni's promise, then I signed it. The woman, named Marta, seemed genuinely grateful for it. How ironic was that? I taught my final discussion, while hovering over the Salt Lake Valley, to a Chilean.

When I emerged from the gateway at the airport I was greeted by my family, who did their best to humiliate me with signs and balloons. I know they meant well. Everyone looked so much older. I had three more nieces and nephews than I had when I left. It was strange. Especially when the little guys started asking what the adults didn't dare: "Uncle Preston, what happened to your voice?"

"What do you mean?"

"Why do you talk so weird? You sound like Speedy Gonzalez."

"Don't you like my Spanish accent?" I playfully asked.

"No," they said flatly.

My dad hugged me. "Welcome home, son. I am so proud of you."

On the way home, my parents informed me that I was supposed to speak in sacrament meeting in three days. When we got home, I walked into the house I grew up in and it seemed enormous. I guess spending two years in little huts would do that. We were not wealthy by American standards, but by Chilean standards, we were downright opulent. Things that I had taken for granted all those years while growing up—hot showers, a refrigerator stocked with food, cars in the garage—meant a lot more to me. I felt a little guilty for having so many material possessions.

Mom told me I could have whatever I wanted for dinner. She made a mean lasagna, but I also asked her to pick up some bananas and avocados at the store. I introduced my family to the wonder of *leche con platano* and avocado sandwiches. Let's just say there was plenty left over for me to eat.

"No wonder you look like you lost weight on your mission," Mom said.

Before friends and family came over to see me, the stake president released me from my mission over the phone. Instantly I felt a mantle of responsibility removed from me. It left me feeling a little empty. Plus, I was exhausted from all the travel. My mom had a doctor's appointment for me early the next morning.

"Mom, I feel perfectly fine," I said when she told me about it.

"Maybe so, but you've been living in South America for two years. You may have picked up a tapeworm or something. We need to get you checked to make sure."

I went to the doctor, who was in our ward, and he asked me a few questions about my mission. He did a brief examination, then he asked, "Now, why are you here? Are you feeling sick at all?"

"No," I answered. "I feel great."

The doctor smiled. "Go home and tell your mom you're in tip-top shape."

If nothing else, that put Mom at ease.

Dad was happy to have me home, but he didn't wait long to question me about my future.

"Do you have any idea what you want to study at Snow?"

"No, Dad," I said. I wasn't even sure if college was for me, though I didn't dare tell him that.

"Preston, it's time to buckle down and get serious," he said. "I'm willing to help you any way I can."

"I don't know if I can afford tuition and books and rent," I said.

Dad excused himself and went into his den and returned with a checkbook.

"I wasn't asking for money," I said.

"I know you weren't," Dad said. Then he sat down next to me. "I want to show you something. Since you graduated from high school, your mom and I and your brothers have been saving money to help you through college. We helped your brothers, and they wanted to return the favor by helping you."

He showed me a bank account in my name. It had enough money to pay for tuition, books and rent for one year. I didn't know what to say. At that point, I realized I had to go to college—in Ephraim. There was no turning back.

On Sunday I entered the church and all sorts of people came up to me to welcome me home. I went to Sunday School a little late and everyone was already seated in their chairs. Instinctively, I shook the hand of everyone in the room, as was customary in Chile. They each looked at me like I had just fallen off of the turnip truck. It was just so strange to be dressed in a suit and yet not be a missionary anymore.

I took the stand along with my Mom and Dad for sacrament meeting. I sat down and began nervously tapping my foot. I wasn't sure I could put three sentences together in English. Then, in the back of the chapel I saw Elder Hanshaw. Our eyes met and we both smiled like jack-o-lanterns. Next to him was his mother. He had called my parents without me knowing to find out when my talk was. His home-coming talk wasn't for another week, so he and his mom decided to drive all night from California to come to mine. I had to start getting used to calling him Gunnar, which wasn't easy at first.

Well, even though I could barely speak coherent English, I survived the homecoming experience. I told about Carlos' amazing conversion story—his broken watch, his bout with alcoholism, his calling in the branch presidency—which I think kept the congregation's attention for a while. The best part was talking to Elder Hanshaw, er, I mean, Gunnar, again. He said he was starting summer classes at El Camino the next week. The football coach remembered him in high school and was going to let him walk-on.

"I know if I don't at least give it a try," he explained, "I'll never hear the end of it from you."

Gunnar and I talked on the phone once a week throughout the summer. My parents had bought a new car while I was on my mission, so they gave me their old minivan. It certainly wasn't going to impress the girls, but I wasn't going to complain. I got a job doing landscaping for the summer and most of that went to pay my long distance phone bill. By September I was driving that minivan to Ephraim to start fall semester and a full load of freshman classes at Snow College.

That next year was one of the most difficult of my life. I had spent the previous two years serving the Lord and trying to serve everyone but myself. All of the sudden, I had to focus on me and some serious issues—my career, my future. I didn't know what I should major in. I knew I needed to find a wife and get married. It all seemed too overwhelming. On top of that, I had nothing at all in common with my roommates. I tried to befriend them, but these weren't guys I wanted to hang out with. They were nothing like Gunnar.

We continued talking on the phone as often as possible. He ended up earning a spot as the third-string quarterback and the coach told him to redshirt. That is, he could practice but not play. Just being back from a mission, it was a good idea.

School at Snow College was fine. After paying for tuition, books, and rent, I realized I'd better find a part-time job. I was hired at a little hamburger-and-milk shake joint in Ephraim. It was the local greasy spoon, the hangout for college kids. It got depressing, though, seeing all of these guys bringing their dates while I was scrubbing the griddle and dumping the garbage. My heart wasn't in it, but it paid the bills. I was lonelier than one sock. My life seemed totally up in the air. Instead of having one goal in my life—teaching the gospel— I had all sorts of things to worry about. A part of me longed to be back in the mission field, where everything was structured and everything was black and white as far as what I was supposed to be doing. Besides, in La Chispa, I was popular and admired. In Ephraim I was just another college kid trying to make ends meet. Sometimes I wished I could be called as a permanent missionary, then I wouldn't have to worry about purse or script.

As I battled my feelings, I wondered where all the blessings were for my two years of hard work. I couldn't help but think about my mission and those people I had left behind in Chile, especially Carlos. I wondered about them, I prayed for them. Every once in a while, I'd receive letters from the people and I'd write them back. Carlos sounded so happy because the missionaries let him perform his first baptism. A part of me wished I was there to watch it.

One day while on campus that fall, I passed by the Snow football team's practice field. The Badgers were doing drills and I stayed and watched for nearly an hour. Naturally, I thought of Gunnar and the time he broke my thumb in Chile. Then it hit me—maybe I could be involved, somehow, with the football team. Not as a player—I had long since abandoned that dream. Certainly I could contribute *something*.

I waited until after practice, until the head coach, Jim Hershey, was alone. I introduced myself and asked if there was anything I could do to help the team.

"What do you have in mind?" he asked.

"Anything. I'm a hard worker."

He told me to come back the next morning and he would introduce me to the equipment manager. "If we have anything to do around here, he'll know," Coach Hershey said.

The team manager could hardly believe I was volunteering for this line of work. Then he realized it would cut down on his work load, so he started treating me really nice. He assigned me tasks like washing jock straps, picking up tape from the locker room floor, and fetching new equipment when something broke. It wasn't glamorous, but I felt like I was part of the team in a small way. I felt like I was serving people again. It felt good. Being the assistant equipment manager didn't pay a dime, but I felt fulfilled. Plus, I got to be on the sidelines during the home games. I called Gunnar and told about this little arrangement and he laughed. "I'm actually a player on the team and I have to do some of the same stuff you do," he said.

I could tell Gunnar was having a tough time, too, adjusting to life without his dad. Then he told me, "I really don't see any point in continuing football. I think I should just focus on school, get my degree, and figure out what I want to do with my life. When I run, I feel like I'm running in buckets of sand. I am so many years removed from serious conditioning. I don't think I'll ever get that back. It's so hard to go out for two years preaching love and peace, then pick up a helmet and play a violent sport."

Well, you know me. I begged him to stick with it. In the meantime, I tried to devise a speech that would convince him not to give up on football.

Not to boast, but I went the extra mile when it came to the Snow football team. I never complained and I always showed up early and stayed late. If nothing else, I think I earned the respect of the coaches and the players. Whenever someone needed some gum, I was there with a pack of Juicy Fruit. It got to the point where I felt comfortable enough telling Coach Hershey about a friend of mine, a former missionary companion from California, he should look at.

"Son," he said, "if I had a nickel for every time I heard that, I'd be retired right now."

After football season ended, winter hit Ephraim hard. It snowed like crazy and since I had nothing better to do, I spent a lot of time in the library studying. I got the best grades of my life that semester, though I still didn't have a clue as to what to major in.

When school let out that spring, I talked to Coach Hershey again.

I tried to describe the way Gunnar threw the ball. I told him about the colleges that were after him before his injury in high school.

"I can't make any promises," Coach said. "I don't have any more scholarships. If he wants to enroll at Snow and walk-on, then I promise I'll give him a good look once he gets here."

Excitedly, I called Gunnar and I asked him about how preparations for the next football season were going.

"They're not," he said.

"What?"

"I'm quitting football. It just isn't important to me anymore. I gave it a shot. I think it's time to move on. It's been several months and I'm still out of shape. It's just not the same anymore. It's not fun. I don't have the passion anymore. I'm surrounded by a bunch of 18-year-old kids just out of high school. I feel so old, like I don't belong. That's one of the things the mission field taught me—there's so much more to life than sports. I want to fall in love, get married, and have a family. I can't wait to have a son I can play catch with in the backyard, like I did with my dad. I can't imagine anything better than that."

Well, I wasn't about to let him give up that easily.

"Why don't you transfer to Snow? I've talked to Coach Hershey. Our quarterback here just finished his eligibility and he'll be transferring to Northern Arizona next season. I'm sure Coach would appreciate getting a new quarterback. You're a lot better than any of these guys here."

Long pause.

"What about you?" he asked, turning the tables on me. "After a year of college, do you know what you're going to do for the rest of your life?"

Long pause.

"No, not really," I said.

"Maybe you should worry more about that rather than about me."

"Are you kidding? All I do is worry. Look, Coach Hershey is really excited to meet you." Okay, maybe I exaggerated the truth.

"Really?" he said.

"Yeah."

Gunnar took a deep breath. "I don't know if I can leave my mom alone again."

He had a point.

"I'll talk to her," he said, "and let you know."

The following day, Gunnar called. "My mom said she thinks it might be good if I give Snow College a try," he said. "She said she would miss me, but that she survived without me for two years. She said I had to do what was best for me and that she'd support me fully. She said I should keep trying to play football."

"So you're coming!"

"Under one condition," he said. "Since you think you know what I should do about my future, I'd like to give you a suggestion."

"This ought to be good," I said.

"You've got a real talent for helping people. And you know as much about medical terminology as anyone. I can see you being a doctor someday."

My first reaction was to laugh.

"I'm not joking," Gunnar said. "You should look into that."

I was flabbergasted. Nobody had ever said that to me before and the thought of becoming a doctor had never entered my mind. Medical school was for smart guys, not for me. It was beyond my wildest imaginations. I remembered that in high school I took a career aptitude test and after it had been evaluated, my guidance counselor suggested that maybe I could be a shoe salesman.

"Hey, guidance counselor," I said to Gunnar, "did you practice a lot last fall without your helmet or something?"

"Like I said, I'm serious about this," he said.

I was 22 now, and I knew I needed to start thinking about the future. But a doctor?

"Do you know how many more years of schooling that is?" I asked. "I'll be in my 30s by the time I get done. Do you realize how old that is? Besides, I have good penmanship. My handwriting is too legible to be a doctor."

Gunnar laughed. "You remind me of a few of the doctors I've known and you'd have a great bedside manner. You might want to sign up for some chemistry and biology classes next semester."

Ugh. I never did like science.

"This is the deal," he continued. "If I come up to Utah and play football at Snow, then you have to take pre-med classes."

I couldn't believe he was doing this to me. "Okay," I said.

The good news was we were about to be companions, er, roommates again.

CHAPTER FOURTEEN

Gunnar and I worked all summer so we could save money. I continued slinging hash at the burger joint in Ephraim and taking summer classes while Gunnar worked construction in California. In late July, I picked him up at the Salt Lake International Airport and we traveled the hundred miles south to the beautiful metropolis that is Ephraim.

We went to our off-campus apartment first so he could drop off his possessions, then we went straight over to campus to register him for fall classes. After that, I figured I'd better introduce him to Coach Hershey. I could tell Coach wasn't exactly impressed when he saw Gunnar and I enter the football office. After all, Gunnar didn't look anything like the Hall-of-Fame quarterback that I had described to him. Coach was sitting in the lobby, wearing his patented sweatsuit (I think it might have been one of the only articles of clothing he owned), shooting the bull with his secretary and the defensive coordinator, Coach Simmons.

"Coach Hershey," I said, "I'd like you to meet Gunnar Hanshaw, your next starting quarterback."

Coach Hershey raised his eyebrows. Gunnar smiled weakly. He wasn't cocky like that, so I figured I should be on his behalf. The two shook hands.

"If you ever go pro," Coach Hershey said to Gunnar, "I'd hire this guy to be your agent. Remind me again where you were last season."

"El Camino Junior College," he said. "I got off my mission a little over a year ago, so I was pretty rusty last year. I've been working hard to get back in shape and appreciate this opportunity to be here."

"We're happy to have you, but I want to stress that we just don't have any scholarships left. You don't have a problem walking-on, right?"

"Coach, I just want to play football and get an education."

I could tell Coach liked that answer. He had me assign him a locker, get him his equipment and assign him a number. He saw what was available and picked No. 22.

"Why 22?" I asked.

"It's symmetrical," he replied.

We had time on our hands since classes didn't start for a month. Fall camp didn't start for a couple of weeks, so we spent most of our time in the weight room (I had my own key). It came as no surprise to me, but Gunnar was fanatical when it came to the weight room. We got up at 5 a.m., ran a few miles, ate a semi-healthy, semi-edible breakfast at the campus cafeteria, then it was off to the practice field to play catch in the blistering August sun. Essentially, we did the same stuff we did when we were in La Chispa, except this time I taped my fingers and wore receivers' gloves for protection.

Man, he had a pretty spiral, even prettier than I had remembered. Gunnar never said as much, but I could tell he thrived in this situation, having to prove himself. He started to get that passion for the game back. I knew he could be Snow College's starting quarterback that fall and I think he knew it, too.

When it got too hot to throw, by about noon, we'd go to the weight room and I'd spot for him. One afternoon, while he was glazed in sweat after a rigorous workout, in walked Danny Wallace, Snow's starting quarterback. He had redshirted as a freshman after shattering nearly every Idaho high school passing record. Coach Hershey had publicly named him as the frontrunner to succeed the departing Rick Patchell.

"That's him," I whispered nonchalantly.

"Who?" Gunnar asked.

"Danny Wallace. Your competition."

"I'd better introduce myself, then," Gunner said. Then he confidently strode toward him and offered his hand.

"I'm Gunnar Hanshaw," he said.

Wallace smiled smugly and nodded. "I've never heard of you. You a walk-on?"

"Yeah."

"What position do you play?"

"Quarterback."

Wallace's smile disappeared. "Good luck," he said in a condescending manner, then walked away.

Fall camp began with a less-than-stirring pep talk from Coach (the Win-One-For-The-Gipper thing was not his strong suit, but then again, what could you say after a 2-9 season?) and team photos. All the walk-ons convened in one area, as if they were segregated from the rest of the team like second-class citizens.

I had so much confidence in Gunnar that the scene just made me chuckle to myself as I filled the Gatorade containers. Snow College didn't even know what it had. I just couldn't wait to see him do his thing.

After stretching and calisthenics, Coach Hershey had all the newcomers run sprints and do some agility drills. Gunnar ran a 4.6 in the 40-yard dash and he pretty much whipped everyone in the broad jump and long jump.

"Maybe we could move Hanshaw to safety or cornerback," I heard one of the coaches say. I wanted to tell him that such a move would be a huge mistake.

Later, the coaches had the players congregate by position and Coach Hershey put Gunnar with the quarterbacks. There were five quarterbacks on the roster and three of them were on scholarship. The pecking order was determined quickly as Gunnar took his place at the back of the line for a throwing drill. Wallace was strutting around like he owned the campus. He was 20 years old with slicked-back hair and sideburns that extended way past his ears. He reminded me of a lot of kids I knew in high school, like he was the coolest thing on the planet. The year before, he and his buddies would buy a couple of six-packs of beer and go up the canyon and party it up. That was against team rules, but, then again, Wallace thought rules were meant to be broken.

Speaking of broken, the only thing I hoped Gunnar would break were passing records. Even though I had never seen him play in a game, I just knew he would be a star.

So what happened on the star's first drill? He took the snap, dropped back, slipped on the grass and fell as he threw a wounded duck into the ground about 10 yards short of his intended receiver. Right in front of Coach, the offensive coordinator and the quarterbacks coach. "Brady!" the quarterbacks coach shouted at me. "Get this guy some better shoes, for crying out loud!"

"No need, coach," Gunnar replied as he picked himself up. "My fault. I just slipped. Sorry."

I made such a fuss about Gunnar, that I guess my reputation was on the line a little bit, too. I worried in vain, though, because Gunnar made up for his miscue rather quickly. On his next turn, he took the snap, took a three-step drop and drilled his receiver on an out pattern right in the gut, knocking the poor guy backwards. A few minutes later, I pretended to be picking up trash on the sidelines so I could eavesdrop on the quarterbacks coach, Coach Robinson, talking to Coach Hershey.

"That walk-on ain't half-bad," he said. "He's got some potential. He's better than most of our scholarship guys."

But during a seven-on-seven scrimmage, Gunnar never had the chance to fasten his chinstrap. He sat there and watched while three scholarship guys took turns taking snaps.

After practice, I tried not to buddy up to Gunnar too much. I had plenty of work to do. Besides, I figured it wasn't cool if everyone knew his best friend was one of the equipment managers. In team settings I kept my distance.

As we walked back to our apartment together, I told him what I overheard Coach Robinson had said. "So why didn't they let you scrimmage?" I asked.

"That's team politics for you," is all he said. "I'll get my chance."

When he did he made the most of it. The next practice Gunnar threw perfect strikes again and again. Of course, Wallace and some of the others quickly pointed out that it was against the third-string defense, many of whom were also walk-ons, but I could tell Wallace was getting nervous, as well he should have been.

As fall camp progressed, Gunnar gradually worked his way up the depth chart. A couple of days before the season-opener at home against Mesa Community College, Coach released the depth chart and Gunnar was the backup, behind Wallace.

Maybe because he felt threatened, Wallace ignored Gunnar. The other quarterbacks genuinely liked Gunnar and so did the other guys on the team. Though he was a walk-on, he was a leader on the practice field, encouraging his teammates, offering his insights, and dispensing advice when asked.

The coaches loved him, too. They liked the fact that he was "mature," having been on a mission. I overheard Coach Hershey talking to Coach Robinson one day in the football office (I was taking out the trash and they didn't notice me) that Gunnar had a photographic memory when it came to football. They'd show him film of a play and he was able to tell what all eleven players did right or wrong. He knew where every receiver should be.

On his nightstand in our apartment he had his quadruple combination and his playbook. Sometimes he studied both deep into the night. Once school started, his nightstand was filled with other books not so enthusiastically read, but he managed to make time for schoolwork along with everything else. We enrolled in LDS institute and we took history and English classes together.

Oftentimes, just like when we were on our missions, we'd stay up late just talking about things. On the eve of the season-opener, all I wanted to talk about was football, but Gunnar reaffirmed his belief that I would make a great doctor someday. I was taking some freshman science classes that fall, but they were tough for me. Never in my life did I spend so much time studying. Gunnar was living up to part of our deal, so I tried my best to live up to mine.

CHAPTER FIFTEEN

Snow won the season-opener, 17-13. Wallace played okay and Gunnar never left the sidelines. I was more disappointed than he was about that, I think.

As rosy as things seemed after that game, the victory masked a number of problems on the team from what I could tell. It wasn't very unified, and I think a lot of that had to do with Wallace. All he seemed to care about was his personal stats. When Snow lost its next three games, he was more perturbed that coaches wouldn't let him throw the ball more. The atmosphere was a little tense already, before Wallace did something really stupid.

During the bye week, when Gunnar and I went to Salt Lake for General Conference, Wallace threw a big beer bash at his apartment. He got himself arrested for underage drinking and disturbing the peace. The police report said he was dangling out of the third-story window in nothing but boxer shorts, yelling obscenities to no one in particular. He spent a night in the county jail.

Coach was furious. He called him into his office the next Monday and suspended him for three games. When I told Gunnar the news about Wallace, he didn't say much. He never was one to rejoice in another's misfortune, even when it benefited him. That afternoon, Coach called Gunnar into his office for a closed-door meeting. When he walked out, he was the new starting quarterback for the next game. Coach told Gunnar that this was a fresh start for the team and that he wanted him to become the team leader.

That week, Gunnar, a 22-year-old freshman, acted awfully loose for a guy who hadn't played—let alone started—a football game since his junior year in high school. It had been five long years.

Only trouble was, the game was to be played in Arizona and the team only took one equipment manager. I was never allowed to go, but I had promised Gunnar I would see his first game. I was racking my brain trying to think of ways I could scrape together enough money to pay for gas, hotel and food. But I was on an extremely tight budget. Besides, the tires on my car were almost threadbare and I knew they wouldn't get me to Cedar City, let alone Arizona.

"What would you think if I asked Coach to go with you guys?" I asked Gunnar.

"It would be worth asking," he said.

"Maybe you could put in a few good words for me."

"Sure," he said.

"After all, I'm the one that discovered you, right?" I joked.

"That's what you keep telling me."

So after mustering all my courage, I marched to Coach's office on Wednesday. I spent the entire morning preparing my arguments in my mind as though I was an attorney about to argue a case before the Supreme Court. I had all sorts of stories to tell, like the times when we played catch in South America. I was ready to resort to shedding tears, if necessary.

Coach's secretary told me he was free for a couple of minutes. The door was half-open and I knocked. He removed his glasses and welcomed me inside. "What can I do for you, Brady?"

"Coach," I began, "you know that I am really grateful to be part of this football program. I have really tried to work as hard as I can around here. Now, since the day you brought me aboard, I haven't asked for much, but I want to ask you for a huge favor. Gunnar is like a brother to me. If possible, I'd like to go with the team to this weekend's game. I'd be willing to ride in the luggage bay. Heck, you can tie me to the top of the bus. I promise I won't eat anything. You won't have to spend a dime on a hotel room for me. I'll sleep on the bus. I'll ..."

Coach began laughing. I thought that was cruel to mock my sincere pleadings.

"Did I say something funny?" I asked.

"He didn't tell you, did he?"

"Did who not tell me what?"

"The other day during my meeting with Hanshaw, within thirty seconds after I told him that he was our starter, he begged me to let you come to the game. He said you two were a package deal. Since

89

you were our most successful recruiter during the off-season, I told him yes."

"You did?"

"I can't believe Hanshaw didn't tell you."

That was just Gunnar. I pumped my fist and shook Coach's hand. "Thank you so much," I said.

"We've got a seat on the bus for you, so you don't have to worry about being a hood ornament. I've got a hotel room for you, too. You'll be sharing with Kurt (the head equipment manager). Now get back to work."

When I caught up to Gunnar at practice, a part of me wanted to slug him and a part of me wanted to hug him. Neither seemed appropriate.

"Why didn't you tell me Coach was letting me go this weekend?"

"I thought it would be more enjoyable for you to hear it from him," he said with an impish grin.

"Thanks," I said.

"It wouldn't be the same without you," he said as he pulled on his helmet and trotted out to the practice field. "Besides, you promised me that when I played in my first game, you'd be there. Remember?"

We took the long bus ride to Arizona Western. The day before, Gunnar and I had received a letter with a La Chispa postmark, forwarded from my parents' home. It was from Carlos. He told us that he had just returned from Santiago where he had been sealed to his wife and two young children. "I wish you could have been there. But while we were there, kneeling at the altar together," he wrote, "we thought of both of you. It was like you were there with us." He also told us he was the Young Men's president in the La Chispa Branch. I was amazed that there were enough young people attending church to have a Young Men's president.

Late that night we arrived at the hotel. Most of the players complained about how dumpy the place was, but compared to some places I lived in Chile, it wasn't bad. We unpacked and went straight to bed. The next morning the team ate breakfast at Denny's and held a brief meeting and a practice at the stadium. The coaches made us spend the rest of the day in study hall. That night, we had another team meeting.

Game day arrived, and I talked a little to Gunnar. He seemed so calm, like he wasn't nervous at all. I felt enough nervousness for the both of us.

Snow won the coin flip and deferred until the second half. The Badger defense gave up three first downs before forcing a punt. The punt was fumbled, though, and Arizona Western recovered. It seemed like it was taking an eternity for Gunnar to make his collegiate debut. Two plays later, Snow had fallen behind, 7-0.

For Gunnar it was a fitting place to start.

He took over at the 20-yard line. He worked out of the shotgun on first down and completed a slant pass to another walk-on, Jimmy Wardcraft, for a first down. Next play, he lined up under center, dropped back and danced around in the pocket for a few seconds. Then he tucked the ball and ran for 46 yards, the longest play from scrimmage all year for Snow.

On first down from the twenty-one, Gunnar rolled right, stopped, and threw across his body to the back of the end zone. Wardcraft hauled it in over his left shoulder and got both feet down before stumbling out of bounds. Touchdown.

"Somebody get this guy a scholarship!" I heard Coach Hershey yell.

Gunnar sprinted into the end zone so fast that he got there in time to help Wardcraft off the ground. Gunner slapped him on the helmet and the rest of the team staged an impromptu group hug.

For the first time all year, the team had unity. It was like an entirely different team, thanks to Gunnar. After returning to the sideline, he huddled the defense together and told them to get a stop, that he knew they could do it.

What do you know? They did.

On Snow's next offensive series, Gunnar drove the team eighty yards, again, for another touchdown—this time on a bullet pass in the heart of the end zone to the tight end, Gary Whiting. Gunnar raised both arms in the air, signaling another touchdown. A star was born. Just as I had predicted.

As I watched the scene unfold, it was as if I didn't recognize this Gunnar Hanshaw. He seemed much different from the laid-back, fun-loving guy I knew on my mission. On the football field, he was a maniac.

By the time he finished for the afternoon, midway through the third quarter, Snow had a 49-7 lead and Gunnar had thrown for 450 yards and seven touchdowns. Not a shabby debut. I think Wallace knew he'd never be the starting quarterback at Snow College again. So he quit the team and withdrew from school.

The team was happy, not only because it had won and halted its losing streak, but also because it was such a blowout, everybody who traveled got to play at least half the game. The bus trip back home went fast. At one point, Coach, being a superstitious man like a lot of coaches, came up to me and said I was invited on the rest of the road trips as long as we kept winning.

Turned out, we didn't lose again the rest of the season. Unfortunately, those three early losses cost us a shot at a bowl game. But Gunnar was named second-team all-conference and freshman of the year. He finished No. 8 in the nation in total offense and passing despite playing in four fewer games than all the other junior college quarterbacks in the country. Most importantly, at the end of the semester, Gunnar received a scholarship.

In spite of all his success, Gunnar was still quite anonymous on campus. He liked blending in, being a face in the crowd. But he started getting a lot of attention—not from the student body but from college coaches. Division I college coaches. One day he received about 20 pieces of recruiting mail from schools all over the place—BYU, Washington State, Oregon, Texas Tech, Northwestern, Kansas State. Coaches from those schools congratulated him on his spectacular season and told him they'd be in touch throughout his sophomore season.

They weren't kidding. He received so much mail from college recruiters that the school gave him his own P.O. box. The secretary had a big box for his mail. He'd walk out of there with armloads of letters, postcards, and media guides. I got more excited about it than he did, I think. A letter signed by Joe Paterno! That was cool.

Gunnar didn't want to get his hopes up only to be let down. One day in the spring I convinced him to compile a top ten "wish list" of schools to attend. At that point, BYU was No. 1 because he knew darn well that UCLA rarely, if ever, recruited junior college quarterbacks. BYU probably wasn't his best bet, because I knew the Cougars had about five quarterbacks in the program and three more on missions. I had to admit that didn't seem like the best fit for him.

That next season, Gunnar didn't participate much in spring drills. Coaches were afraid he'd get injured, so mostly he watched a lot of film and helped the backup quarterbacks develop. In the summer, he and I got a job on campus doing landscaping chores—planting flowers, mowing lawns, pulling weeds. It didn't pay real well, but it was enough to help entertain us on the weekends.

One Friday night we went to a movie in Ephraim and it occurred to us that something was wrong. As we looked around the theatre, we realized we were the only two without dates. Every other guy in there had a girl on his arm.

"I like you and all," Gunnar said, "but I think we could do better. We're pretty pathetic."

Though I had been back from my mission nearly two years, I couldn't imagine myself being on a date, let alone married, or being a father. There was only one way to achieve those goals—and it wasn't by going to movies with Gunnar. I remember wishing that the Church would present you with the perfect girl upon your honorable release from missionary service. No such luck.

Gunnar knew my apprehensions about dating and he tried calming my nerves. "It's just like missionary work when you think about it," he said. "You start by finding, then you follow that commitment pattern. You build a relationship of trust, you invite, then if she's the right one, you commit her. You've done that a million times."

"Yeah," I said, "but not with the future mother of my children."

We decided we'd better get started. Gunnar hadn't dated much since his mission, either. He was still a little skittish after that infamous "Dear John" letter on his mission. Anyway, we decided to set a goal for ourselves. We would go out on a date the next Saturday night—a little over a week away. What we were going to do we had no idea. We thought we'd get dates first then worry about that later. Finding a date was no trouble for Gunnar. He asked out a blonde, the ward Relief Society president, by simply calling her. She immediately said yes. After Gunnar hung up the phone, I swear I heard her shriek with joy from her apartment across the way.

As for me, well, I decided to be a little more creative than a phone call. I was no good on the phone. Come to think of it, I wasn't much better face-to-face, either. For some inexplicable reason, I was a little afraid of girls. Maybe it had to do with the fact I never grew up with sisters, so I didn't understand them. Whatever the reason, it puzzled me that on my mission I could walk up to anybody and start a conversation. But back home, the thought of talking to a girl and asking her out petrified me. Maybe it was because as a missionary, I was representing the Church and I had total confidence. After my mission, I was representing myself. So why couldn't that confidence with girls transfer over?

I fretted for a couple of days before I took the ward directory and began going through the list of prospects. There were a couple of girls I thought were attractive, but I had no idea what they thought of me. My top choice was the gospel doctrine teacher. She was pretty and probably dated a lot. I purchased a box of donuts and wrote a brief note on it: "I 'donut' know what you've got going next Saturday, but it would mean a 'hole' lot if you'd go out with me."

I was nothing if not clever.

I placed the box on the doorstep on Friday afternoon with her name attached to the note, and got out of there post haste. Then I waited for a reply. I didn't tell Gunnar what I had done, just in case it didn't work out. Friday and Saturday passed with no response and Gunnar kept asking me if I had asked someone yet. Sunday morning, I had a pit in my stomach and I didn't even want to go to church, particularly gospel doctrine class.

When we arrived at church, as fate would have it, she and her roommates arrived at the same time. I held the door open for them, in fact, and she smiled at me briefly and said hello, but that's it. I wondered what was up with that girl. She didn't even have the decency to call me. She was making me suffer. Either that or she was completely blowing me off.

By the time we got to gospel doctrine class, I was feeling mad, hurt and rejected. I would have preferred her calling me and saying, "I wouldn't go out with you in your wildest dreams."

After an opening prayer, she took her place in front of the class. "Before we start this morning," she began, "I have some personal business I want to take care of first. I received a box of donuts this week ..."

As soon as she said that, my heart briefly stopped beating.

"...It was a really cute thing, with a cute note attached and an invitation. The only problem is, it wasn't signed. I don't know who it's from."

I wanted to just die right there and then. How could I have been so careless?

"Does anyone know who those are from?" she continued. "I'm really curious."

I figured I had better raise my hand. The eyes of everyone in the room were on me. I'm sure I turned several various shades of colors, from amber to maroon to scarlet.

"Thank you so much," she said in my general direction, with a surprised look on her face. "I'm sorry," she said, "but I can't remember your name."

At that point I longed to be back in one of Cesar Sepulveda's meetings in Chile. I thought she would at least recognize me. We had had a couple of conversations at ward parties and apparently I made quite an impression on her.

"Preston Brady," I said.

"Oh yeah, Preston. Well, I'd really love to go, but I'm going to visit my Grandmother on Saturday. Sorry. But thanks for the donuts. That was a really cute idea."

"Thanks," I said, sweating profusely.

I wanted to change wards immediately. Everyone felt sorry for me, I think, and tried not to make eye contact with me. "This is something you can tell your grandkids about and laugh," Gunnar said to me with a smile.

"You're presuming that I'll someday have grandkids," I replied. "I've got to find a date first."

The good thing that came out of it, though, was after the class, a girl came up to me and said, "I think that was so cute what you did. I hope I'm not being too forward, but if you need a date for Saturday, I'm available. Your roommate, Gunnar, asked out my roommate."

Sounded good to me.

She wasn't a real pretty girl, but I said yes. At least if our dates were friends, it might make things more comfortable.

For the date, Gunnar and I went to a fast food restaurant and bought chicken, potatoes, biscuits and drinks. We took the girls up to a picnic spot in the canyon. Things went smoothly, at first. After eating, we took a stroll along a creek. I felt at ease, until we heard a loud grunting noise behind us. It was a large moose, foaming at the mouth. Apparently we were in his territory and he seemed perturbed. Before we knew it, the massive animal began charging us at a rapid pace. Gunnar and I grabbed our dates' hands—that was a first for me, let alone on a first date—though it wasn't like it was a romantic moment in my life because we were running for our lives toward my car. We sped out of there.

With our picnic plans ruined, we went to an ice cream parlor in Ephraim. We were having a pretty good time. They asked how long we had known each other. We explained how we were missionary companions. When they asked where we served, we proudly answered, "Chile."

"You probably had a lot of baptisms," my date said.

"Well, the people there are really humble, and they've been prepared to receive the gospel," I said.

"Yeah," Gunnar's date said, rolling her eyes, "but don't most of them get baptized then never go back again?"

I didn't like the direction this conversation was going.

Gunnar tried to be nice. "The Church is relatively young in Chile," he explained. "There are some who fall away, sure, but there are a lot of strong members there."

"I think a lot of missionaries just care about statistics, not people," the girl said.

At that moment, I had lost my appetite. "You know what?" Gunnar said, looking at his watch. "We really need to get going. We've got to, um, do our laundry."

So we left four half-eaten banana splits on the table and took the girls home.

That was the end of our dating experiences for a while.

CHAPTER SIXTEEN

That summer we took a few classes so that we could graduate with an associate's degree in December. We spent an inordinate amount of time in the library studying. After work and school, we'd head over to the practice field and throw the football around. He ran me ragged, running all sorts of pass patterns, but at least I got some exercise. He also worked out with those teammates that stuck around for the summer.

I realized that if Gunnar continued to play like he did as a freshman, he would have a great shot at earning a scholarship with a Division I school. His sophomore season would be like an extended audition. If he played well, he could wind up in the big-time. If he didn't, his career likely would be over. He did his best to downplay the whole idea.

"If it happens, it happens," he'd say. "I just need to stay healthy and things will work out."

I took it upon myself to ensure that Gunnar was well taken care of during the summer. We never ate fast food. We bought a lot of fruits and vegetables, especially bananas and avocados so we could drink *leche con platano* and eat avocado sandwiches. Instead of watching David Letterman at night, we broke down film of the previous year's games.

Toward the end of the summer, I met a girl named Crystal at a stake dance. It was a '70s themed dance and she was dressed appropriately. Someone presented her with a sash that said "*Miss 1976*." At one point, the DJ played a slow Bee Gees song and Crystal asked me to dance. That was the first time a girl had ever asked me to dance. When the song finished we talked briefly. "You have a great smile," she said. Before I knew it, she was writing down her phone number for me.

Though I later learned Crystal was only 19, Gunnar encouraged me to pursue her. A week later, I kissed her for the first time. In fact, it was the first time I had ever kissed a girl. She became my first girl-friend. Dating was a whole new world for me, but I enjoyed it.

By September everybody in town was excited for the season to start. Signs went up in store windows, wishing the Badgers luck and some talked openly about a junior college national championship. A friendly reporter from the *Deseret News* came down and wrote a nice feature story on Gunnar.

When fall camp began, coaches protected him like he was the last spotted owl in the world. He wore a red jersey during practices, and no one was allowed to lay a finger on him.

In the season-opener, Gunnar led touchdown drives on Snow's first six possessions. At halftime, the Badgers were up 42-0 and he had nearly 300 yards passing and 150 rushing. That was pretty much the story of the season. Gunnar never played a full game on account of the lopsided scores. Still, he led the nation in passing and total offense.

The backup quarterbacks on the team were almost in awe of him.

"Hey, Gunnar," one said the next week after a practice, "I'd like to pick your brain sometime."

"But if you pick my brain," Gunnar joked, "it will never heal."

He spent countless hours after practice working with the other quarterbacks, poring over the playbook and game film with them.

Meanwhile, interest from Division I schools shot up significantly as the season wore on. He had pieces of mail from, by my count, 75 schools, including some back East. Occasionally he'd get phone calls from coaches out of the blue. One time, when Gunnar wasn't home, I had a five-minute conversation with Joe Paterno.

By late October, Snow had a 7-0 record and was ranked No. 3 in the nation. Gunnar not only led the junior colleges in passing, he was in the top 10 in rushing as well. He was skilled at breaking tackles and staying upright, crediting his balance to his surfing days. He didn't go down after being hit once—opposing defenders quickly learned they had to wrap up on him.

The Badgers were busy preparing for the Big Game against No. 1 ranked Dixie State College, the archrivals from St. George.

Not only was it important in determining the conference title, it also had national title and in-state rivalry implications.

With a number of major college assistant coaches in attendance, Gunnar had a terrible game. By his own admission, he stunk. He threw three interceptions and fumbled once. Dixie won, 21-17. Gunnar was heartsick, knowing his chance at a national championship was blown. Unfortunately, several schools lost interest in him that day and stopped recruiting him. Some coaches were impressed with his lustrous stats, but when they saw him play, they felt he was too small to play on the Division I level. Though he struggled against Dixie, he bounced back and played well the rest of the season, including a victory in a bowl game.

The one coach whose interest in Gunnar never lessened was Arizona State offensive coordinator Dan Guthrie. In his early 40s, he was considered an up-and-coming coach. ASU had the top-rated offense in the nation that season. Coach Guthrie even came to visit one evening at our apartment and he was well-prepared. I have to give him credit for doing his homework. He wasn't a Mormon, but he knew a lot about the Church. He asked about Gunnar's mission and told him about the great institute program at Arizona State. He even quoted statistics about how many Mormon students attended the school and mentioned the names of prominent LDS athletes who had gone to ASU. And, of course, he praised Gunnar up and down about how impressed he was with who he was as a player and as a person.

"Do you practice on Sundays?" Gunnar asked him.

"No," Coach Guthrie said. "That's a day of rest. Players need a day off after a football game on Saturday."

Gunnar was sold. He told Coach Guthrie he didn't believe in playing, or practicing, on Sundays.

When he came home from his recruiting visit to Tempe, he was on cloud nine. Gunnar met with the head coach, who offered him a scholarship. Instead of accepting the offer, he calmly thanked him and told him he would think about it. The coaches told him that was fine. "I need to pray about this and make sure this is the right thing," he told me.

Other scholarship offers had come from a variety of schools—

Oregon State, San Diego State, Stanford, Marshall, Montana, Utah and Northwestern. But ASU rose to the top of Gunnar's list because he liked Coach Guthrie a lot. He seemed like an honest, straight-shooting guy. Gunnar liked that. He wasn't pushy. He didn't bash other schools, or other coaches, to build up himself, like many did. He didn't promise him that he would start, like some did, but said he would have a chance to compete for the starting job. Gunnar didn't want anything handed to him. Still, he studied ASU's roster and their quarterback was a senior, meaning the job would be up for grabs. Not since his spectacular junior season in high school did he dream he'd have the chance to play in the Pac-10 Conference. But that chance was suddenly staring him in the face.

As for me, I continued dating Crystal that fall. We went to movies and on long drives up the canyon. Sometimes I felt bad that I was leaving Gunnar behind so much, since he didn't really date. He mostly focused on football and school work. Things were going pretty well between Crystal and me.

Once when we were eating at a restaurant, she asked me what my plans were after graduating from Snow. I told her I didn't have a clue.

"You could work at the Norbest Turkey factory here in the valley like my Dad," Crystal said. "Maybe I could talk to him about getting you on there."

I just gave her a blank stare. I tried to imagine myself married to her, working in the turkey industry. The only time I wanted to be around a turkey was Thanksgiving.

"You know," I said, "I probably won't stay in Ephraim when I'm finished with school. It's a nice town and all. I don't know what it is I'll do, but I don't see myself doing it here."

She looked at me like I was the rudest person on the face of the earth. I thought she was going to stab me in the heart with a butter knife. Even though I bought her a chocolate milk shake for dessert, she didn't speak to me the rest of the night. I took her home and as she was getting out of the car she said, "I don't think we should see each other anymore."

Crystal was the first girl I ever really liked. I thought I was falling in love with her. So over the next couple of weeks I was lonely.

During Thanksgiving break, I knew I had to get out of Ephraim. Gunnar and I went to Gunnar's house in southern California. While we drove, we talked non-stop.

"Is it over between you two?" Gunnar asked. "Or do you want to get back together?"

"I want to. I miss her," I said. "But I think she wants to get married and settle down in Ephraim. Why couldn't she just have left things the way they were? Why don't girls come with instruction manuals?"

"Wouldn't do any good," Gunnar said. "Every one of them is different."

"What do you think about Crystal?"

"She's a sweet spirit," he said.

"Seriously."

"Seriously? She's pretty, she's smart. You couldn't go wrong with her. I hope it works out for you two."

"What about you? Are you going to Arizona State?"

"It would be nice to play in the Pac-10," he said. "I could get used to being a Sun Devil, even though I always rooted against them as a kid. How about you?"

I had already figured out the drive time from Ephraim to Tempe. Then again, I didn't know where I would be the following fall. I was so consumed with Gunnar's football career, I barely gave any thought at all to where I would be.

"Yeah, I guess I could become an ASU fan," I answered.

"You don't sound all that excited," Gunnar said.

"I am excited for you," I said. "It's just that I'm sorry we won't be together anymore."

"Does that mean you're not coming with me?" he asked.

"I don't know. I don't know anything right now."

"I guess I always thought I wasn't going to anywhere without you. I always thought we were a package deal. If you end up getting married, I understand."

"Don't base your decision on me. You do what's best for you. Besides, even if I didn't get married, there's no guarantee I'd get into ASU."

"You'd get in. We're graduating in a couple of weeks. Coach Guthrie told me if you come with me, you can help out with the team as an equipment manager."

I had never imagined going to school at ASU, or at any big school, because my high school grades weren't very good. Plus, since I wouldn't be on scholarship, I knew out-of-state tuition would be expensive.

"I've already checked it out," Gunnar said. "ASU has a great premed department. If you're going to be a doctor, you're going to have to get your bachelor's degree and then apply to med school."

We didn't talk about it the rest of the way to Gunnar's house. Thanksgiving Day, Gunnar couldn't wait any longer. He had made up his mind and had to talk to Coach Guthrie. He dialed the number. Coach Guthrie was in the middle of carving his turkey.

"Sorry to call you at home and interrupt your time with your family, but I wanted to let you know I've decided to go to ASU."

Through the telephone receiver, I could hear Coach Guthrie yell with excitement.

If only I could figure out what I should do with my life.

When we returned to Ephraim, I decided I would tell Crystal how I felt about her, hoping that she would want to accompany me to Tempe.

"I'm so glad you called," she said. "I really want to see you."

Wow, I thought. That was easy. Maybe she had missed me as much as I had missed her. Maybe we really were in love. I planned to take her home over Christmas break, then maybe we could have a June wedding at the Manti Temple. In the fall, we could go to ASU. All day long leading up to our date, I planned what I was going to say and how I was going to declare my feelings for her.

Gunnar wished me luck as I headed out the door. I was so nervous I couldn't eat. I picked her up and we drove to a quiet place on campus to talk. After I parked the car and turned to her, she placed her hand on top of mine. It all seemed so romantic, like a storybook.

"Preston," Crystal said, "I have something very important to tell you."

Great! I thought. *Maybe she would reveal her love for me first!*

"When we broke up, I was miserable for days," she said. "But now, I'm as happy as I've ever been in my life. I had a dream where I was getting married in the Manti Temple."

My heart started pounding. Maybe she was about to propose to me, I thought.

"What I have to tell you is very important," she continued. "Preston, I'm getting married in March."

I was about to tell her that March was no good for me, that I'd prefer June.

"I met this guy named Josh last week and we have fallen in love. I hope you'll understand."

"Congratulations," I said unenthusiastically. "That's great. I'm happy for you."

"You have been such a good friend to me. I'm sorry if I've hurt you. I never wanted that to happen." Then she hugged me for the last time. "You're such a good guy. I knew you'd understand. Thank you. Maybe you and Josh can meet sometime. Maybe you can be friends!"

"That's okay," I said. "I've got plenty of friends already."

Crystal laughed. I dropped her off at her apartment, where Josh was waiting for her. I never saw her again.

When I came back to our apartment, Gunnar was studying. "Back so soon?" he asked.

"I crashed and burned," I said.

"Then you need a *leche con platano* to put out the flames," Gunnar replied, heading for the kitchen. We spent about an hour talking and drinking *leche con platanos*. After a while, Gunnar had me laughing and forgetting about what's-her-name.

"How could I be so stupid?" I said. "How could I let a girl do this to me?"

"Well, there is a bright side," Gunnar said. "There's nothing stopping you now from coming with me to Arizona State."

Indeed. I began the process of applying to ASU, hoping I'd be accepted. Gunnar was going to go to Tempe the first of January for the start of winter semester. I knew if I were accepted, tuition would be expensive. I hoped there was enough money in the account to cover it.

One day after classes, I drove home to Salt Lake amid a snowstorm to talk to my Dad. He was surprised, but happy to see me.

"You're going where?" he asked as he brought me a cup of hot chocolate.

"Arizona State," I said.

"That's a good school, but are you going there for you or for Gunnar?" he said. "Preston, you need to think about your future. You can't ride his coattails through life."

"I know," I said. I didn't dare tell him my secret plans about med school. I was afraid he'd laugh.

"There are a lot of members of the Church in Tempe and there's a good institute program," Dad said. "I think going out-of-state will be good for you."

Were my ears deceiving me? Did my Dad actually think I was making a wise decision?

"The trouble is, Dad, I have to pay out-of-state tuition …"

"Now, Preston, you don't worry about that," Dad said. "I want you to focus on your studies. We'll take care of the money. Do you know what you want to major in yet?"

I merely shrugged.

"I want you to know I'm proud of you finishing up at Snow," he said. "That's a good first step. Now you need to buckle down and think about your career. That's one of the most important decisions you'll ever make. Speaking of important decisions, have got your eyes on any special young ladies?"

"No, Dad," I said, "but I'm working on that, too."

While I felt relieved that Dad was happy with my progress, I still felt an enormous burden, like I still wasn't measuring up to the high standards my older brothers had set.

The night after we finished our final exams, Gunnar and I ordered a pizza, made *leche con platanos* and turned on the TV to watch SportsCenter. One of the first things out of the mouth of the commentator at the top of the show was this: "Sources tell ESPN that a news conference will be held at the University of Alabama tomorrow and it is expected that Arizona State offensive coordinator Dan Guthrie will be introduced as the school's next head coach."

We both about choked on our pepperoni and sausage.

Gunnar immediately tried calling Coach Guthrie's home to see if it were true, but hundreds of people must have been doing the same thing, because it was busy for a couple of hours.

"The biggest reason I'm going to ASU is because of Coach Guthrie," Gunnar said. "I don't know what to do."

It was an agonizing night for him. Was his commitment to ASU or to Coach Guthrie? I mean, he did like the Tempe campus, Sun Devil Stadium, and the football program, but would his departure affect his decision? The beginning of national letter-of-intent signing day for junior college players was just 24 hours away. He had already filled out the forms and all that was left was to fax it to the ASU football office.

The following day we had ESPN on from the time we woke up in the morning and we were happy to learn that the network was going to carry the Alabama press conference live. Ten minutes before it began, Coach Guthrie called Gunnar.

"Guess you've heard the news that I'm leaving Arizona State for Alabama," he said.

"Yeah," Gunnar said. "I heard."

"I know this must be confusing for you, but this is a great opportunity for me and my family. I'm here in Tuscaloosa. Can we talk after the press conference?"

"I'd like that."

We sat directly in front of the TV with the sound turned way up. The proceedings began with the athletic director saying something about how this was a landmark day in the history of the University of Alabama football program. (The Crimson Tide were coming off of a very un-Tide-like 4-8 season.) Then he introduced Coach Guthrie, the third coach at Alabama in six years. He beamed as he donned an Alabama cap and talked about his dream coming true. He waxed eloquent and philosophical about the challenges that lie ahead.

There had been major recruiting violations and scandals at Alabama, resulting in NCAA probation. That meant scholarship reductions and no bowl appearances. The sanctions were about to be lifted and Alabama was looking toward Coach Guthrie to right the ship. Coach Guthrie, a no-nonsense guy with good, down-home values, was hired to rescue the program and return it to prominence. He was a devout Methodist, a family man. He vowed integrity, honesty and commitment. He promised to do everything in his power to make the program respectable again, one Bama fans worldwide could be proud of. He didn't promise any national championships or even SEC championships. He didn't promise to beat archrival Auburn. But he did promise to make Bama football entertaining— that the forward pass would be used on a regular basis. "Footballs will fill the sky," he said. His talk of installing a "wide-open offense" at a place that had earned a legendary reputation because of its conservative running game made the locals think he was a little *loco*. The West Coast Offense wasn't something Tide fans believed much in, but Coach Guthrie had a solid track record, having produced an exciting, high-scoring offense everywhere he had been. I wondered what Bear Bryant must be thinking.

After hearing Coach Guthrie's speech about an exciting offense, I knew that he needed a quarterback. One like Gunnar Hanshaw.

When the press conference ended, the ESPN commentators expressed mixed feelings about the hiring. They all agreed that Coach Guthrie was one of the finest up-and-coming coaches on the college football landscape, but they also pointed out this would be his first head coaching job. And what about the intense pressure to succeed? They talked about the fact he wasn't an "Alabama" guy, with no previous ties to the program or to Bear Bryant. Would he be accepted by Bama fans?

"He will be," one commentator said, "if he wins. If he doesn't, he'll be gone quicker than you can say Tuscaloosa."

I wondered how this would all affect Gunnar. Coach Guthrie called back later that day, just as he had promised.

"I'm sorry how this has played out," he said. "I've put you in a bind. When you committed to me, I had no idea Alabama would be making me an offer like this. You've made a verbal commitment to Arizona State and I wouldn't blame you for honoring that. But, at the same time, I feel like we have a good relationship and I'd like you to be my first recruit at the University of Alabama."

Gunnar was quiet for a moment upon hearing another recruiting pitch. "Coach, I'm happy for you and your family," he said, "but I've got to think about it."

"I understand," he said. "This is a big decision for you. Do what you feel is best. When you decide, call me. Just know that I have a scholarship set aside for you here at Alabama."

Gunnar felt he had to hurry and decide, too, because it was crucial for him to enroll in school for winter semester or else he'd be way behind. He prayed long and hard that night for guidance.

The next day on the national letter-of-intent signing day for junior college players, we sat down and I started compiling a list of pros and cons for attending the University of Alabama. Among the pros: it was part of the Southeastern Conference, where football is king. Among the cons: it was part of the Southeastern Conference, where football is king.

On top of that, I wasn't sure that I'd be able to go with him to Alabama.

"Nothing's changed," Gunnar said. "If you don't go, I don't go. I've told that to Coach Guthrie. He told me he could speed up the acceptance process so you could start school with me in January. I told him about your interest in sports medicine and he said if you come, you can be an assistant trainer. How cool is that?"

"Cool," I said.

Still, it was one thing to go to school in Arizona; it was quite another to go to Alabama.

Gunnar spent most of the day in his bedroom with the door shut. I didn't want to bother him. When I returned to our apartment after doing some Christmas shopping, Gunnar emerged from his room.

"Preston, how long of a drive is it from Ephraim to Tuscaloosa?" he asked.

"A few days, if you stop at nights."

"Will your car make it that far?"

"I suppose so … Why? Are we going?"

"Go Bama!" he shouted.

"Roll Tide!" I replied.

I pulled out an Alabama hat that I had found at a sports shop at the mall. "Here's an early Christmas gift," I said, handing it to him. He thanked me, adjusted the brim and placed it on his head.

"How does it look?" he asked.

"Like you were born to wear that hat," I said.

Gunnar called Coach Guthrie and told him he'd accept his scholarship offer—again. Soon after, he faxed a copy of his letter-of-intent to Alabama.

I was excited for Gunnar, and I was excited I would be part of Crimson Tide football. Still, I wasn't sure about going to school in the Deep South. Other than the Miami airport, when I left for and came home from Chile, I'd never been there before. In fact, all I knew about the South came from the *Dukes of Hazzard* reruns.

Gunnar called one of the coaches at Arizona State and apologized profusely, telling him he was headed to Alabama. In a completely unforeseen turn of events, we were going to Tuscaloosa, sight unseen. Just like when we went to La Chispa, we were going on faith.

CHAPTER SEVENTEEN

Someone at the University of Alabama, I think it might have been Coach Guthrie's secretary, called a couple of days later to inform me that I had been accepted for winter semester. Apparently, Coach Guthrie had pulled some strings to push it through quickly. I wasn't sure I would have gotten in that quickly on my own, though I had pretty good grades at Snow. I was even on the honor roll and I wasn't exactly taking basketweaving classes.

The toughest part for me was calling my Dad to let him know my change in plans. I figured he was going to flip out. And I was right.

"*Alabama?*" he said, after he picked himself up off the floor. "Why, of all places, would you go there?"

All of that confidence in me he had before seemed to disappear.

"It's where Gunnar's going. Alabama is one of the most storied football programs of all time."

"That's great for Gunnar, but explain to me how that is going to help you?"

"It's going to be a great experience, I think. They're letting me be part of the football team. I'm going to be an assistant trainer."

"Preston, at some point you need to forget about football. What about dating and getting married? How are you going to find a nice Mormon girl down there?"

"I don't know," I said. "But I have prayed about this and I feel good about it."

Dad knew he had no comeback for that one.

"Mom and I trust your judgment," he said. "You're old enough to make your own decisions."

Since he wasn't much of a sports fan, I knew it was futile to explain that Tuscaloosa was a college football Mecca. I always loved the way the Voice of College Football, Keith Jackson, said "Al-a-*bama.*" Sure, I was thrilled. Alabama. When some people hear that word, they think of that country band. I always thought of college football. Don't most people base their college choice on the school's football program?

In early January, we loaded up my car and began the long drive to Alabama. We traded off driving duties and when it got real late, we pulled over to a rest stop and slept in the car. A few days after we left, we finally arrived. Tuscaloosa is nicknamed the Druid City because of the abundance of large oak trees that populate the area. There were acres of rolling land and plenty of forests and lakes. Though I missed the mountains of Utah, I enjoyed the surroundings.

It was a gray, bitterly cold day. "That humidity goes right through ya," a man said to us when we asked for directions to campus. Then he noticed our license plates. "Utah?" he said. "Y'all are a long ways from home. Y'all lost or sumptin'?"

Yes, we were, so we asked for directions to campus. "Go down yonder a piece and turn left at the Piggly Wiggly. Y'all can't miss it."

"Thanks," we said. I knew I'd have to incorporate y'all into my vocabulary right away.

The people were warm, as nice as can be, though they looked at us funny when we told them where we were from. They wondered what possessed us to go to school in Alabama, especially me, since I looked nothing like a football player. I looked like something that might have fallen out of an offensive lineman's pocket. A few people recognized Gunnar's name from some newspaper articles. I was just his little sidekick, which I didn't mind a bit.

After buying our books and getting familiar with the campus layout, Beau Whittle, a defensive back on the team, introduced himself to us. He wanted to show us some southern hospitality, I suppose. "You Mo'mon boahs want sumpin' to eat?" he asked. "Y'all look 'bout as hongry as starve-gutted dawgs."

I hadn't a clue what Beau (or most of the people, for that matter) was saying. For the first few weeks at Alabama I was wishing, just like I did when I first arrived in Chile, that some of these people came with English subtitles. But I liked the Southern way of talking. Even when someone in Alabama got really mad, it didn't sound that bad because it was quite melodic, even pleasing to the ear.

From what we could gather, Beau was inviting us to lunch.

"Sure," we said.

"I'm just jokin' around with you two," he said. "I don't really talk like that. I was just indoctrinatin' y'all."

We really were hongry as starve-gutted dawgs. Beau took us to a little place called Dreamland Barbecue (folks in the South call it "bobbycue"). It was hidden away, tucked down a back road. From the outside it looked like a pathetic shack with a creaky screen door out front.

This is why they say you shouldn't judge books by their covers. Inside there were autographed photos of famous people, mostly sportscasters, players, and coaches, adorning the walls as well as Alabama football memorabilia. It was the combination of a sports bar and barbecue pit.

There was also a sign that said, "Ain't nothin' like 'em nowhere." We presumed the sign was referring to the ribs. We sat down at a table and a waiter wearing a T-shirt and white apron stood in front of us.

"How many slabs y'all want?" he asked flatly.

"Can I see a menu?" Gunnar asked. The waiter looked at him like he was about to toss him out on his ear.

"No menus here," Beau laughed. "We get ribs here. You don't want nothin' else. Don't even ask about side dishes." Then he looked at the waiter. "We'll have three slabs, please."

Minutes later, while I was staring at all the pictures and memorabilia, the waiter brought us plastic utensils and Styrofoam plates and cups and a new roll of paper towels. Then he gave us a plate with two stacks of white bread and two plastic cups of barbecue sauce. Beau started pouring the sauce on his plate and grabbing a piece of bread. He mopped up the sauce with the bread and scarfed it down like he had been raised by wolves.

"C'mon," Beau said when he saw us watching him. "Dig in! It's gonna be gone in a minute if you don't hurry."

The sauce tasted a little spicy, a little sweet, and a little vinegary. After my first bite, I understood why Beau was eating like that. It was the best sauce I had ever tasted. Then the waiter brought out our slabs. The meat was tender, but not too tender. We went through that entire roll of paper towels during that meal. About halfway through, my lips started to tingle, then burn. Two days later, I could still taste the sauce on my lips. I was never much of a connoisseur of food, but these ribs were unbelievably good. They weren't just finger-lickin' good. They were elbow-lickin' good, too. Sure enough, the place was aptly named. It *was* Dreamland.

We met most of the players that first week. Almost every single one of them made it a point to introduce himself. Most of them were friendly, polite, and kind. They were always saying "Yes, sir" or "No, sir."

A reporter from a Tuscaloosa newspaper interviewed Gunnar and wrote a big story on him. From that day on he lost his anonymity. Everybody recognized him.

On our first day on campus, we walked into the weight room and were amazed. It was spacious, filled with weights and treadmills. Photos of past Alabama greats adorned the walls. Inside his locker, Gunnar taped pictures of his family, including one of him in his high school uniform standing with his dad. He also had a sign with Alma 26:22 on it.

Then a foreboding behemoth of a man lumbered up to Gunnar and introduced himself as E.J. Jefferson. He was 6-foot-6-inches tall and 340 pounds. He looked like he walked off of an NFL Films production. When he wasn't in the weight room, I think he spent his leisure time benchpressing Volvos.

"So you're The Mormon Gunslinger," Jefferson laughed out loud, his gut giggling like a bowl full of Jell-O. *Mormon Gunslinger.* He coined that nickname that day. Nobody knew at the time what he started. "I ain't never seen a quarterback so small," he said.

"I ain't never seen anyone so big," Gunnar replied.

"I ain't never met a Mormon before, neither."

"What do you think so far?" Gunnar asked.

"'Pends on what you can do on the field."

"What position do you play again?" Gunnar joked. He knew exactly who he was. Jefferson didn't know Gunnar was joking, though. He was offended. After all, he had been a second-team All-America selection the previous year and was hoping to be a Lombardi Award candidate the next season.

"Left tackle!" he barked. "And if you ever get into a game, I'm going to be guarding your lilly-white, Mormon backside."

"Well then," Gunnar replied with a smile, "I guess you're my new best friend."

I didn't take that personally.

That night, Gunnar and I took Jefferson to Dreamland, where, in one sitting, I think he ate an entire herd of cows.

Because of that kind gesture, Jefferson became Gunnar's friend for life. For those offensive linemen, it doesn't take much to win them over. Especially if it involves barbecue ribs.

CHAPTER EIGHTEEN

Looking back, we had no idea what we were getting into at Alabama, where the passion for college football is unmatched anywhere. We knew it was a big deal, but we were naïve as to *how* big.

In Tuscaloosa they like to say, "At a lot of places, they just play football. At Alabama, we live it." Truer words have never been spoken. At Alabama, fans pay a large amount of money *just for the right* to buy season tickets. Then they pay a large amount of money on top of that for their tickets. Everything in Tuscaloosa seemed inextricably connected to Alabama football. It was hard to believe I was going to go to school there.

One place Gunnar and I knew we had to visit was the Paul W. Bryant Museum, located on (where else?) Bryant Drive. As expected, everything in this place revolved around Bear Bryant, the legendary coach. It seemed everyone who had any sort of connection with The Bear liked to tell you all about it, even the people whose best friend's wife's second cousin twice removed had been his barber.

Gunnar learned quickly that the key to endearing himself to the folks in Alabama was to show he knew about, and respected the Crimson Tide tradition. So we took a crash course on the subject. We started by touring the Bear Bryant Museum.

Bear Bryant's trademark houndstooth fedora was an honored symbol of Alabama football. The Bear coached at Alabama for 25 seasons, won 232 games, lost 46 and had nine ties. That's a winning percentage of 82 percent. In all, he won 323 college football games (prior to Alabama he had coached at Maryland, Kentucky and Texas A&M). No wonder he cast a long shadow. How many coaches have their own museum?

Of course, we heard a lot of Bear stories that day. He was born to a poor farmer's family in southern Arkansas—the eleventh of twelve children. One day he was with a group of friends who visited a local theater to see a wrestling bear. His friends challenged him to wrestle that bear for a dollar. After a minute or so, the bear removed a muzzle from its mouth and started chewing on Bryant. He flew off the stage, but he earned his nickname.

One of the displays inside the museum was a re-creation of The Bear's office. There was a bronze bust of him and a replicated press box with recordings and highlights of some of the greatest moments in Alabama football history. That day, I think, I was converted—into an Alabama fan, that is.

Bryant didn't so much talk as he did growl. Once he was asked about the value of a football team on a college campus. "It's kinda hard," he drawled, "to rally around a math class."

The Bear presided over Alabama football during an era that saw the integration of black players, an era that saw popularity of college athletics grow immensely on a national scale. He once said that when he retired from the game, he probably wouldn't live long after that. As it turned out, he was prophetic. He announced his unexpected retirement at the end of the 1982 regular season and in late January, a month after Alabama defeated Illinois in the Liberty Bowl in The Bear's final game, he died of heart failure.

Of course, legends don't really die. They live on forever in the hearts and minds of those who revere them. Tuscaloosa is irrefutable proof of this. Alabama fans continually look on the horizon for another legend to carry forward the tradition.

Before that trip to the museum, I thought I knew a lot about Alabama football. I knew about the Crimson Tide's slew of national championships and 83,000-seat Bryant-Denney Stadium, but I learned even more that day. The Crimson Tide began their program in 1892, long before they were known as the Crimson Tide. I always thought that was an unusual nickname for a school in a landlocked city like Tuscaloosa.

In 1907, a sports writer named Hugh Roberts used the term "Crimson Tide" while reporting on an Alabama-Auburn game. According to the account, the contest was played in a sea of mud and Auburn was heavily favored. The game ended in a 6-6 tie and the Crimson Tide title stuck.

And what was up with that elephant mascot—named "Big Al"—that roamed the sidelines at Alabama sporting events? What does an elephant have to do with Crimson Tide, or Alabama for that matter? Well, I found out that in 1930, Atlanta sports writer Everett Strupper covered an Alabama-Mississippi State game. Here's what he wrote:

> "At the end of the quarter, the earth started to tremble, there was a distant rumble that continued to grow. Some excited fan in the stands bellowed, 'Hold your horses, the elephants are coming,' and out stamped the Alabama varsity.
> "It was the first time that I had seen it and the size of the entire eleven nearly knocked me cold, men that I had seen play last year looking like they had nearly doubled in size."

After that, it became common practice for sports writers to refer to 'Bama linemen as "Red Elephants."

Right away, Gunnar and I were in awe of Alabama football. National championships weren't just hoped for at Alabama. They were expected. To think he was going to don the same crimson jersey as Lee Roy Jordan, Bart Starr and Ozzie Newsome gave me butterflies. I was sure Gunnar was feeling the pressure of about a dozen red elephants on his back.

"Preston," he said as we walked out of the museum, "we're not in Ephraim anymore."

CHAPTER NINETEEN

After settling into our off-campus apartment, we made a visit to the local Piggly Wiggly store and stocked up on bananas and avocados. We didn't have much time to acclimate to our new surroundings. School started a couple of days after our arrival and Gunnar and I both felt a little lost on a 1,000-acre campus amid 19,000 other students. It was a beautiful place to go to school, with lush green trees and historical landmarks.

Alabamians are a very religious people. They take their religion just as seriously as their football. Once, I saw an interesting statistic that said Alabama had the second-highest percentage of Southern Baptists per capita in the nation. I looked in the phone book and there were pages and pages of churches listed in Tuscaloosa. There was one LDS Church. We were a couple of Mormon boys in the heart of the Bible Belt. At BYU we would have been one in a crowd. You can't throw a quadruple combination without hitting a returned missionary in Provo.

At Alabama, we were definitely conspicuous. We felt a little like missionaries again, sans the nametags, white shirts and ties.

One night we received a visit from the bishop of the Tuscaloosa Ward, Saul Clements. He must have been the only man in Alabama who didn't care at all about football, or about sports in general. And Gunnar loved that about him.

"So you boys are from Utah and California. What are y'all doin' here at Alabama?"

"I've been asking myself that question all week," Gunnar said with a laugh. "Actually, I'm here to play football."

"Oh, you're a football player," the bishop said. "What position?"
"Quarterback."

"That's kind of an important position, isn't it?"

"Kind of," Gunnar said.

Then instead of a million questions about football, like the ones he had been answering since our arrival, he went on to other matters. He asked us all sorts of questions about our families and our lives. When he found out we were returned missionaries, his eyes lit up.

"Boys," he said, "it just occurred to me how we can put you to work in the ward."

"What would you like us to do, bishop?" I asked.

"We'd like to call you two to work with the youth in the ward. We need two people to teach early-morning seminary. The couple that had been doing the past few years moved to Florida last week. Would you be willin' to take on that responsibility?"

We looked at each other. There was only one way to respond: "Absolutely, bishop."

My dad, the seminary teacher for four decades, was thrilled when I called to tell him. He thought there was still hope for me.

Bishop Clements was relieved that we accepted the calling, but our schedule had just gotten a lot more hectic. So much for sleeping in. We taught a group of six teenagers, three boys and three girls, and we met bright and early at the church five days a week. The toughest part about it was trying to keep the kids awake at that hour. Either that or our lessons were boring. Most mornings, we brought donuts.

At Gunnar's prompting, I signed up for a couple of athletic training and pre-med classes. Gunnar and I attended institute classes, too.

Most of the players were God-fearing and good Christian people. One of the most interesting players on the team was Reginald "Preacher" Stargell, the starting middle linebacker. Gunnar and I met him one day during strength and conditioning drills. His dad was an ordained minister and he wanted to be an ordained minister, too, and play in the NFL. After that, he said he wanted to get into politics, maybe become the governor of Alabama. He had a John 3:16 tattoo on his left shoulder and a WWJD? (What Would Jesus Do?) tattoo on his right shoulder. He wore a gold cross around his neck. A copy of the Holy Bible rested in his locker, where it could be seen by all, and he wasn't shy about pulling it out and quoting scripture. He had a fire-and-brimstone approach about everything. From day one, he didn't seem to care much for Gunnar.

119

"I hear you're a Mormon," Preacher said.

"That's right."

"I've heard of that church. It does some good for some people. But it's misguided, you know."

Gunnar laughed and said, "Now that's a misguided observation." But Preacher wasn't laughing.

Anyway, we couldn't wait for the start of spring drills. The NCAA allows teams to schedule fifteen practices during the off-season to prepare for the upcoming season. Coach Guthrie wanted to establish his new philosophy and mindset during the spring, so he was tough on the players. He was even tough on us trainers. I was a little nervous since it was my first experience as a trainer. They gave me a little bag that contained athletic tape, Band-aids, aspirin, scissors and other equipment.

I worked under Billy Ray McCarty, who basically taught me all I know about sports medicine. He could tell you Bear Bryant stories nobody else ever knew. He was extremely patient with me, someone who had no prior experience, and he took me under his wing. He showed me how to tape ankles, apply bandages and how to get blood stains off the training room floor, among other things. His counsel to me and the other assistant trainers was this: "You don't do this for the attention or the glory. But without us, there is no Alabama football."

That's why I took it upon myself to do everything in my power to make sure every player was as healthy as possible. How could I expect the players to do their best if I didn't? So, I worked as hard as I could. When I pushed the water cart, I sprinted. The guys gave me a hard time about it. Some of them called me "Jolt" because they joked that I was all hyped up on caffeine, though they knew, because I was a Mormon, that wasn't the case at all.

I reported to the football complex a couple of hours earlier than Gunnar every day to prepare and I tried to learn all I could from Billy Ray. Prior to the first practice, he called me into his office. "Preston, I have a special assignment for you," he said.

"You want the nutritional supplements alphabetized, right?"

"Naw. It's a little more important than that. We got a wide

receiver, Ricky Fontaine, who's got a special health condition. He's diabetic."

"I didn't even know you could play football if you had diabetes," I said.

"Oh, you can play, if you've got trainers and doctors watching you like a hawk. Ricky has type 1 diabetes. We've got to monitor his blood sugar levels regularly. He has to have several insulin injections every day. He needs to be well-hydrated, like a houseplant. You need to bring the needles to practice and make sure he's okay all the time. The boy's life will be in your hands. Can you do it?"

I swallowed hard and said I could.

The guys used to rib Ricky all the time about his illness and called him Alabama's token, slow, white wide receiver. Ricky had a good sense of humor. I think it made him feel like part of the team. I'll never forget the day he met Gunnar.

"You're a Mormon?" he asked.

"Yeah, I'm a Mormon," Gunnar replied.

"I'm Ricky Fontaine," he said with a straight face, "I'm a diabetic."

Each day I lugged Ricky's needles and insulin to practice so he could give himself a shot whenever he needed to. It was amazing to me how nonchalant he was about it he was. I've never liked needles, but to him jabbing a long, sharp metal object into the major vein in his arm was no big deal whatsoever. While doing it, he'd crack a joke about being the biggest pin cushion on campus. And of course, I always brought a cooler of water for him to drink.

The first ankle I ever taped? Fittingly, it was Gunnar's. When I was done, he said, "That's too tight." He made me do it over again, just to mess with me.

As Gunnar walked onto the practice field that first day, with his crimson Alabama helmet with the number 22 in white on each side, an army of media types corralled him for an impromptu press conference, knowing that he was expected to be the starting quarterback. Television cameras, microphones, notepads, and pens were shoved in his face. There were several 300-pound men with an affinity for unmatching clothes with what looked like half of their free press box buffet from the previous season on their ties.

Gunnar looked around awkwardly as the media surrounded him. "How are y'all doin'?" he asked to no one in particular.

"Good," chorused the reporters.

"Hey, I'm getting good at this Southern stuff, huh?"

That comment drew laughs from the assembled throng. As he patiently answered their questions, he talked about the legend of Bear Bryant and the tradition of Alabama football, and what a privilege it was to be there. The hardest part was over. It was on to practice.

Gunnar took snaps with the first-team offense and he impressed everyone with his strong, accurate passes. He looked better than any of the other quarterbacks Coach Guthrie had to work with, but he was having a little trouble with the new playbook. There was a lot of new terminology to learn. Thankfully, Gunnar had plenty of good young talent around him, and the players seemed to accept him. I always told him he could have been a politician with the way he made friends.

Gunnar didn't have much luck befriending Preacher, though. The quarterbacks all wore yellow jerseys, signifying that they couldn't be touched during practice. Preacher would slip a couple of times just to shove Gunnar in the back. When the media asked him about it he said, "How's he gonna be ready for the SEC if he ain't used to it in practice?"

Though I was an assistant trainer, I was the lowest rung on the ladder, so I still did equipment manager stuff. I helped put each player's jersey in their locker before practice. A couple of reporters asked Gunnar why he wore an unorthodox number for a quarterback. He told them he liked the symmetry of 22. Truth was, it's the number his dad wore when he played minor league baseball. It was a tribute to him. In high school, Gunnar wore No. 2. But since his dad's death, he felt as though he was playing for both himself and his dad. Hence, No. 22.

Coach Guthrie knew his team's fortunes that first season largely rested in Gunnar's hands. It couldn't have been easy for Coach Guthrie. Alabama fans are notorious for being impatient. To them, there is no such thing as a rebuilding year. Every day, he heard about how he needed to beat Auburn. During spring practices, people publicly questioned everything Coach Guthrie did, including the car he drove and his preference in aftershave. They were especially skeptical of the decision to place so much trust in Gunnar, a junior college transfer from Utah.

What made it even more difficult for the locals to swallow was that there were a couple of highly touted, homegrown quarterbacks on the roster already. They questioned the wisdom of Coach Guthrie's approach to throw the ball at will. That had never been done at Alabama. One thing he learned early on was that if the Bear didn't do it, then, at least in the eyes of the fans, it probably wouldn't work. Though he had been dead for years, the Bear still had an enormous effect on folks' opinion.

With all of the busts, murals and reminders of the Bear everywhere, Coach Guthrie had to have felt almost guilty about installing an offense that went against everything the Bear believed in. No more two-back sets. Instead, four or five wide receivers lined up. He used a lot of shotgun and spread formations—no more was Alabama a bastion of conservative football.

For the most part, his teammates accepted Gunnar and they considered him a novelty as much as they did a quarterback.

"What's up with you Mormons, anyway?" E.J. Jefferson asked one day in the locker room while flipping his towel at a couple of his teammates. "I know you guys like women, because y'all have a bunch of wives. But I never see you chasin' women. Are you not allowed to chase women?"

"Oh, we can chase women," Gunnar replied. "We're just not allowed to catch 'em."

E.J. laughed.

"At least not until we get married," Gunnar continued. "By the way, contrary to popular belief, wives are one to a customer in our Church."

"What's up with those missions, man?" Jefferson asked. "What do you do, hide out for a couple of years and work out?"

"Not exactly."

"I read there's a bunch of stuff y'all can't do."

"That's true," Gunnar said. "You can't swim, you can't date, you can't watch movies . . ."

"Sounds like a prison sentence," E.J. said.

"Yeah," Gunnar joked, "but the food's a lot better."

Once, defensive backs Alonzo Passey and Jerome Lincoln started asking Gunnar personal questions. "So if you've been a Mormon all your life, that must mean you're a virgin."

"That's right," Gunnar said. "My goal is to wait until marriage."

Passey and Lincoln shook their heads and laughed heartily. "Man," Passey said, "you don't know what you're missin' out on. Tell me you're kidding."

"I'm not," Gunnar said. "It's what I believe."

E.J., who was overhearing the whole thing, stepped into the circle with his mammoth frame and glowered down on Passey and Lincoln. "Let the man be," he said. "Why do you think he runs circles around you and kicks your butt at practice? He has a lot of energy stored up."

Gunnar and the other players laughed. That was the last time anyone brought up that topic with him.

By the end of spring practice, Coach Guthrie named Gunnar as the starter, which surprised nobody. He and I celebrated by making *leche con platanos* and avocado sandwiches, of course.

Preacher wasn't too happy about Coach Guthrie's decision. I honestly think he couldn't stand the thought of his team being led by a Mormon.

"Hey," he said one day in the locker room, "do you believe in the Bible?"

Gunnar and I could smell a set-up. It was like Cesar Sepulveda all over again.

"I do," Gunnar said.

"You believe it to be God's word?"

"I do."

"Then what's up with this other book you try to pass off as scripture, this Book of Mormon?" Preacher asked.

Preacher feverishly thumbed through his Bible. "Don't you know it says right here that there shall be no other books of scripture?"

"Well, Preacher, I could pick up that same Bible and show you where it says there would be other scriptures," Gunnar said. "But I don't believe in Bible-bashing."

"C'mon, now, we're just having a friendly discussion about religion," he said. "Does this make you uncomfortable?"

"Yeah, it does when I'm dressed in nothing but a jockstrap," Gunnar said.

"You 'fraid of learnin' the truth about Jesus?"

"No. This just isn't the time or place..."

"You say you believe in Jesus, but the Bible says you shouldn't be ashamed of His gospel."

"I'm not ashamed, but if you keep hounding me like this, I may say something to you I'd be ashamed of."

Then E.J. stepped in. "Let it go, man," he said to Preacher. "The man has his religion, you have yours. This is a free country. This ain't no church. It's a locker room."

Some other teammates didn't exactly warm up to Gunnar at first, either. On weekends they held parties and Gunnar would usually say he couldn't go because he was too busy. "Does he think he's too good for us?" I overheard some of them say.

Gunnar played well in the "A-Game" intersquad scrimmage held at the end of spring practice. He threw a couple of touchdown passes and looked sharp. Even some of the curmudgeon sportswriters gave him a chance of doing well in the fall.

When I wasn't with the football team or teaching early morning seminary, I was either in class or studying. I took biology, chemistry and physics courses as well as an English class. At first, I struggled with my science classes. They were a lot harder than the ones I took at Snow. I was in over my head and on the verge of drowning that first week. I told Gunnar I was going to drop those classes, as well as the idea of becoming a doctor.

"Don't give up so soon," he said. "What if we had given up in La Chispa? C'mon. I'll help you. You have a great memory. You just need a new approach."

Just like he promised, Gunnar managed to find time to help me with my homework, as busy as he was. He came up with this ingenious memorization system for me (he had learned it from his Dad).

He knew I could remember anything if I could relate it to sports. We learned the entire periodic table of the elements by associating names and numbers of athletes to the names and numbers of the elements. With Gunnar's assistance, I formed sports-related association images with the definition. Those word images were absurd—so absurd that I could never forget them, not even to this day. Once on a biology test I was asked to define photosynthesis. When I see the word photosynthesis, I immediately envision in my mind's eye an imaginary baseball player named Clor O. Phil dressed in a green 1970s Oakland A's uniform. He stands at home plate surrounded by giant plants in the stadium, all holding cameras with flashes. Clor smacks the ball over the fence and rounds the bases as the flashes pop. When he arrives back at home plate, he is congratulated by Bernie Carbo (who was a real baseball player) holding a giant glass of water for him.

From that absurd image, I could immediately answer, with relatively little effort, the question: "Photosynthesis is the process by which chlorophyll-containing cells in green plants use light as an energy source to synthesize carbohydrates from carbon dioxide and water."

Get it?

Neither did anyone else, but it worked for me. I finished the semester with straight A's. For me, that was a minor miracle. I mailed a copy of my grades home to my parents and suddenly they thought I was a Rhodes Scholar candidate. Science ceased to be intimidating for me, thanks to Gunnar. Later, I used that device to memorize the nervous system as well as the names of all the bones in the human body.

When winter classes ended, we decided to stick around Tuscaloosa for the summer so we could prepare for the upcoming season. Gunnar and I did janitorial work on campus to earn money. We also took a couple of classes.

Springtime is beautiful in the south. The kudzu was in full bloom. If you don't know what kudzu is, then you probably haven't been to the South. I remember seeing fields and buildings covered in the plant, a fast-growing vine that has practically taken over the southeastern United States. It was everywhere. It's not native to the South, however. It was introduced from Japan in the 1800s and took on a life of its own. Some people loved it, some people hated it. Some used it to make Kudzu Quiche and Kudzu decorative items for their homes. Some people spent hundreds of dollars trying to eradicate it with herbicides.

Anyway, everything was going pretty well—except for our social lives. We were both so consumed with school and football, we didn't have much time for stuff like dating. Our experiences with girls at Snow College weren't exactly encouraging. In Tuscaloosa, the only place where we could meet LDS girls was at our ward or at the institute. Not a large selection to choose from. Not that there weren't some wonderful girls there, but it was a little awkward asking out girls in the ward. Since there was only one ward in Tuscaloosa, it could have made for a difficult experience if things didn't work out. So when Bishop Clements announced a multi-stake Young Single Adult dance in Birmingham, we knew that was our heaven-sent opportunity to meet new girls. Gunnar made me promise not to bring up anything about football. He didn't want girls flocking to him just because he was a football player.

We decided we should start our quest for social lives by getting haircuts. Not that our hair was long or anything, but it was getting a little shaggy in the back and hung over the ears a little. As we drove around town, we saw a sign that said, "Haircuts, $5."

"Pull over!" Gunnar shouted.

"A five-buck haircut?" I asked, looking at the establishment's front door.

Turned out, it was a cosmetology school, which explained the cheap price. We weren't picky, though. We walked in and sat down in a waiting area. Within a few minutes, a receptionist asked if she could help us.

"We'd like to enroll," Gunnar said.

"You're joking, right?" asked the receptionist.

"Do you have a problem with male hairstylists?" Gunnar replied.

The woman froze as the phrase "discrimination lawsuit" probably flashed before her eyes. Gunnar cleared things up.

"Actually, we're here for haircuts," he said.

The receptionist sighed. "I'll be right with you. Now, you do understand these are just students, not licensed professionals, right?"

"Do we have to sign a waiver?" Gunnar asked.

She glanced at the mop on top of his head. "I wouldn't worry about that with your hair," she said. "It'll be a few minutes."

We sat down in the waiting area. I picked up the local newspaper and there was a story on Alabama football. The season was still four months away, but I don't think a day went by that the Tuscaloosa papers didn't have something on the Crimson Tide.

The receptionist got on a loudspeaker. "Miss Murphy! Miss Thatcher!" she squawked. "You've got a couple of walk-ins up here in front."

Miss Murphy and Miss Thatcher walked through a door and let me tell you that they were lovely girls. Genuine southern belles, except we didn't notice it right away since they were wearing black smocks. They invited us into the back and we followed them. I think we would have followed them anywhere. I sat down toward the front while Gunnar kept walking toward the back. For some reason, I forgot all about him.

"My name's Kali," my hairdresser said in a melt-your-heart Southern accent. "What kind of cut would you like today, sir?"

"Nice and short," I said. I could tell she was a little nervous. "You ever done this before?" I asked.

Kali was standing behind me and she looked in the mirror and smiled. "No, sir. You're the first live person I've cut hair on. I've logged about 20 hours on mannequins. Now's your chance to escape."

"That's okay," I said. "I don't mind being a guinea pig."

"I hope after we're done you still don't mind," she said. "I'll do my best. Let's start with a shampoo, if that's okay."

Okay? That was the best suggestion I had heard in years. She leaned me back in the chair and ran warm water on my head. Then she put some shampoo in her hand and started running her fingers through my hair. For the first time in my life, I wanted to rinse and repeat.

"How's that feel, sir?" Kali asked.

"You don't need to call me 'sir,'" I said. "It makes me feel like I'm 40 years old."

"Sorry. That's what they taught us to say. What's your name?"

"Preston."

"You're not from around here, are you?" she asked.

"No," I said. "I'm from Utah."

She just about dropped her clippers on the floor.

"Is everything alright?" I asked.

"Everything's fine. Utah, huh? Now that would explain the way you talk," she said with a smile. "Not that there's anything wrong with the way you talk."

She tipped me up again in the chair and started whacking away. I studied her blue eyes and light brown hair through the mirror and I could tell she was trying hard not to make eye contact. I tried to put her at ease.

"Where are you from?" I asked.

She didn't respond, but just kept on clipping away, oblivious to me.

"You really must be used to cutting hair on those mannequins," I said. "I imagine they don't talk much."

Kali stopped what she was doing. "Oh, I'm so sorry," she said, "I'm just concentrating so hard on this…"

"Sorry," I said, "to interrupt you."

"No, no it's okay. I just want to do a good job. I'm hoping to work at a salon. In fact, my friend, who's cutting your friend's hair, and I would like to open our own salon someday."

"You're off to a great start," I said.

She turned on the clippers and within seconds she gasped and let out an "Oooops!"

I'm no cosmetologist, but I figured that couldn't be good.

Kali apologized profusely. "I am sooooo sorry," she said in that adorable accent. "I accidentally had the clipper setting too short. I can't believe I did that. I'll make sure you get your cut for free …"

"That's okay," I said. "Really." Really, I didn't mind at all. Though I barely knew her, she seemed to be everything I wanted in a girl. Too bad she's not a Mormon, I kept thinking. She was close enough to me that I could smell her perfume. Then she leaned forward, her face inches away from mine. She was close enough to me that I could have kissed her. But I didn't believe in kissing on the first date, especially when the girl wasn't aware this was a date.

"Oooops," she said again, with one finger on one side of my head and another finger on the other. "Your sideburns are uneven."

I noticed she kept cutting my sideburns, trying to even them, and before I knew it I had no sideburns at all. Not that I wanted to point this out. Not long after that, she let out her third "oooops."

She was over her oooops quota, even for a beginner. Then she put down her clippers, and bowed her head. She began to quietly cry. I didn't know what to do.

"Something wrong?" I asked.

"Everything," she said. "I've really butchered your hair. I'm so sorry."

"It's not that bad," I said, looking at it in the hand-held mirror. "In fact, I like it."

"That's nice of you," she said, "but you're lying."

Okay, so I looked like I had been attacked by a weed whacker, but I wasn't about to tell her that. I just felt so bad for her. "Tell you what," I said. "I've changed my mind. Why don't you just give me a buzz cut."

She stopped crying. "Really?"

"Yeah. I hear it gets awfully hot here in the summers. Plus, the lower maintenance for my hair, the better. With a buzz, I could cut about 30 seconds off the time it takes me to get ready."

She giggled and pulled out the clippers and started shearing away like I was a sheep that was going to be entered in the State Fair.

When she was done, I thanked her and she walked me up to the front, where I handed the receptionist a five dollar bill. Then I gave Kali a $5 tip. Before I knew it, I was on the receiving end of a gentle hug.

"Thank you so much," she said. "You've made my first hair cutting experience really nice."

Then she hurriedly backed away and apologized for getting hair from her smock all over my white shirt. "Don't worry about it," I said. "It's my hair anyway."

Gunnar and his hairstylist, Danielle, showed up and he was also sporting a buzz cut. It looked as though he had hit it off well with her, too. The four of us must have chatted there for about 20 minutes, until the receptionist ordered them back to work.

"What do you think this is, girls, a singles bar?" she asked.

"Since you guys were so patient with us," Kali said, "we'd like to make it up to you by taking you out to lunch sometime."

Gunnar and I couldn't believe it.

"Sounds great," I blurted out. "When and where?"

"How about tomorrow at noon," Kali said. "We'll meet you at the Subway across the street."

We didn't care where we went for lunch. It didn't matter.

As Gunnar and I walked to the car I said to him, "I didn't know you were getting a buzz cut today."

"Neither did I," he said. "I didn't have any other choice once she started hacking away, but that was the best haircut I've ever gotten."

I couldn't have agreed more. While their hair cutting skills were lacking, they made up for that in sweetness. They looked even prettier without their black smocks. Really, we didn't know anything about them. Our lunch went well, so a couple of nights later, we took them bowling. We never did make it to that multi-stake Young Single Adult dance.

We had a lot of fun with Kali and Danielle. Gunnar liked the fact they didn't know he was a football player, and he felt Danielle liked him for who he was. He wanted to be sure that girls weren't going out with him for ulterior motives. Clearly, these girls didn't seem to care about football. Still, Gunnar and I were concerned that they weren't members of the Church. We were always taught not to date non-members and we knew nothing was going to stop us from marrying in the temple. What if we fell in love with these girls, though?

After bowling, we dropped them off at their apartment and they invited us inside. Gunnar and I took a seat on the couch next to each other, not knowing what to expect. The girls sat across from us.

"You guys are *different*," Kali said.

We didn't know if that was a compliment or not.

"Thanks, I think," I said.

"What do you mean by *different?*" Gunnar asked.

"Not once have you guys tried to grab us," Danielle said. "Not once have you used foul language. You don't drink alcohol. You open doors for us. That doesn't happen very often."

"You don't happen to be Mormon, do you?" Kali asked.

"Yes," I said, "we happen to be Mormon."

Kali's face lit up. "I knew it!" she replied. "So am I!"

Another answered prayer.

Kali darted out of the room and returned moments later with a dusty copy of the Book of Mormon. "I haven't been to church in years, though," she said.

"Why don't you come with us tomorrow," I said.

"I'd love to," Kali said.

"I'm not a Mormon," Danielle said, "but can I still go?"

"We'll swing by at 9:50 to pick you up," Gunnar said.

They accompanied us to the Tuscaloosa Ward. Kali loved being back in church again. Danielle had a lot of questions and seemed sincerely interested. After our meetings, we invited them to our apartment for Sunday dinner. Kali very candidly told us why she stopped going to church. She and her family were baptized when she was nine. At 12, her parents divorced and both of them stopped going to church, but she said she always believed in what Mormons taught. She still tried to live those teachings she remembered from Primary.

Danielle told us she grew up a Catholic, just like so many people we had run into in Chile. She believed in God, but always had questions that went unanswered.

So we spent the rest of the day basically teaching them the discussions. After every principle we taught, Danielle would say, "That makes perfect sense." She was amazed that we could answer all of her questions.

That night we took them to a fireside. As we walked into the building, Kali grabbed my hand. It had to rank up there as one of the highlights of my life. I couldn't believe a girl as pretty as her would be interested in me. I nonchalantly turned around and noticed Danielle had Gunnar's hand in hers.

As Gunnar and I lay awake in our apartment that night, trying unsuccessfully to sleep, he announced, "I've got a confession to make."

"What?" I asked.

"This may sound crazy, since I've only known her a week or so, and especially since she's not a member, but I think I'm in love with Danielle."

"I know what you mean," I said. "I think I love Kali."

Over the next few weeks, we went out with them almost every night. We helped them by letting them give us manicures and pedicures. Now if that isn't love, I don't know what is. Though Danielle was not a member, it didn't bother Gunnar too much, because she sure acted like one.

One evening we went out to eat with them and while we were waiting for our food, an old guy in an Alabama ballcap approached our table.

"You're Gunnar Hanshaw, aren't you?" he asked.

"Yes, sir," Gunnar said.

"Can I have your autograph?"

"Sure," Gunnar said sheepishly. "But shouldn't you wait until I play in a game first?"

"We have confidence in you," he replied. "We gotta beat Auburn this year, or else I dunno how I'm gonna show up to work anymore."

Gunnar took the man's pen and signed his napkin.

After the man left, Danielle's eyes were boring a hole right through Gunnar.

"What was he talking about?" she asked.

"Oh, I play a little football," Gunnar said. Then he sipped his water.

"He's the quarterback," I chimed in.

"You're the quarterback at Alabama?" Danielle asked

"One of them," Gunnar said.

"Why didn't you tell me?" Danielle asked, a little perturbed.

"I didn't think it was that big of a deal," Gunnar said.

"I just can't believe you'd keep a secret like that from me."

Danielle stood up, excused herself, and marched into bathroom.

Kali looked at me. "You're too small to play football, right?" she said.

"Yeah," I replied. "I'm just one of the assistant trainers on the team."

"I'm going to check on Danielle," Kali said.

They didn't return for a long time. Gunnar and I felt bad, but we really weren't trying to hide anything from them. When they came back we tried to explain that to them, but it was too late. They asked us to take them home. It was a long, quiet ride.

They wouldn't even let us walk them to the door. They said they could find it without our help.

Gunnar and I sat there in the parking lot, wondering what had just happened. What had we done wrong? Here we had two beautiful girls and suddenly they were gone. We weren't sure if they'd ever talk to us again. All over Alabama football?

"Do you suppose they're Auburn fans?" Gunnar wondered aloud.

We decided to be stubborn and let them come to us. I guess Kali was mad at me by association. We were sure they would come to their senses. Two weeks went by with no contact, until Gunnar and I went to get a bite to eat and saw Danielle and Kali on a date with two other guys. That about killed us. We missed them so much. Besides, we had to find out what the problem was. It brought back some painful memories of my relationship back in Ephraim with Crystal. I didn't want to make any mistakes with Kali.

That next morning, we showed up at the cosmetology school each carrying a dozen of red roses. Kali and Danielle finally appeared after 30 minutes. They looked prettier than we had remembered. They took the flowers without saying anything, then we asked if we could talk to them later. They reluctantly agreed.

That night, we met at their apartment. Danielle and Gunnar sat on the couch. Kali and I went into the kitchen. "I'm so glad you came over," she whispered. "I've missed you. I'm not really mad at you. Danielle just needs to talk to Gunnar."

One relationship saved, one to go.

Kali and I tried to be as quiet as possible in order to overhear their conversation. "I'm really sorry I didn't tell you that I played football," he began. "I didn't know it would be that important to you."

"Gunnar," Danielle replied, "I don't like guys who play mind games."

"I wasn't trying to play games," he said. "You have to understand, though. I don't want to be known simply as a football player."

"Maybe I overreacted," Danielle said. "It's just that it came as such a shock when I found out you played football. You seem too nice to be a football player."

Danielle explained how her father had played football at the University of Texas. He injured his knee and back but he never missed a game. After college, he vigorously pursued a professional career, but never made it. His failure drove him to alcoholism. Danielle blamed football for his problems. He died when she was nine years old. Finally, she said, she found a guy she really cared about and to find out that he, too was a football player, was hard to cope with.

"I'm so sorry about your father," Gunnar said.

"I know you're not like that," Danielle said. "I feel safe and secure with you."

They kissed.

Everything was back to normal. Actually, everything was much better than normal. The next week, Danielle listened to the formal discussions from the missionaries. By mid-summer Gunnar baptized her and I confirmed her a member of the Church. It was like we were back on our missions. Except Gunnar was allowed to kiss the new convert.

CHAPTER TWENTY

Needless to say, we saw a lot of Kali and Danielle that summer. One weekend the girls went on a little trip to Danielle's hometown in Texas. Gunnar and I were bored and spent Saturday just sitting around our apartment watching TV.

I had been riding Gunnar hard about the upcoming season, telling him how he was going to be famous, how he was going to win the Heisman Trophy. He'd just smile and say, "What are you trying to do? Jinx me?"

I wouldn't let it go. I was so confident in Gunnar's abilities. Well, he got me back.

Gunnar loved playing practical jokes on people. When he was training new American missionaries in Chile, he'd tell them that in order to hail a cab or a bus in Chile you had to lift your leg at a 90 degree angle. Then he'd tell his young companion to order a taco and a burrito at a restaurant. The companion would receive the strangest looks because in Chile, a taco is the heel of a shoe and a burrito is a little donkey.

Well, Gunnar continued his practical joking at Alabama, too.

On Sunday morning I was really thirsty for some reason. I must have drunk about four glasses of orange juice before going to church. We were in sacrament meeting and right after the sacrament was passed, I needed to go. Badly. I felt like my bladder was going to explode.

Bishop Clements was notorious for calling on ward members out of the blue to speak extemporaneously on a gospel topic. He warned us that we should all have a talk prepared, just in case. Every once in a while, if the bishop felt so inclined, he would randomly call on someone. I didn't consider it a big deal. President McPherson used to do that when we were on our missions.

Well, when I came back from the bathroom after draining my bladder, I sat down next to Gunnar.

"Preston," he whispered, "you're up next."

"Up next for what?" I asked innocently.

"You're speaking after this girl."

"Really?"

Gunnar nodded. "He announced it while you were in the bathroom."

I opened my scriptures and scrambled to find my notes from a prepared talk. Then I remembered that I left my notes at our apartment. Suddenly, I had trouble swallowing. My brain froze up and I couldn't even remember the topic I was going to speak on. As my turn grew closer, I managed to piece together something coherent off the top of my head.

When the girl at the podium wrapped up her talk, I jumped up and bounded up to the stand. Looking back, I guess the bishop was looking at me a little strangely. To be honest, I don't remember a thing I said. Which is good. I rambled on and read a couple of scriptures, and I'm sure it sounded disjointed toward the end. All I know is that Gunnar was leaning over, trying not to laugh out loud. Everybody else was looking at me like I was attempting a hostile takeover of the ward.

Then it dawned on me as I walked back to my seat that Gunnar had zinged me good. I sat down again on the bench next to him. "Good job," he said with a straight face.

Bishop Clements figured out was had happened and thanked me for my unsolicited talk. "Now we'd like to hear from Brother Hanshaw," he said.

Gunnar gave a little two-minute sermon on forgiveness.

By late July the excitement for the upcoming season was palpable. When fall camp started in early August, it was broiling hot. And, oh, the humidity!

Gunnar was ready to play football. What he wasn't ready for was all the media attention. After every practice, he had interview requests from every newspaper, radio station and TV station around the state of Alabama.

"Fans here in Alabama won't be happy until there's another

national championship in the trophy case," a reporter said. "Do you feel you are good enough to deliver that?"

"Let me complete a couple of passes first," Gunnar said.

A couple of weeks into fall camp, some reporters got desperate for material. One guy, a columnist named Chip Merriweather actually asked Gunnar—I'm not making this up—the following question: "Do you like peas?"

Gunnar laughed, thinking it was a joke. Then he realized the man was deadly serious.

"Yeah," Gunnar replied, "I like peas."

"Do you eat them with a fork or with a spoon?"

I don't know Gunnar's response because I left before he could say anything. I was embarrassed for the entire journalism profession.

One reporter did a feature story on Gunnar and quoted E.J. Jefferson calling him "the Mormon Gunslinger." The press ate that up.

Despite the fact Alabama was coming off of a 4-8 season—and had a new coach and a new quarterback—optimism was everywhere. Fans hoped this was the dawning of a new era of Alabama football and a return to prominence. After years of probation, scandals and sanctions, Alabama was finally eligible for a bowl game and Crimson Tide fans fully expected to go to a bowl game that season. Despite the scholarship reductions the past several seasons, Alabama was loaded with talent.

Some media and fans didn't think Gunnar was the answer. "What is this idiot Guthrie doing, anyway, bringin' in this Mormon kid who spent two years in South America?" said one radio host. "He hadn't proven squat before they gave him a scholarship. He put up big numbers at a junior college in Utah. Whoop-de-doo! Here Guthrie is, in the South, the richest area for talent anywhere and he brings in this guy?"

Much of the weight of the season rested squarely on the shoulder pads of Gunnar Hanshaw.

CHAPTER TWENTY-ONE

Kali and Danielle graduated from cosmetology school—thanks in no small part to Gunnar and me. We always let them practice on us. That's why we wore hats almost exclusively during the summer. Soon they both got jobs working at a local hair salon. That kept them busy while we were busy with football.

Gunnar and I found it nearly impossible to sleep the week before the season-opener against Southern Miss. The game was played at Alabama's home-away-from-home, Legion Field in Birmingham. The Tide was favored by 21 points and Gunnar was the starting quarterback. I still had to pinch myself. It seemed too good to be true.

The night before the game we checked into a local hotel, as was customary for home games. Coach Guthrie didn't want any distractions, and he wanted to ensure we were all in our rooms by curfew. Gunnar and Ricky were assigned as roommates, which was good because the three of us liked to hang out together. We continued the usual pre-game ritual that we had at Snow. We fixed *leche con platano* and avocado sandwiches. We just made Ricky's *leche con platano* without sugar.

"How did you guys like spending two years in the jungles of Chile?" Ricky asked.

"Actually, there are no jungles in Chile," Gunnar said. "You're thinking of Brazil."

"What was it like, then?"

"Chile is this long, narrow country," Gunnar explained. "It's like a shoestring that runs along the western coast of South America for a few thousand miles. Up north, you have some of the world's driest deserts. Down south, it's cold. They have penguins and icebergs. In the central part, where Preston and I served, a lot of it was very similar to California with mild climates."

"You must really believe what you teach if you're willing to go all the way to South America."

"We do," I said.

"I've never been religious, but I admire you two," Ricky said. "Sometimes I wish I could believe in something that strongly."

We spent probably a half-hour talking about the Book of Mormon with him and promised to get him his own copy.

Ricky told us that he grew up in Montgomery as a huge Tide fan. He would dress up as Bear Bryant for Halloween every year. Though he was gifted athletically, people always told him he could never play football at Alabama because of the diabetes. He walked-on at Alabama and earned a scholarship his second year. He was determined to prove he could play at this level.

That night in the hotel, I kept waking up about every hour with nightmares of me spilling Gatorade bottles or tripping on the field. The next morning, since I was an assistant trainer and had access to the stuff, I swallowed a couple of spoonfuls of Maalox.

The team bus arrived at Legion Field about three hours before kickoff. We walked past a city of RVs parked outside the stadium. Some were barbecuing, some swilling beer, at 10 a.m., no less. A wall of crimson-clad fans lined up in front of our entrance into the stadium, cheering the players and coaches.

I wasn't surprised that so many people recognized Gunnar, though a couple of fans mentioned he was smaller than they had imagined, or at least smaller than the 6-foot-2 that he was listed in the media guide. He was actually just barely over 6-feet tall. I know because I helped with the players' measurements, but fudging on a player's height is a time-honored tradition in sports.

"Gunnar Hanshaw! The Mormon Gunslinger!" hollered a large, bearded man clad in a crimson-red T-shirt and crimson-red shorts. "Bring the pride back to Bama!"

Sure, and find a cure for cancer and establish world peace while you're at it, I thought.

Gunnar smiled. "I'll do my best," he said.

We walked into the locker room and right away I spotted Gunnar's locker. In front of it, I had placed his No. 22 jersey with "HANSHAW" on the back. It was beginning to sink in. Gunnar was the starting quarterback at the University of Alabama. He and

Coach Guthrie were about to make their long-awaited debuts.

The game day atmosphere was everything I had expected. Among the spectators were four students who had painted their faces, chests, backs, and arms red. Each had a white letter on their chests, spelling out the word T-I-D-E. Big Al was prancing around among the cheerleaders—he was quite nimble for an elephant—and the Million Dollar Band was pounding out a rousing rendition of the school fight song.

No, we weren't in Ephraim any more.

Though I worried about the high expectations, I knew Gunnar would come through. By the end of the day, I thought, everyone would be talking about him.

Turned out, I was right. But not in the way I had hoped.

It was a muggy, hot afternoon in Birmingham. From the comfort of the locker room, while Gunnar dressed, I reminded him over and over again to get plenty of fluids in his system. "You don't want to cramp up," I said.

He acknowledged me, but I don't think he listened. He was on a different planet. I could tell he was going over every imaginable situation out on the field. Nerves took a toll on him. While guys in the locker room were listening to rap music on a big boom box, he had his head in the toilet, vomiting.

After warmups, the team reconvened in the locker room one final time. Coach Guthrie wore an Alabama cap, tweed slacks, and a red golf shirt with the word, "Alabama" stitched above the right breast. The team gathered around him.

"Men," he began, "this is the beginning of a new era in Alabama football. This is a proud program. You're here at Alabama for a reason—you're great football players. Now let's go out and show it!"

With that, the players roared. They formed a mosh pit and started bouncing up and down. "Go Bama!" E.J. Jefferson shouted.

"Roll Tide!" the rest of the team responded in unison. I was so excited I wanted to go out there and lay a lick on somebody myself.

But that was nothing. When we ran out onto the field to the roar of nearly 80,000 fans, my whole body was tingling like I had been dipped into a vat of Selsun Blue. Hearing the band play the fight song, seeing the cheerleaders carrying giant Alabama flags, looking up at the azure sky, it was like a dream. I only wish Gunnar could have enjoyed the moment like I did. I think he had to block all of it out. He had other things on his mind—like the actual game.

Alabama lost the coin toss at midfield and that was a bad omen. Southern Miss opted to kick off and defend the south goal.

The Tide began on its own 20. On the first play from scrimmage, Gunnar dropped back and fired a pass about 10 feet over the head of his intended receiver. On second down, his pass was tipped at the line of scrimmage and fell incomplete. Bama fans started squirming in their seats.

Then, on third down, he threw a slant pattern that was picked off by a Southern Miss linebacker and returned for an easy touchdown. Gunnar tried to make a tackle on the play but before he could, a defensive lineman knocked him flat on his backside. It was as if someone had pushed the mute button on the crowd. The place went quieter than a library on Christmas Day. One minute into the game and the Tide trailed 7-0.

Welcome to Alabama.

Gunnar caught an ear full from the coaches, not to mention the fans on the first few rows sitting behind our bench. Just when I didn't think it could get any worse, it did. He threw another interception on a post pattern. He underthrew the pass, something I hardly ever saw him do.

That's when the boos began cascading down from the stands. I just felt sick for Gunnar. So I swallowed a couple more spoonfuls of Maalox. Coach Guthrie threw down his headset as he approached him. "You've got to learn that the next-best-thing to a completion is an incompletion. Don't ever force the ball into traffic. You know better than that."

Gunnar sat down and talked on the headset with the offensive coaches up in the booth. He looked a little dazed as I brought him a cup of Gatorade and just before he was going to drink it, he started talking to one of the wide receivers, so he never did. It was time to return to the field.

"Hey Hanshaw!" shouted one guy who was missing his front teeth. "Don't you belong at BYU?"

Alabama forced Southern Miss to punt on its first offensive possession. On the Tide's first running play, Gunnar botched the handoff to the running back and the ball squirted free. Southern Miss recovered at the Alabama 13. Three plays later, Southern Miss took a 14-0 lead. Three series, three turnovers. The booing level ratcheted up a couple more decibels and even more so when Gunnar took the field for the fourth time. I looked up in the student section and saw a banner unfurled: "TIRED OF WAITING. BRING IN WAITLEY!" It was in reference to Koy Waitley, a sophomore quarterback from Birmingham.

On third down and six, Gunnar sprinted out and faked a pass. He had 20 yards of green grass in front of him. Just when he was about to tuck the ball under his arm, he crumpled to the turf, short of the first down. At first, the crowd started booing again. Then they realized he was injured and couldn't get up, so they cheered.

It was as if his career had ended before it really began. I rushed out to the field with Billy Ray, the head trainer, to attend to him. Gunnar complained of cramping in his left calf. I wanted to say "I told you so" for not taking in enough fluids, but I figured that wasn't a good time for that. Billy Ray and I helped him off the field and the crowd cheered again as Waitley stepped onto the field.

"I'll be okay," he kept saying to the coaches on the sidelines, but soon his health didn't appear to be the issue anymore. When Alabama got the ball back, down 21-0, Waitley completed a pass, then the tailback gained 14 yards. The Tide wound up scoring a field goal, but they spent the rest of the afternoon swimming upstream. Gunnar sat on the bench helplessly, getting taunted by fans. Alabama lost, 31-17.

The most difficult part of that experience for Gunnar was facing the glaring media spotlight afterward. "How would you characterize your play today?" a reporter asked.

"I stunk," he told them. "I was really bad and I'd like to apologize to the Alabama fans. I'm sorry I let you down today. No one is more frustrated than I am. But I promise you that I'm going to work even harder to make sure that doesn't happen again."

Preacher told the press that Gunnar was in over his head and that Waitley was Alabama's quarterback of the future.

Understandably, Gunnar was quieter than usual that night. I didn't know what to say to him. Kali and Danielle tried to be positive.

"You look good in that uniform," was about the only constructive thing they could come up with. The only time I saw Gunnar get upset was when Danielle and Kali told us that some fans around them were yelling mean-spirited things about him.

"You shouldn't have to listen to that," he said.

"Don't worry," Danielle said. "I can take care of myself. I told those jerks to sit down and shut up. They didn't make a sound the rest of the game."

Luckily, Gunnar didn't read the newspapers. Good thing. I'm a newspaper junkie, so I couldn't stay away, though it was painful for me to read the next day. One headline in the *Birmingham News* on Sunday morning simply blared, "*EMBARRASSMENT.*" One column was headlined, "*'Gunslinger' Fires Blanks.*" You can probably guess the gist of those stories.

Gunnar wasn't prepared for the barrage of criticism that followed that week. On campus, some students told him to transfer to Auburn.

At practice on Monday, Coach Guthrie implemented a new rule—the offense had to do 50 pushups for every turnover committed. Alabama had four against Southern Miss, which didn't do much for his popularity with his teammates.

What everyone had already known became official that day— Gunnar had lost his starting job to Waitley, who started the rest of the season. Coach Guthrie called Gunnar into a meeting after practice to tell him he had decided that because Waitley had two more full seasons of eligibility remaining and Gunnar had only one, that Waitley should be groomed for the future. So Gunnar dutifully carried a clipboard and an Alabama cap backwards on the sidelines most of the rest of the season.

As a small consolation, he went from backup holder on extra points and kickoffs to the starting holder. Though bitterly disappointed in his own performance, Gunnar was supportive of the coaches' decision.

"So, Gunnar," a reporter asked, "how does it feel to go from starter to backup after only one game?"

To which I wanted to say, "How does it feel to go from human to subhuman after only one question?"

But I didn't, because I try to be a good Christian. It wouldn't have been good publicity for the Church.

Those fans and media types who questioned the decision to start a quarterback with no Division I experience felt justified. They poured out of the woodwork, producing their snide "I-told-you-so" columns. Chip Merriweather, whose name is a contradiction because of his perennially pessimistic outlook on life, wrote how he felt hoodwinked by the hype (which he helped create, by the way) of Gunnar Hanshaw. "Returned missionaries," he wrote, "just can't be successful at this level of football. It can't be done. A Buddist monk fresh off the boat from the India would have fared better than Hanshaw did on Saturday."

As difficult as it must have been for him, Gunnar obtained a tape of the Southern Miss game and watched his miserable performance over and over again. He winced every time he turned the ball over. In practice, he worked hard and I thought he consistently looked like the best one out there, in my humble, and biased, opinion. Of course, nobody asked me.

The next week, at Bryant-Denney Stadium in Tuscaloosa, Alabama won its first game of the year against Middle Tennessee State. The Tide jumped out to a 31-0 halftime lead and cruised the rest of the way. Gunnar got into the game in the fourth quarter (he was on the receiving end of a smattering of boos) and drove the team 42 yards for a field goal. Because the score was so lopsided, Coach Guthrie didn't let him throw a pass.

The euphoria of a dominating victory over a weak team didn't last long. Alabama lost its next six games. The Tide got steamrolled by East Carolina, South Carolina, Arkansas, Ole Miss, Louisiana State, and Georgia. It got so bad that fans were longing for the mediocrity of the previous year. It seemed everything Coach Guthrie did backfired. The team's youth and inexperience cost it time and time again. Every time the pressure was on, this team self-destructed.

Gunnar got into a few games, but he wasn't very effective, either.

I read the newspapers and listened to the sports talk radio stations—at least until I couldn't stand it anymore.

A group of fans set up a Website on the Internet called **fireguthrie.com**. On message boards, fans insulted not only Coach Guthrie, but also his family and his pets. Some lunatic sent him a letter demanding that he step down or else harm would come to him. Another one threw a brick through a window at his home with a message that said, "Resine (sic) Now!"

Some fans turned on Gunnar, too. They sent him letters saying that Mormonism was wrong, that it's through grace that we're saved. They sent him anti-Mormon pamphlets and strongly urged him to repent. Some told him to go back home to his "Mormon cult." Some people in town would simply call his name and when he turned they'd shout something really intelligent like, "You suck lemons!" Except they left out the part about the lemons. Coach Guthrie and Gunnar were the lightning rods for everything that went wrong that season.

Not that I want to paint Alabama fans with the same broad brush. There were a lot of them who expressed their support and were real nice to Coach Guthrie and Gunnar, but the negative ones seemed to overshadow the rest, unfortunately.

"Find Jesus," said one caller to an all-sports radio talk show, "then maybe you'll find a receiver."

Fans complained that Coach Guthrie had never coached east of the Mississippi before and therefore was not qualified. They said he had been overrated at Arizona State. He wasn't one of "Bear's Boys." As for Gunnar, he was a California kid. Some fans didn't think Coach Guthrie and Gunnar were worthy of the honor of being part of the Alabama football program.

"This ain't the Pac-10, coach!" shouted a fan at the Mississippi State game.

Everybody in the state is a football critic. Coach Guthrie had as high a profile in Alabama as the governor.

It was a miserable season, to put it mildly. Of course, Gunnar was well-acquainted with adversity, so he tried to make it work for him. He dragged me, and sometimes the early-morning seminary class, to local hospitals every once in a while, visiting people and showing interest in them. He focused on the less fortunate.

"My dad taught me that the best way to combat discouragement," he said, "is to seek someone out who is in worse shape than you. It's funny how, when you do that, your problems don't seem so big."

That was true. Spending time with the sick and poor put everything in perspective. It was kind of like being on a mission again.

Gunnar told me that after he tore up his shoulder in high school, he spent a couple of weeks feeling sorry for himself. Other than going to school, he rarely left his house. He thought his life was over. His dad was obviously concerned and he started taking him to orphanages, soup kitchens, and nursing homes around town. At first, Gunnar didn't want to, but during that time spent with his dad, they would talk about life, about the future. Then Gunnar asked him for a father's blessing. For him, it was one of those turning points. It made him realize how little football mattered, in the eternal scheme of things. So, whenever Gunnar felt like the world was closing in on him, he'd go find someone to serve and those feelings disappeared.

The other thing that saved Gunnar and me that season was the support of Danielle and Kali. They made The Longest Season tolerable. We spent a lot of time with them at our apartment, doing homework and studying scriptures. They fixed us countless meals—they could outcook Andy Griffith's Aunt Bea. Fried chicken, collard greens, fried oakree, cobbler, fried apple rings, boiled grits, fried grits, cornbread biscuits, smothered okra, ham hocks, black-eyed peas, and sweet potato pie.

And if that weren't enough, they gave us free haircuts.

Though I thought it was nonsense, deep down Gunnar felt personally responsible for the season going south, especially after all the preseason expectations. One morning I accompanied him to campus so he could work out. We saw a light on in the football office, so we went inside. Coach Guthrie was sitting on the couch in the lobby, staring at a wall filled with trophies and plaques. The man who once seemed so confident, so certain of success at Alabama, was discouraged and searching for answers.

"Coach," Gunnar said, "sorry I let you down."

"Don't blame yourself," Coach Guthrie said. "A team is more than just one player. I've made as many mistakes as anyone. But we'll all get past this—together."

Then he got up and walked away. That was Gunnar's junior year at not-so-sweet-home-Alabama.

After doing the predictable barrage of stories about what it's like to be one of the biggest busts in Alabama football history, what it's like to go from Golden Boy to benchwarmer, the media pretty much left him alone. As always, he never backed away from his obligation to talk to the press, even amid difficult circumstances.

Some of the questions were, in my mind, pretty insensitive. Not to mention dumb, but Gunnar would always smile politely and respond respectfully. "It's really hard. I didn't come here to fail," he said. "But this program is bigger than just one player and I believe in Coach Guthrie. He'll turn things around and I hope to play a role in that."

In the Louisiana State game, when Coach Guthrie pulled Waitley near the end of a blowout loss, he sent in the freshman, Dillon Redhage. Reporters asked Coach Guthrie if that meant Redhage was now the second-string quarterback over Gunnar. Coach Guthrie replied, "At this stage, I've got to prepare for the future."

Ouch.

Though the season was an unmitigated disaster by almost any standard, Alabama fans knew they could salvage it in a small way if the Tide could win the Iron Bowl in the season finale. That's what they call the annual rivalry game between Alabama and its mortal enemy, Auburn. It's the mother of all rivalries. It's one of those rivalries for which you have to live in the state of Alabama to under-stand. But let me tell you, it's intense. I thought the BYU-Utah rivalry was bad, but it doesn't even compare.

Billy Ray told me a story of an Alabama fan who was stabbed and killed by an Auburn fan during a fight over the game. The Crimson Tide fan, who was married to the Auburn fan's ex-wife, was charged with murder. Talk about a sign of the apocalypse.

It's not a game that fans watch then forget about. I can attest that from the day Gunnar and I arrived in Tuscaloosa, we heard mention of the previous season's Alabama-Auburn game every single day, without fail. People looked forward to the game year-round. It was astonishing to me how much this game affected the lives of thousands of people in this state.

I heard all the jokes about Auburn from the Alabama fans:

* *"Your mother tells all her friends you're in prison, rather than admit you're going to school at Auburn."*

* *"Best line in an Auburn bar: Nice tooth."*

* *"Did you hear about the skeleton they just found in an old building at Auburn? It was the 1951 hide-and-seek champion."*

* *"What is the difference between an Auburn cheerleader and a fish? One has whiskers and smells; the other is a fish."*

* *"Did you hear about the tornado that touched down at Auburn? It caused $3 million in improvements."*

* *"I had an Auburn fan in my family tree ... and he's still hanging there."*

Of course, Auburn fans told the same jokes, just substituting Auburn for Alabama.

Against that backdrop, we stepped off the bus at Legion Field in Birmingham. You could feel the intensity and excitement instantly upon our arrival, even though the Auburn Tigers were favored by three touchdowns that day. After all, Auburn had only one loss and was ranked No. 4 in the country. For the Tigers, a win would send them to the SEC title game. They had everything to play for. Of course, it was televised nationally.

Auburn players were pretty cocky the week leading up to the game. They were quoted as saying they didn't feel bad one bit for the way Alabama's season had gone. They said that since this would be the Tide's final game of the season, they were eager to give them a whipping that would give Alabama players, coaches, and fans nightmares during the off-season.

E.J. Jefferson, who was our most outspoken player, confidently said Alabama would give Auburn a fight to the finish. "It's going to be a slobberknocker," he said.

Alabama played its best game of the season that night. It was tied at 13 at halftime and the Tigers knew they weren't going to walk over Alabama like they had hoped.

Midway through the third quarter, Waitley injured his ankle badly while trying to escape the Auburn pass rush. I ran out with Billy Ray and we checked out the injury. While the Alabama defense was on the field, Waitley was throwing on the sidelines and Coach Guthrie removed his headset and asked Billy Ray what his status was.

"Look for yourself, Coach," he said.

Waitley could barely walk, let alone run an offense. Then he called Gunnar over to him. "Hanshaw," he said, "this is your game. This is your second chance. Let's see what you can do." When I heard that, I started praying like crazy.

Based on what Coach Guthrie had said earlier, I had presumed the freshman would go into the game, but there was Gunnar, strapping on his helmet and jogging into the huddle.

Billy Ray and I were busy attending to Waitley again, so I couldn't see what happened, though I heard the contingent of Bama fans cheering after Gunnar had scrambled for a seven-yard gain and a first down. After a play Gunnar would help up other players, even the Auburn guys, then pat them on the back.

The Tide ended up punting on that drive, but I think Coach Guthrie liked the experience and mobility Gunnar brought to the team. He was much more relaxed and confident than he had been in the season-opener. Alabama's defense kept forcing Auburn to punt, giving the offense good field position. Gunnar drove the team deep into Tiger territory, but the placekicker, John David Bender, shanked a 32-yard field goal.

Late in the third quarter, Alabama's defense suffered a brief but costly letdown. Auburn's All-America running back, Julius Blackmon, ran for a 76-yard touchdown to give the Tigers a 20-13 advantage. Once again, Gunnar drove the Tide downfield, only to watch John David Bender miss another chip-shot field goal. Auburn eventually stretched its lead to 27-13.

Gunnar rallied the troops, though. You never would have guessed he was the third-string quarterback. He was able to elude the Auburn pass rush, but he had a tough time finding open receivers. I could tell he just didn't want to make any mistakes. Early in the fourth quarter, he handed off to tailback Jamal Page on four consecutive plays and Alabama drove inside Auburn's 20-yard line.

The Tigers were expecting another handoff because on the next play, Gunnar faked the handoff and ran a naked bootleg left, meaning he had no blockers in front of him. Just as the safety bore down on him, he found tight end Zeke McCallister at the back of the end zone for a touchdown. Gunnar ran in for the two-point conversion to make the score 27-21.

Alabama's defense stiffened and forced Auburn to punt with 1:07 remaining. The Tide had one last chance, starting on its own 34 yard line. On first down, he completed a 28-yard pass, then scrambled for 14 yards. Two plays later, he found wide receiver Rayshard Joyner over the middle to put the ball at the Tiger three-yard line. My heart was pounding out of my chest. With six seconds remaining, Alabama used its final timeout. If Gunnar could somehow get Alabama into the end zone, and kick the extra point, the game would be over.

Gunnar came over to the sidelines and talked to Coach Guthrie for a minute to set up a final play. As he trotted out onto the field, the crowd went nuts. I couldn't even hear myself pray.

At the line of scrimmage, Gunnar barked instructions to his receivers and began to call an audible. He stood under center, mishandled the snap and dove to the ground. A huge pile formed on top of the loose ball at about the five-yard line as time expired. The officials tried pulling the massive players off, but it didn't matter who had the ball. The game was over. Auburn fans stormed the field, exulting in victory and taunting Alabama fans. An apple chucked from the stands grazed Gunnar's shoulder pad as he sprinted off the field.

Beau Whittle caught up to Gunnar as they headed into the locker room and put his arm around him. "That was the gutsiest effort I ever saw," Beau said, patting him on the back. "I don't care what the coaches or players or fans think. You're our quarterback."

That meant a lot to Gunnar. As always, he put on a brave face for the media. They surrounded him outside the locker room and peppered him with questions.

"What happened on the snap exchange at the end?"

"It was my fault," Gunnar said. "I was trying to call a pass play based on what I saw from Auburn's defense. I was so busy trying to call the audible, I forgot the snap count. Our center snapped the ball when he was supposed to. It's my fault."

"Considering the type of season you and your team had, and considering how close you came to winning, would you consider this a moral victory?"

"We don't believe in moral victories at Alabama," Gunnar said. "We lost. Even though a lot of people expected us to get blown out today, we were fully expecting to win. Still, I'm proud of my team-mates and the way they rallied out there today. We didn't quit—ever. That's what Alabama football is all about."

"Was your performance today a statement, in terms of what's going to happen with the quarterback race next year?"

"I was just trying to help us win the football game," he said. "We lost and there's a lot of guys in this locker room who are hurting right now. But I hope we remember this feeling during the off-season, that it will inspire us to do better next year. We're a young team, so hope-fully the fighting spirit we showed today will carry over."

In the local paper the next day was a huge, color picture of Gunnar walking off the field dejectedly. Above it was the headline, "*Gun-Shy.*"

No wonder he never looked at the newspapers.

CHAPTER TWENTY-TWO

The day after the Auburn game, Gunnar was a little despondent. After church I walked into his room and noticed him looking at photos of his dad and his mission.

"I don't think things could have gone much worse than they did this season," he said. "There were times this season when I thought that maybe I don't belong on this level. I thought I should just be glad that I have a scholarship. I thought that maybe the real reason why I—we—came to Alabama was to meet Danielle and Kali. But as terrible as the Auburn game went, there were times when I thought, 'Hey, I *can* play at this level.' That's why I'm not going to worry anymore about my stats or awards or even about whether I start or not. That's irrelevant. I haven't been putting the Lord first in my life like I should have, like I did on our missions. That's going to change."

Following a season of anxiousness and frustration, Gunnar was at peace. He studied the scriptures more diligently than ever and I noticed him spending a lot more time on his knees in prayer. On Saturdays, when we didn't have early-morning seminary to teach, Gunnar still woke up at five in the morning. What he did at that hour I was never sure, because I stayed in bed. What I saw when I woke up, bleary-eyed, was Gunnar doing pushups. I'd roll over and go back to sleep for another hour. By the time I had got up and showered, he was watching game film on our TV. Nobody worked harder than he did.

Not long after the season ended, Coach Guthrie hired a new strength and conditioning coach, Bubba Tankowitz. He was a former Marine (he liked to remind the players of that fact) with a crewcut and arms like battleships. He was a strict disciplinarian, a General Patton with a whistle.

Still, Gunnar took it a step farther. He gathered the other quarterbacks and receivers and tight ends every afternoon for workouts.

They would work on plays on their own, running them over and over again. Even though Gunnar wasn't officially the starter, he kind of took matters into his own hands. Besides, Waitley had to undergo ankle surgery and was unable to practice. Gunnar kept saying this was his senior year and his last chance to play in a bowl game. He didn't want to miss out on it.

An interesting thing happened during the off-season. Gunnar tried to be more of a vocal team leader. As a junior, he felt happy to be a part of the team. Going into his senior campaign, he felt ownership in the program. I remember him frequently encouraging the other players by saying, "The glory days of Alabama football are now!"

Gunnar, E.J. Jefferson and Preacher were the ones who set the tone for the rest of the team. Gunnar and Preacher peacefully co-existed, the defensive guys followed Preacher and the offensive guys followed Gunnar.

At the end of the semester, Coach Guthrie implemented what he called the "Alabama Football Olympics Night," under Bubba's direction. It was held at the Alabama basketball arena and about 1,000 fans turned out to watch the Tide players run sprints and lift weights in a competitive situation. If nothing else, it brought the team closer together and it made the drudgery of lifting weights a little more entertaining. It served as a motivator. Gunnar, Preacher, and E.J. Jefferson each earned "Iron Man" awards based on the proportionate amount of weight lifted per pound of body weight. Gunnar also received "Gold Medals" in the 800-meter and 1600-meter runs as well as the standing long jump. He also had the lowest percentage of body fat and was honored for being in the best physical condition. Not bad for a returned missionary, huh?

One afternoon after a conditioning workout, I was picking up athletic tape off the floor when Gunnar approached the kicker, John David Bender. John David had been kicking himself for his poor showing in the Auburn game. Gunnar noticed he was cleaning out his locker.

"How's it going, John David?" Gunnar asked.

"Terrible," he said.

"What's wrong?"

"I can't kick the ball straight to save my life. The coaches want me to work with the team sports psychologist. I'm fixin' to quit the team."

Kickers are a different breed. While the rest of the players are knocking each other silly, you can usually find the kickers off by themselves. That gives them a lot of time to think, and for some kickers, that's not a good thing.

"You can't quit," Gunnar said. "We're a team. I hold, you kick. We're a team."

"Look, I'm not like you," John David said. "You have your source of inner-strength. I don't. I've done judo and yoga, I've recited self-affirmation phrases in the mirror and listened to wildlife sounds with subliminal messages. None of it helps. Why do you Mormons have to be so darn happy all the time? What's your secret?"

That was the start of Gunnar's weekly Book of Mormon classes. John David, Ricky, Gunnar, and I were the only ones who attended at first, and we spent about 30 minutes a week reading different passages. We taught John David and Ricky how to pray. They even went to church a couple of times with us. Every once in a while, they'd ask Gunnar to tell them funny and inspirational stories from his mission. While they walked out to the practice field or to team meals, they'd invariably say, "Tell us another one of your mission stories."

When Preacher caught wind of our Book of Mormon get-togethers, he began his own weekly Bible Study class. Attendance for his class was much better, I'll admit. He'd get up in front of his teammates and deliver stirring sermons. That summer, I wasn't sure if we were becoming a better football team, but we sure were exercising our freedom of religion.

John David wasn't the only one of Gunnar's summer reclamation projects. Turned out, I was on his list, too.

One unseasonably warm afternoon in February, after I had accompanied him on a five-mile run around Tuscaloosa (I actually only made three of those miles on foot, the final two in a car), we were eating lunch when Gunnar snapped, "What are you doing?"

"Eating lunch," I answered, my mouth full of pimento sandwich.

"I mean about your future," he said. "Are you going to med school or not? I was thinking about you as I was running. Now I'm not going to tell you how to live your life, but I can see you as a doctor as plain as day. It bugs me to see you so wrapped up in football. I appreciate all you've done for me, but we've got one year left and I don't want to see you graduated and still wondering about your life."

Gunnar's little speech almost staggered me. A few months earlier I had declared myself an English major and I received a boost of confidence after doing well in a couple of science classes. I had promised Gunnar to look into med school, but I was scared about the process. So I guess I was procrastinating.

"Um, well," I stammered, "I'm taking the MCAT (Medical College Admission Test) in August."

"I didn't know that," Gunnar said, backing off.

Neither did I, until that moment. In fact, I couldn't believe those words spilled out of my mouth. At that moment, I made up my mind, thanks to Gunnar. Later in the week I gathered up as much information as I could about the MCAT and I started preparing, though standardized tests scared me.

Meanwhile, Coach Guthrie drew a lot of attention for some comments he made to the Tide Pride booster club. He was asked by a booster how it was possible to be above board in recruiting and still compete for national championships. "We won't cheat, period," Coach Guthrie said. "I'd rather go 1-10 and run a clean program than go 10-1 and be crooked. I know we can win and run a clean program. We will do it."

Reactions were mixed. Some admired his integrity. Others were angry that the coach would acknowledge that a 1-10 season could be a possibility (that's a federal offense in Alabama). Most people thought he was off of his rocker.

When spring drills started in March, Waitley had made a lot of progress recovering from ankle surgery but he still wasn't at full strength. Waitley participated in most of the drills, but not all of them. Billy Ray spent a lot of time rehabilitating him and Gunnar went out of his way to help, too. Together they studied film and the playbook and talked about the offensive philosophy. The press called it a quarterback controversy as if the two guys hated each other. In reality, they were good friends.

In my humble opinion, Gunnar looked and acted like the starter. Unlike the previous year, Gunnar had earned the respect of his teammates. In the annual "A" Day Game, an intrasquad game that attracted several thousands of fans, Gunnar threw a couple of touchdown passes. But afterward, Coach Guthrie said he didn't believe a quarterback should lose his starting job due to an injury. So Gunnar remained the backup on the depth chart put out by the Alabama football media relations staff. That only kept him hungrier during the off-season.

During the spring, Gunnar and I signed up for a class called "The Anthropology of Mormonism." It wasn't a lecture course, the professor told us, but a discussion course. He would get in front of the class and ask a question from the previous day's readings from LDS or LDS-related books, hoping to spark a spirited debate, I guess. Gunnar and I always had to clear up misconceptions about the Church and a few times we bore our testimonies, before the professor told us proselytizing was prohibited. We explained the concept of eternal families.

"So what you're saying is," a guy on the front row asked us afterward, "if I'm not baptized into your church, I can't be saved?"

"It's not *my* church," Gunnar said. "It's the Church of Jesus Christ. Look, we don't want to tear down what you already believe, we just want to build on what you already have."

Gunnar and I did our class project on the Prophet Joseph Smith and our classmates were impressed, I think. We received an "A." Anything less would have been downright embarrassing. The best thing about that class, though, was that a girl who sat next to us started taking the missionary discussions. Within a couple of months, she and her entire family was baptized into the Church.

NCAA rules say players can practice and prepare for the upcoming season as much as they want during the summer, but it must be done on their own. Almost every single player remained in

Tuscaloosa that summer. No coaches are allowed to supervise or even observe the workouts, except for Bubba, the strength and conditioning coach. Officially, they're called "voluntary" workouts. Players could opt not to participate. As a result, coaches could opt not to play them the next fall. Unofficially, they're called "mandatory" workouts. Just don't tell the NCAA about that. Anyway, they kept me busy.

One morning in June the players were doing drills outside in the sweltering Alabama heat. It felt like being inside a sauna. In addition to shuttle runs and sled-pushing, Bubba loved doing unorthodox drills. One of his favorites was to have players crouch down on all fours and go as fast as they could around the practice field. Bubba called them "Bear crawls." Not only were they moving like bears, they had to think about The Bear, as in Bryant, while doing them. I think it was something that he must have picked up in the Marines.

Near the end of one grueling session, Bubba announced, "Everybody take a Bear crawl!" As usual, the players groaned loudly. "Okay," he added, with a twisted smile on his face, "make that two Bear crawls! You've got 10 minutes. If the last player doesn't finish in that time, everybody must take an extra one. Your time starts now."

The players didn't say a word. They simply assumed the position and started Bear crawling. Who says football players are dumb?

Just after they started, Billy Ray told me he had an important phone call in the office. "I'm leaving you in charge," he said.

I didn't take that lightly. I was feeling pretty important. As an assistant trainer, I usually kept my eye on the stragglers, those who were struggling a little. From a distance, I noticed Ricky panting heavily and stopping every once in a while, which was unusual for him. A couple of players gave him a hard time, telling him to pick it up. They understandably didn't want to do more Bear crawls. Something told me Ricky was in trouble.

I jogged over to him, wondering if I had provided him with enough fluids. Had I accounted for the more severe heat and humidity? Did he administer his insulin injection? Just before I could ask him how he felt, he collapsed and lay motionless on the grass.

The drill came to a standstill and the players started to gather around Ricky and just looked at me.

"Help him, man!" I remember E.J. Jefferson shouting at me.

Everything became blurry for me. I was no doctor, just a humble assistant trainer. I panicked. "Somebody go get Billy Ray!" I yelled, knowing that if I didn't do something quick, it would be too late.

I bent down as all the players crowded around me. I checked his pulse and his heart. Both were faint. Come to think of it, I was faint myself. Billy Ray's words, "He's your responsibility, his life is in your hands," echoed loudly in my ears. All I could do was pray, "Don't die, Ricky. Don't die. Don't die."

Suddenly, I looked up and saw Gunnar standing over me. He never had any formal medical emergency training, but he knew exactly what to do.

"Will you help me give him a blessing?" he asked rhetorically.

All I could do was nod.

Gunnar placed his hands on his head and I placed mine on top of Gunnar's hands. He was calm as a summer's day. I don't remember a thing that was said, but by the time he was done, an ambulance had arrived and rushed him to the hospital.

Ricky lived, no thanks to me. I know it was that blessing that saved him. Nobody said it, but I think the rest of the team knew it, too. Including Preacher. After that, the players' respect for Gunnar grew tenfold. Several players asked questions about the blessing and about the Church. Attendance in Gunnar's Book of Mormon class soared to as many as eleven.

Later, rumors circulated around campus about how Gunnar raised Ricky from the dead. When the press asked about it, Gunnar had to explain all about priesthood blessings.

For me, the experience with Ricky was a sobering one. The whole thing made me doubt my capacity to become a doctor. How could I freeze like that under pressure? A tendency to lock up in pressure situations is not a good quality for someone in the medical profession.

When I told Gunnar about hat, he said I should chalk it up as a learning experience. "Performing under difficult circumstances is something you have to practice, like anything else," he said. "Remember how I froze up in the season-opener against Southern Miss last year? It happens to everyone from time to time."

"It shouldn't happen when it's a life-and-death situation," I said.

"You'll become a better doctor because of that experience," Gunnar said.

I wasn't so sure if I was cut out to be a doctor. I couldn't figure out what he saw in me. I certainly couldn't see it.

A couple of weeks later, Gunnar and I were at the Piggly Wiggly, stocking up on bananas and avocados and other essentials, when we overheard two people speaking Spanish. We immediately turned and saw two Hispanic men acting a little suspicious. They had stuffed their jackets with cigarettes and magazines. I guess they figured that two guys like us wouldn't understand Spanish because they didn't attempt to lower their voices. We were shocked by what we heard.

"You walk up to the counter with this sack and tell them to put the money in there," one of them said. "I'll hold the gun. As soon as they empty the cash register, we're getting out of here. Finish getting what we need and we'll meet here in ten minutes."

Knowing we didn't have much time, we borrowed a phone from the store manager and called the police. At first, the police thought we were pulling a prank, but Gunnar insisted that we overheard everything in Spanish.

"And how do you know Spanish?" the police officer asked.

"I went on a church mission to Chile for two years. Believe me, sir, I wouldn't make something like this up."

"What's your name, son?"

"Gunnar Hanshaw."

"The football player?"

"Yep."

"We'll send someone right over."

We waited around the store and saw several people come in, but no police officers. Time was running out. Then we noticed the two Hispanic men making their move. When they reached the cashier, one said very calmly, in broken English, "Put your money in this bag. We have a gun."

Suddenly, a man who had been browsing the magazine rack for a few minutes drew a gun and ordered the men to drop the weapon and hold up their hands. Turned out, the guy was an officer in street clothes sent by the police department. He radioed for help on his walkie-talkie and soon the place was teeming with police. They handcuffed the two men, who wondered how their plot had been foiled.

The police and the store owner thanked Gunnar for his good detective work and for being an alert citizen.

"I didn't really do anything," he said. "I just happen to speak Spanish."

The media had a field day with it, to the point that it was blown way out of proportion. According to some press reports, Gunnar had tackled the suspects and wrestled the gun away from the gunman. It sounded good, but it wasn't true. That didn't stop people from believing it, though.

Meanwhile, we both had another issue to resolve that summer, namely with Danielle and Kali.

I've heard of some mission presidents who strongly encourage their missionaries to get married as soon as possible when they return. In our exit interviews with President McPherson, he told us not to rush into anything, but to look carefully for our future wives. He explained that it would be the most important decision we would ever make. Nearly four years after completing our missions, we both had found the women we loved. So why wait any longer?

Danielle was coming up on her one-year anniversary of being a member of the Church, which meant she could get married in the temple. Gunnar and I enjoyed being roommates, but we were ready to move on. We spent hours trying to figure out how we were going to accomplish this.

We wanted the girls to be surprised. That's why we didn't take them ring shopping. When the four of us were hanging out together, we'd get them to talk about what kind of rings they liked. It didn't take much prompting.

Gunnar and I visited a local mall to look for rings. Believe me, we got some strange looks from people seeing two guys enter a jewelry store together. Fortunately, one of the dealers recognized

Gunnar and told him he was one of his favorite Alabama players. It was probably just a shallow line to get our business. But it worked.

The rings weren't extravagant, but we still had to borrow a substantial amount of money from our parents to make the purchase.

When the rings were finished a couple of weeks later, we picked them up and we picked up Danielle and Kali at their apartment early one Saturday morning. We had told them to get dressed up and that we were going on a little road trip. Several hours later we were at an Atlanta restaurant.

The girls were unusually quiet, wondering what we were up to.

"This is fun," Danielle finally said when our meal arrived at our table, "but did we come all the way to Atlanta just for lunch?"

"Sure," Gunnar said. "I hear these are the best fries in the South."

"We're a little overdressed for lunch, dontcha think?" Danielle said. "It's not like this is some exclusive French restaurant."

"Is that what you had in mind?" Gunnar asked.

"Well, when you told us to dress up," Danielle replied, "I thought maybe we might be doing something special."

"We've got one more stop to make," I said.

"Knowing you two," Kali said, "it's probably a baseball game."

The girls weren't complaining, though. They enjoyed the mystery of it all.

After lunch we drove to the Atlanta Temple grounds and piled out of the car. They became even more intrigued. "Let's walk around," Gunnar said.

So he and Danielle went one way, Kali and I the other. When Kali and I found a secluded spot on the grounds with nobody around, we stopped walking and gazed at the temple. My heart was racing.

"Beautiful, isn't it?" I asked.

"It is," she said. "Preston, it's about 90 degrees out here and yet you look like you're shivering. Are you okay?"

"Everything's fine," I said.

"It's so peaceful here," she said.

Then I awkwardly dropped to one knee.

"What are you doing?" Kali said with a trace of panic in her voice. "Are you okay? Do you need a doctor?"

"It's okay," I said, looking up into her face. Then I swallowed hard and took her left hand and told her I loved her. I reached into my suit coat pocket, pulled out a box and gave it to her. With trembling hands, she opened it. She was speechless.

"Kali," I said, "will you marry me?"

At first, she just stared at me in disbelief. Her eyes welled up with tears, which began dripping on my arm as she stared at the ring.

"I love you, too," she said, grinning. "Yes, I will marry you."

I stood up and hugged her. Then she pulled away. "I've got to tell Danielle," she said. "Don't tell me Gunnar is proposing to her, too?"

For his sake, he better be, I thought.

Just then we saw Danielle and Gunnar walking toward us, and both were beaming and practically floating on air.

"Does that answer your question?" I said.

The girls ran toward each other, as fast as they could in heels, and hugged. They tried their best to maintain the proper decorum. It was hard for them to avoid screaming with excitement while maintaining a sense of reverence on the temple grounds.

We returned to Tuscaloosa and told Bishop Clements the good news. We also told him not to make a big deal about it. The following day during sacrament meeting, he announced our engagements and followed that up by saying, "Boy, oh boy, did y'all see those rocks on their fangers?"

We planned to have a double wedding, of course, at the Atlanta Temple in mid-July, just before football season. Though we did everything else together, we decided to draw the line at honeymooning together. It was expensive for our families to come all the way to Atlanta, but they were happy to come.

From that day on, the burden of planning the weddings fell to Danielle and Kali, which in itself was a relief for us. While we were attending classes and preparing for the upcoming season, the girls picked out china patterns and sent out invitations. About the only thing we showed up for was getting our pictures taken for the invitations. My parents and Gunnar's mom came to Alabama a week before the wedding to get to know their new daughters-in-law.

Gunnar was about to become the only married player on the team. A bunch of players wanted to throw Gunnar a little bachelor's party. Of course, their idea of a bachelor's party and ours were polar opposites. Gunnar said he would show up if they promised to keep it low-key, with no girls jumping out of cakes. We went to an apartment of one of the players and there were several cases of beer on the table. Then E.J. ordered us into the kitchen, where he showed us a couple of gallons of milk. "That's for you guys," he said.

So Gunnar and I drank milk out of the container while almost everybody else drank cans of Budweiser. We left before the passed-out bodies started piling up in the living room.

Anyway, our wedding day was glorious. Kali and I were married first, after which we had all of our pictures taken. An hour later, we attended Gunnar's and Danielle's wedding. That night, we had a giant reception at a stake center in Birmingham. Hundreds of friends from Alabama attended, including quite a few players on the team. I think some of them were a little offended that they weren't invited to the wedding itself, so we tried to explain the situation as diplomatically as possible.

Not only were Gunnar and I with the southern belles of our dreams, we'd get free haircuts the rest of our lives. We couldn't imagine how we could have been any happier. Who would have guessed we'd find our eternal companions in Alabama, of all places?

After the honeymoons—I won't offer any details about mine—we came back to Alabama and moved into our respective apartments in Tuscaloosa. Conveniently, they happened to be right next to each other.

"Are you sure you guys can live without each other?" Kali asked me with a smirk.

"Aside from a serious case of withdrawals during the honeymoon, I think we'll be okay," I said with a smile. "Can I invite Gunnar for sleepovers?"

"Not on school nights," Kali said.

CHAPTER TWENTY-THREE

About the time we got back, the radio talk shows and newspapers started diving headfirst into football. Some of the discussion revolved around Alabama's schedule, which featured a non-conference game at Notre Dame in addition to the regular Southeastern Conference deathmarch against Georgia, Ole Miss, Tennessee, Arkansas, Mississippi State, Vanderbilt, Louisiana State and, of course, Auburn.

Coming off another losing season, standards weren't as high as usual. Things couldn't get much worse, folks in Tuscaloosa figured. A mere winning record would have been welcomed. Still, there was some optimism. That season, Alabama had a huge senior class, which included Gunnar. Many of those seniors had arrived in Tuscaloosa four years earlier as part of what was considered a blockbuster recruiting class. The year they signed with Alabama, the Tide was coming off of probation. Unfortunately, after their freshman season ended, Alabama was placed on two-year probation again due to NCAA violations that occurred when they were in junior high. Instead of transferring, they decided to stick it out. Bama fans respected them for that, but the fact remained that they were in jeopardy of becoming the first class of players to go four years without a single winning season. That hadn't happened since the 1950s, when J.B. "Ears" Whitworth was the coach. He happened to be the guy who preceded the Bear. In case you're wondering, no, there are no "Ears" Whitworth busts on campus or any streets named after him.

Mostly, though, the hot topic was Alabama's quarterback "controversy." It was clear not everyone was sold on Gunnar, despite those flashes of brilliance he showed in the Iron Bowl. Among the fans, Waitley was still the favorite. Because of the hard work of the trainers during the off-season, including myself, Waitley had a clean bill of health entering the season. During the beginning of fall camp, Coach Guthrie named Waitley the starter going into the season-opener against Southern Miss.

Meanwhile, Gunnar was elected by his teammates as a team captain, along with E.J. Jefferson, Beau Whittle, and Preacher.

I had been married only a few weeks when I had to take the MCAT, the Medical College Admission Test. Kali, who was very supportive of my quest to get into med school, quizzed me during our honeymoon. When we returned, she helped me while I shaved and ate breakfast. I studied on my own late at night. I used those memorization methods Gunnar had taught me. I felt good about my preparation, but by the time I went into a classroom to take the test I was shaking as if I had some neurological disorder. I took my booklet and started. I looked around the classroom and had this over-whelming feeling that I didn't belong. *You have no business taking the MCAT*, I kept hearing a voice say. It might have been three of the worst few hours of my life. It was torture. The test is broken up into four sections—verbal reasoning, physical sciences, biological sciences, and the writing sample. I did poorly on each.

My mind kept drawing blanks. I'd look down at the page and all of the words blurred. I spent a lot of time chewing on my No. 2 pencil. On the written portion of the exam, nothing I wrote made sense. I think I may have written part of it in Spanish. I got about two paragraphs into it when the proctor announced time was up. I slinked out of there feeling lower than an earthworm. I knew I had flunked the MCAT. There went my shot at going to med school.

Kali was at work at the salon that afternoon. I returned to our apartment to find balloons and streamers and a cake. She wrote a note that she left on the kitchen counter. "You're finished! Congrats! I can't wait to come home and celebrate. I love you!"

I just went to our bedroom and lay on the bed, feeling sick to my stomach. I just felt like a complete failure. A couple of hours later, Kali, Gunnar, and Danielle arrived. They were in a festive mood. I wanted to change my name and move to Guam.

"Preston, congratulations!" Gunnar said. "You're on your way to med school!"

Kali burst into the bedroom. "Something wrong?" she asked.

"I don't want to spoil the party here," I said, "but I didn't pass."

Gunnar and Danielle stepped into the room.

"What do you mean?" Kali said. "You don't get the results for two months."

"Trust me," I said. "It was like all the information I have learned leaked right out of my ears. I won't be going to med school. Sorry to let you all down."

There was about 10 seconds of silence, which felt like 10 hours.

"We'd better go," Gunnar said. "We'll see you tomorrow at church."

They left, leaving Kali and me alone. She sat down next to me, took my hand, lifted my face off the bed and looked into my eyes.

"Preston, I am so proud of you," she began. "You haven't let anyone down, least of all me. No test can measure the kind of man you are. That's all that matters. I love you."

That's when she wrapped her arms around me and lay my head on her shoulder. Then I just cried and cried, until her shirt sleeve was soaked. All I kept thinking was, *What did I do to be blessed with a wife like this?*

The next day, after church, Gunnar brought up the MCAT issue with me. Typical Gunnar, he encouraged me to try it again, insisting that I was smart enough to pass it. I told him I'd think about it.

I still wasn't myself for a couple of days, but life went on. I decided to take a page from Gunnar's book and immerse myself in someone else's problems. One day after practice, my duties as an assistant trainer had me working on Preacher's ankle. He had slightly strained it during a seven-on-seven drill. Since he didn't like Gunnar much, he didn't like me, either. With most players I had a cordial relationship, even a friendship. I'd listen to their complaints and concerns, as if I were some sort of bartender. When players entrust you with their health and well-being, I guess they figure they can pour out their heart to you as well. Working with Preacher was another story. While taping an ice pack to his swollen ankle, we didn't communicate much. He got up and left for the day, but he left his backpack in the trainer's room by mistake. I decided I'd better return it to him. But as I grabbed it, I didn't realize it was open and books fell all over the floor. As I picked them up, I saw that there were a few books about "witnessing" to the Mormons. Apparently he was feeling threatened by the numbers turning out to Gunnar's Book of Mormon study group, though it wasn't many.

One was called, "How Shaky A Foundation." In smaller letters it said, "How to reach our well-meaning but dead-wrong Mormon friends."

I hurriedly stuffed them back into the bag, tracked Preacher down and handed it to him.

"Thanks," he muttered.

Later that day I told Gunnar about what I had found. One of those who attended Gunnar's class was Rayshard Joyner, the fastest guy and the best receiver on the team. He was also one of the smartest and most humble. Raised by his grandmother in a small Alabama town, Rayshard learned to read the Bible and knew what it meant to be a Christian. He never said anything bad about anyone and although he was exceptionally gifted as an athlete, he was as humble as could be.

Not surprisingly, Gunnar and Rayshard became good friends, though not only because of their quarterback-receiver relationship. After that incident with Ricky Fontaine, Rayshard made it a point to talk about God and religion. Rayshard said he had attended many different churches and never felt comfortable in any of them. He took a few of the discussions that summer and I really thought he was going to be baptized. But then he stopped coming to our Book of Mormon studies, and explained that he wasn't interested in hearing any more discussions. He told us he was too busy. But Gunnar and I, using our missionary training, knew we decided to find out what was really happening.

Turned out, Preacher had started talking to Rayshard, who began reading anti-Mormon literature. So we confronted Rayshard about it.

"Look," he said, "I like the stuff your religion teaches, I like the Book of Mormon and the way you guys pray and worship God. The gospel you teach really makes sense and speaks to my heart, but I can't belong to a church that embraces racism."

Gunnar and I knew what was coming, though we never had any experience with it in the mission field. We never encountered any black people in Chile.

"Rayshard, we don't embrace racism. Not at all," Gunnar said.

"I understand your church didn't give priesthood authority to blacks until 1978, is that right?"

"That's right."

Rayshard, normally a very calm person, was upset. "I also understand you Mormons think that we blacks are cursed with dark skin, is that right? Just like it says in your Book of Mormon."

"No," Gunnar said, "we don't believe that. We are all Heavenly Father's children. I know it's difficult to understand why God did not allow blacks to hold the priesthood before 1978. Truth is, I don't know why and I don't think anyone does, either. But we believe what happened in 1978 was the result of a revelation from God to a modern-day prophet."

Rayshard shook his head. "I just can't affiliate with a church that is prejudiced. I don't think you two are prejudiced, but I've been reading a lot about the history of your church and I don't like what I'm reading."

"As long as you're investigating the Church, remember to give equal time to both sides," Gunnar said. "You're reading all about one perspective of the priesthood ban. There's another side. Remember how you feel when you read the Book of Mormon and when you pray. Go to Heavenly Father and ask Him about it."

"I don't know, man," he said with a sigh. "I feel disillusioned. I thought I had found something special with the Mormons. I guess it's like they say. 'If it's too good to be true, it usually is.'"

He never attended another Book of Mormon class or talked with us about the Church.

We were disappointed, of course, but Gunnar and I realized Rayshard would have had to confront the issue sooner or later. "It's better that he find out about this before he got baptized," Gunnar told me.

Preacher posted fliers around the locker room about his Bible study class. Gunnar and I decided to drop in and pay Preacher a visit. There were only a handful of players who came on a regular basis, so our presence was noticeable. You should have seen the look on Preacher's face when we showed up, armed with our scriptures.

"Hope it's okay that we come," Gunnar said.

"Of course," Preacher said smugly. "The Lord never turned anyone away."

Preacher began by having everyone sing a couple of verses of "Amazing Grace." Then he preached a little sermon and we read from the Bible. Preacher always threw a few jabs our way, but we never let him know that it bothered us. We'd just smile a lot and talk about how much Jesus Christ meant to us.

"You mean you guys believe in Jesus?" one player asked us.

"Of course we do," Gunnar said. "We belong to the Church of Jesus Christ of Latter-day Saints."

"Oh," the player replied. "I thought you guys worshiped someone named Mormon. That's what Preacher said."

It didn't go over too well with Preacher when the class members asked Gunnar to prepare something about his beliefs for the following week. "We welcome all kinds of beliefs here, even false ones," Preacher said, gritting his teeth.

The next week when we met, Gunnar brought out a cassette tape player and played the Mormon Tabernacle Choir version of the hymn, "Come, Come Ye Saints." The black players all yawned and laughed and said the Mormons needed some "soul" in their music. Then he told the story about the pioneers' trek across the plains to Utah and how "Come, Come Ye Saints" was written during that trek across the country. Then the players asked to listen to "Come, Come Ye Saints" again. Gunnar passed out copies of The Book of Mormon and together we read about Christ's visit to the Americas. I swear you could have heard Preacher rolling his eyes. When Gunnar finished, Preacher asked if he could make a comment. Gunnar relented, but it was much more than a comment. It turned into a full-fledged ten-minute sermon about the errors of Mormonism, how man cannot be saved simply by not sinning. He wanted to ignite one of those Baptist-vs.-Mormon, grace-versus-works debates. Gunnar kept his cool, as usual.

"You're denying Jesus," Preacher said. "Only Jesus can save us from our sins, no matter what we do." When he finished, sweat dripped from his bald pate.

Now I had about a dozen scriptures out of the Bible that I was prepared to read Preacher, to set him straight. But before I could open my mouth, Gunnar simply bore his testimony of Christ, then he excused himself.

A few days later, one player told Gunnar that no matter what Preacher said, he thought Gunnar was acting the most like a Christian of the two.

Heading into the season, Preacher was the defensive star, Gunnar was the backup quarterback. Preacher was on the cover of the media guide, touted as a Butkus Award and an All-America candidate. Gunnar was just hoping to get into a game.

CHAPTER TWENTY-FOUR

Days before the season began, the coaches posted hotel room assignments for the year. Gunnar was paired with Jamal Page, a troubled running back. He was a prep All-American in high school in Mississippi, but his three previous years at Alabama were filled with troubles. He fathered two children by two different women, he had been arrested for DUI and theft, he missed an entire year with a serious ankle injury, and he was on academic probation. He also liked to refer to himself in the third person. "Ain't nobody better than Jamal," Jamal would say during practices.

Coaches would say, "C'mon, Page, give it a full effort!" To which Jamal would respond, "Jamal plays hard when Jamal wants to play hard."

Other than that, everything was fine with him.

When he arrived on campus he was hailed as the school's top recruit in years, destined to break all of the Alabama rushing records and go on to the NFL. Instead, in three years, due to injuries and off-field mistakes, he had taken a total of 32 handoffs, which is about the same number of times he had nearly been kicked off the team. As a senior, he had lost interest in school and football. As a cocky freshman, he believed he would play a couple of years, maybe win the Heisman Trophy, then make millions in the NFL. Once a "can't-miss" prospect, he turned into a big mess. The only thing worse than his situation was his attitude.

During two-a-days he'd mope around and say derogatory things behind the coaches' backs. He had a reputation for being lazy in the weight room. In the summers he would attend the voluntary workouts but you could tell he was never fully committed. Then when he'd get his chance in practice, he'd run the wrong play. It was too bad because there were times he'd show a glimpse of his tremendous potential. He had a graceful gait when he carried the football and he was so instinctive with the way he could elude tacklers. Coaches kept him in the program over the years hoping that one day he would be able to display his talents on the field, but Coach Guthrie had stomached about enough of him.

That's why I don't think it was any coincidence that Page and Gunnar were assigned to room together on road trips. Coach Guthrie wanted to help him, but not at the expense of the entire team. I overheard Coach Guthrie telling one of the other coaches one day that he was giving Page one more chance to shape up. If he didn't, he would be gone.

"Jamal's bein' assigned to a babysitter?" That was Jamal's reaction upon finding out Gunnar was his roommate.

Gunnar and I weren't superstitious or anything, but we decided that on the Thursday night before every game, we would drink *leche con platano* and avocado sandwiches. That meal reminded us of our success in the mission field and we hoped it would transfer over to other aspects of our lives.

At the completion of fall camp in preparation for the season, Coach Guthrie told Gunnar that he was going to redshirt Dillon Redhage and that Gunnar was going to be the backup.

"You've earned it after working hard this summer," he said. "I want you to prepare for every game as if you'll be the starter."

Like Gunnar, I had learned a few lessons from the previous season. I remembered how he had cramped up due to the humidity in his first game the previous year. One of the papers I had to do for one of my summer physiology classes was study the effects of humidity-caused cramping. During my research, I found an article in a sports medicine journal that said pickle juice was an effective antidote. I decided to do my own little experiment on Gunnar. Something told me he would be playing at some point in the season-opener.

That morning, I got up early and went to the hotel restaurant and made an unusual request.

"May I have a small glass of pickle juice please?"

They gave it to me, without asking any questions. Then I went to Gunnar's room. Gunnar answered the door and let me in. I gave him the pickle juice and told him to drink it.

"What's this for?" he asked.

"For cramping," I said. "I read it in a trainer's magazine. Pickle juice reduces the chances of cramping up."

He looked at the juice and at me. "Okay, you're the trainer," Gunnar said.

And he gulped it down and nearly threw it up.

Jamal was getting out of the shower about then and had overheard us. "Jamal can't handle bein' surrounded by Mormons," he said.

Before a game, Gunnar and Jamal had two different ways of preparing. Jamal would do pushups in nothing but a towel while listening to rap music. Gunnar would pull out his Spanish copy of the Book of Mormon to read Alma 26 while listening to his Mormon Tabernacle Choir tape. He said it inspired him.

Anyway, we arrived at Legion Field that afternoon for the game. After running out onto the field and seeing the same opponent, Southern Miss, brought back some nightmarish flashbacks of the previous season's opener. I could tell Gunnar was itching for a chance to play, even if it was in the fourth quarter with the outcome decided.

On the third play from scrimmage, Gunnar was granted his wish, though a lot sooner than he had expected, and not in the way he had hoped. Waitley went down in a crumpled heap at the 28-yard line, tearing the anterior cruciate ligament in his left knee. Right away, it was clear he was done for the season.

Coach Guthrie turned to Gunnar, who grabbed his helmet and went to work. It didn't take him long to shred Southern Miss's defensive secondary. On second down he completed a 45-yard pass to Rayshard Joyner, who made a spectacular diving catch. A couple of plays later, he threw a 19-yard touchdown strike to Rayshard.

When Southern Miss had the ball, Gunnar asked me about Waitley, who was taken to the locker room and told me to tell him how sorry he was. So I did.

Gunnar wound up tying a school record with seven touchdowns passes that day in just three quarters, and Rayshard caught three of them. Dillon Redhage's redshirt status was burned and he played the final quarter. The final: 63-zip. In one afternoon Gunnar seemed to erase one year of frustration. Nobody was happier for him than me.

Of course, Preacher found a way to spoil Gunnar's Kodak moment.

After the game, he gathered players on both sides at midfield for a postgame prayer. Gunnar shook hands with the opposing players and as he walked off the field, he tossed his sweatbands to a couple of little kids. Then he headed for the locker room. Though Preacher was busy offering the prayer, he took notice. Before hitting the showers, Preacher confronted Gunnar.

"Hey, Mormon, don't you believe in giving thanks to Jesus? You think that was all you out there?"

Gunnar tried to ignore him.

"Here you are professing to be a religious and spiritual guy, yet not once in the year that you've been here have you prayed with us on the field."

"Everyone has their own way," Gunnar said. "Other people have other beliefs and I respect those and I hope people respect mine. Praying at midfield is not my style."

"Oh yeah? What *is* your style?"

I had a feeling that would get Gunnar going.

"Look, my religion teaches that anyone can worship anywhere, anytime, in any way they want. You can do what you want. For me, I follow what Jesus taught in the Bible. Didn't He teach that we should pray in secret, not to be seen by men?"

"What, are you calling me a hypocrite?"

"I didn't say that. You did."

Preacher shoved Gunnar into a locker door and bloodied his lip.

"And I suppose you'll turn the other cheek, too," Preacher said as he walked away. Gunnar pressed a towel to his mouth and finished dressing.

E.J. Jefferson pulled Preacher aside and told him to cool down. Then he swore everyone to secrecy. "How 'bout we say nothin' to the press about this," he said. "What happens in the locker room stays in the locker room."

It was timely advice, because it was time to meet the media.

Suddenly, Gunnar found himself in the good graces of Bama fans everywhere, except for Preacher that is. Every newspaper and

TV station in Alabama fired questions at Gunnar while, a few feet away, Preacher was being interviewed, too.

The press wanted to talk about the record-setting day, but Gunnar emphasized that the win was a team effort. He credited his offensive line, his receivers, his running backs, his coaches.

"And our defense is awesome," Gunnar said, loud enough for Preacher to hear. "Pitching a shutout like that was fun to watch."

"So can you perform like this in two weeks when you play at Notre Dame?" columnist Chip Merriweather asked. I think he was talking about Gunnar in particular, but Gunnar only wanted to talk about the team.

"We've got to see if we can play this way next week against North Texas first," he answered.

Meanwhile, Preacher was busy praising, too. "That was all God," he said. "We played hard and God did the rest. I've got to thank the Lord for allowing us to win today."

In every answer he gave, he had to mention the Lord. I thought it was interesting that by doing so he seemed to be bringing attention to himself, not the Lord. At least, that's my humble opinion.

Gunnar told me later he actually liked the fact that Preacher rode him so much. He said it inspired him not to let his guard down when it came to living the gospel.

Then came the question of the day to Gunnar from a reporter. "What happened to your lip?"

"I got hit awfully hard by a linebacker," Gunnar said with a smile. "It's part of the game." He didn't say it was a linebacker on his own team.

Gunnar came out of the locker room nearly an hour after the game had ended to find about 100 kids lined up with pens and game programs in hand. His eyes first scanned the crowd, and he found Danielle. After giving her a hug, he spent a good part of another hour shaking hands and signing autographs, all the while smiling.

I kept busy doing trainer stuff while Danielle and Kali waited patiently in the background. By the time we left, it was dark. Gunnar wanted to go visit Waitley at his apartment. He was scheduled to undergo knee surgery the following week. We spent a few minutes with him and Waitley congratulated him and wished him well for the rest of the season.

After that the four of us went out to eat. Well, Danielle, Kali and I ate. Gunnar signed more autographs and relived the game with fans. It was nearly 11 p.m. by the time we got home. Gunnar was growing on people like kudzu.

Though we had church early the next morning, I couldn't sleep. I was too keyed up. While Kali slept, I stayed up until 2 a.m. that night watching SportsCenter over and over again, just to make sure Gunnar's performance wasn't a dream.

At church, everyone wanted to talk to Gunnar. When he entered the chapel, all eyes were on him. Everyone patted him on the back and talked about the game. Even Bishop Clements, who didn't know a touchdown from a touchback, mentioned Gunnar during sacrament meeting. During Sunday School there was almost more talk about the game than about the Old Testament.

After church I bought a couple of local newspapers to see what they were saying about Gunnar and the Tide. "*'Gunslinger' Leads Bama to Victory,*" screamed the *Tuscaloosa News* on the front page. Not the front page of the sports section. The front page of the entire newspaper.

"That boy can play football," E.J. Jefferson was quoted as saying. "That's why we call him 'The Mormon Gunslinger.' Did you see him complete a couple of those passes right between three defenders? There was only one place he could put the ball and he did it. He's kind of different, you know? I mean on and off the field. He's a nice guy. He wears Dockers and sensible shoes off the field, but on the field, he's a terror. I kept seeing that look of fear in the eyes of Southern Miss's defensive backs. The guy doesn't drink. The worst thing I ever heard him say is 'heck.' I don't understand the Mormons at all, but Gunslinger, he can play football. He's the whole package. He can run, he can throw, he's got eyes in the back of his head, you know? I don't know what happened to him during the off-season, but he's a totally different quarterback than he was last year."

When the national polls came out, Alabama received a few votes. A few national Internet sites mentioned Gunnar's remarkable performance, though they also pointed out the following disclaimer—that it was against Southern Miss.

After practice one day that week, Beau Whittle approached me. "What's Gunnar's secret?" he asked.

"Secret?" I asked.

"Yeah. He's the same guy, but such a different quarterback than he was a year ago. What got into him?"

I thought for a moment and figured I would play along. I got close to his ear and whispered, "*Leche con platano.*"

Beau furrowed his brow. "*Lazy come flat you know*? What does that supposed to mean?"

I explained about *leche con platano* and told him the ingredients.

"Is that a Mormon thing y'all do?" he asked.

"No," I said. "It's a Chilean thing."

"Where can I get some?"

I told him that Gunnar and I met to drink it on Thursday nights and invited him over. Beau drank his first glass and immediately poured himself another. "Shoot, this stuff tastes better than beer," he said, wiping away his *leche con platano* mustache from above his lip.

"It's good for you, too," I said.

Against North Texas, Gunnar was in a no-win situation. Everyone expected perfection from him. Well, Gunnar delivered near-perfection, again. He completed 16 out of 21 passes for 312 yards and three touchdown passes (he also ran for two more) — in three quarters. Meanwhile, Alabama's defense just as impressive and the Tide earned a 41-0 shutout. Beau Whittle immediately became convinced of the mystical qualities of *leche con platano*. He recorded two interceptions and a sack. The rest of the season, he drank *leche con platano* the night before a game. He introduced other teammates to it as well.

Preacher was not one of them. "Lord willing," he said to reporters, picking parts of North Texas players out of his teeth, "we're going to have the best defense in the nation this year!"

Of course, after the North Texas rout, all that the reporters wanted to ask questions about was the Notre Dame game in South Bend, Indiana, the following week. Once again, it was a mob scene outside the locker room. After autographs, Gunnar and I went back to our apartment with Danielle and Kali to avoid the crowds.

CHAPTER TWENTY-FIVE

The week of the Notre Dame game was completely nuts. Alabama finally cracked the Associated Press Top 25, at No. 25. The Fighting Irish were ranked No. 6. As with all of Notre Dame's home games, this one would be on national television.

Gunnar was looking forward to going on the road for the first time that season. It gave him an opportunity to play some practical jokes. The previous year, he was never in the mood for joking around. His senior season was a different story. One time he brought a pumpkin pie into the trainer's room, sat down and started eating it while a couple of teammates looked on, drooling. After he took a bite he looked up and said, "This tastes kind of funny. Hey, would you guys like some?" And they'd line up and grab a fork and dig into it. What they didn't know was instead of whipped cream on top, he had put shaving cream.

While the team was at the airport in Tuscaloosa, waiting for the charter flight to South Bend, he had various coaches and players paged over the public address system. Once they were on the plane, he told the captain that it was Ricky's birthday when it really wasn't.

I suppose it was kind of a stress-reliever for him. And the stress piled up on him the week of the Notre Dame game. He had dozens of media interview requests from newspapers and magazines from around the country. The media wondered what Gunnar and the Tide could do against "real" competition. Gunnar expected to field questions about the Irish's defense. He did, but he also got a number of unexpected questions.

"Being a Mormon," Chip Merriweather asked, "does this game hold any special significance, to play against a Catholic school?"

Gunnar was blindsided by that one. But, like the great quarterback he was, he masterfully sidestepped the rush. "To be honest with you, it never crossed my mind that I'm a Mormon going against a Catholic school," he said with a chuckle. "It's a football game, not a theological debate. It's a game between two programs with a lot of mystique, tradition and history."

"What do you think of the Catholic Church?"

"I don't know what this has to do with Saturday's game," Gunnar said.

"Didn't you proselytize to the Catholics on your mission?"

"I met and worked with a lot of Catholics during my mission for the Church of Jesus Christ of Latter-day Saints. They're good people."

(Gunnar constantly tried to emphasize that he was a member of The Church of Jesus Christ of Latter-day Saints, while explaining that it was the same thing as the Mormon Church. Some reporters got the name of the Church right while others didn't bother to get it right. Some called it the Church of the Latter-day Saints. "Mormon" was a lot easier for people to understand. I suppose that The Church of Jesus Christ of Latter-day Saints Gunslinger just didn't have the same ring to it as The Mormon Gunslinger.)

"Did you convert some Catholics on your mission? How many?"

I could tell Gunnar was becoming bothered, but he tried not to let it show. "Yeah, I saw a few Catholics who joined our Church," he said. "But you guys are blowing this all out of proportion. This is a football game between two very prestigious schools. That's it."

Reporters then asked about Gunnar's mission, about what he could and couldn't do, about what he learned, about how hard it was to come back after a two-year layoff. It gave him a chance to talk about missionary work and the Church.

When we arrived in South Bend, the media who cover Notre Dame was there waiting, looking for sound bites for the 11 o'clock news. Of course, Gunnar was the one everyone wanted to talk to. Preacher was not too pleased about that. Gunnar was already on the Heisman Trophy watch list. He was leading the nation in passing and total offense. He was about to step onto the biggest stage of his career to that point—Notre Dame Stadium.

In the morning I bought a copy of the *Chicago Tribune*. One smug columnist wrote about Gunnar, "You've heard of a young gun. Well, this guy's an old gun." He wrote that Gunnar had served a two-year mission for "the Church of the Latter-day Saints." He added that Gunnar was married, spoke fluent Spanish, and "didn't drink anything stronger than Sprite."

We had some free time that morning so Gunnar and I walked around the campus, which was filled with large cathedrals. I kept pinching myself. I couldn't believe I was there. We kind of stood out, since we were wearing Alabama paraphernalia. Students and faculty members were very nice to us and wished us well. We saw the so-called "Touchdown Jesus," a 132-foot-high stone mosaic on the south side of the library. It depicts Christ with upraised hands and it is visible from inside the stadium. On the other side of the library we found "We're No. 1 Moses," a bronze statue that depicts Moses in flowing robes at the foot of Mount Sinai. Moses is chastising the Isrealites and the right index finger on his right hand is extended upward.

During the walkthrough at Notre Dame Stadium on Friday, I decided to do a little sightseeing. I saw the sign outside the locker room that says, "*Play like a champion today.*" I was also allowed to step into the Notre Dame locker room. I could almost hear the echoes of the famous "Win One For the Gipper" speech. There was an aura surrounding the place that was so thick, it felt like I was covered in a film of blue and green and gold. It reminded me of my first day in Tuscaloosa.

At the end of the walkthrough, Coach Guthrie gathered the team together and had them kneel down in the end zone. He stood among them in the shadows of the goal posts with his own Gipper speech prepared.

"This is the place where Paul Hornung, Joe Montana and The Four Horsemen played. Some of the most memorable games in college football history happened right where you're kneeling. But what I want to tell you is, none of that matters. We're not playing against ghosts or legends. We're playing against a team that we've studied extensively on film. They're football players, like you. We have no reason to be intimidated by this atmosphere. The most important thing I want you to do is enjoy this moment and play as hard as you can. This game will be one you'll remember the rest of your lives. Let's make some memories of our own tomorrow."

With that, the team huddled up around Coach Guthrie. Jefferson yelled, "Go Bama!"

"Roll Tide!" screamed his teammates.

Gunnar was busy the rest of the night with team meetings. Curfew was 10 p.m. I called his hotel room just after that to wish him luck.

"Do me a favor. Don't get into any fights with that leprechaun mascot of theirs," he joked.

Billy Ray and I shared a room as usual. He fell asleep quickly, but I couldn't even close my eyes. I did some physics homework, flipped through Notre Dame's 423-page media guide, then watched a little TV. In the morning while I dressed, one of the pundits on ESPN's College GameDay predicted Notre Dame to rout Alabama. "The Tide are overrated. They've played one of the weakest schedules in the nation. Their quarterback is a senior, but he's inexperienced when it comes to big games. Look for the Irish to roll over the Alabama pretenders."

That really fired me up.

I looked out the hotel window to see four buses lined up. We boarded and headed to Notre Dame Stadium, accompanied by a police escort. It was a sunny September morning, a gorgeous day for college football. When we arrived, thousands of Irish fans were already there in the parking lot. Some were barbecuing beef and drinking out of their hip flasks. Even from outside the stadium there was a palpable sense that something big was about to happen inside.

While the teams warmed up on the field, fans filled the stands. Amid the sea of navy and gold there was a relatively small faction of brave Bama fans clad in red. We went inside the locker room, where the players received final instructions from Coach Guthrie. After we ran out of the tunnel to a smattering of cheers, I stayed close by and waited for the Fighting Irish to emerge from the same tunnel. When they did, the crowd let out a thunderous roar, the players' golden helmets sparkled in the sun and the band struck up a rousing rendition of the most famous fight song in college football.

Cheer, cheer for old Notre Dame,
Wake up the echoes cheering her name,
Send a volley cheer on high,
Shake down the thunder from the sky.

At that moment, I knew it couldn't get much bigger than this.

Notre Dame won the coin toss and deferred until the second half. James Whitten took the opening kickoff all the way out to the Irish 41, quieting the crowd. Gunnar strapped on his helmet, took the field, went under center and dropped back to pass on first down. He couldn't find any open receivers so he tried to sprint out, but he slipped and fell without being touched. On second down, he handed off to Page, who was swarmed under by a host of navy-and-gold uniforms. It was a three-yard loss. On third-and-18, Gunnar's pass attempt sailed way out of bounds, nearly into the front row of seats. It marked the first time Alabama had to punt that season with Gunnar as the quarterback.

As if we didn't know it already, Notre Dame was no Southern Miss or North Texas.

The Irish kicked a 20-yard field goal on their first possession. Gunnar returned to the field and completed a four-yard pass but was sacked twice. The Tide had to punt again. At the end of the first quarter, after four possessions, Alabama had minus-three yards of total offense and no first downs. The offense that exploded against the first two opponents couldn't budge against Notre Dame, which held a 10-0 lead.

It appeared Gunnar had found his stride in the second quarter on a 33-yard completion to Rayshard Joyner, but he threw his first interception of the season on the following play. Gunnar didn't see the free safety cheating on the outside and he picked off the pass and returned it for a 68-yard touchdown. At halftime, it was 17-0.

It looked like Bama's bubble had burst. There were a lot of heads hanging in the locker room. Except for Gunnar's.

"We're going to beat these guys!" he said. "We've played a bad half of football but we're only down by two touchdowns and a field goal. Let's score on our first possession and then we're back in this thing!"

Not to be outdone, Preacher arose. "They've got their Touchdown Jesus and we have our own. Nobody believes we can win this game. Let's shock the world!"

Just before returning to the field, Gunnar approached Coach Guthrie with a suggestion. "When we get the ball, let's try a red-halfback-fly," he said. It was a gimmick play Coach Guthrie ran at the end of almost every practice, for fun.

"This is no time for trick plays," Coach Guthrie said.

"Coach, it might loosen the guys up. We're all a little tight. Plus, I don't think Notre Dame will be expecting it."

"I'll think about it," Coach said.

On Notre Dame's first play from scrimmage in the second half, Preacher nearly sawed a little wide receiver in half. As the Irish player lay writhing in pain on the ground, Preacher went down to one knee, with his head bowed, as if he were thanking the Lord for the power and ability to maim. Notre Dame then punted to Alabama, giving the Tide field position at the 'Bama 39.

Coach Guthrie pulled Gunnar aside. "Okay we'll run red-halfback-fly," he said. "If this doesn't work, I'm telling everyone you called it."

Gunnar smiled and huddled up with the rest of the offense.

"Red-halfback-fly," he announced to his teammates.

"Don't be kiddin' Jamal," Jamal Page scoffed.

"I'm serious," Gunnar said. "That's the play."

"Does Coach Guthrie know about this?" asked E.J. Jefferson.

"He's the one who called the play," Gunnar said.

"Jamal can't do this," Page said. "Jamal can't throw passes in a game. Jamal's a running back!"

"It works every time we run it in practice," Gunnar said. "Now let's run the play."

Just as they had practiced it, Gunnar handed the ball off to Page, who ran right a few yards. Then he stopped, turned and threw the ball to the opposite side of the field. You could almost hear the sound of the entire city of Tuscaloosa shouting, "What is Jamal doing?"

What Jamal was doing was throwing a pass to Gunnar. It was a little behind him, but Gunnar caught it at the Alabama 34 yard line.

Suddenly, he was running all by himself. Just when a couple of Irish linebackers appeared to have an angle on him, instead of going out of bounds, he juked and bolted down the middle of the field, causing Coach Guthrie to gain a few more silver hairs. "Go down! Go down!" he yelled to Gunnar.

Of course, Gunnar couldn't hear him and even if he did, he probably wouldn't have listened anyway. He loved running in the open field. He kept eluding tacklers, weaving back and forth until he reached the end zone. Talk about an electrifying way to open the second half.

"Maybe Jamal should be the quarterback," Jamal said to Gunnar as they high-fived and returned to the sidelines.

Just as Gunnar had predicted, the play loosened the players up. In fact, it loosened them up a little too much. E.J. lumbered down field on the play and performed an Irish jig on the goal line. The referee whistled him for excessive celebration, which was tacked onto the extra point attempt. But John David Bender split the uprights anyway to make the score 17-7. It didn't surprise me in the least. Tucked inside John David's right shoe was a piece of paper with the scripture 2 Nephi 9:41 written on it. In part, it says, "Behold, the way for man is narrow, but it lieth in a straight course before him."

Hey, whatever works.

The Tide defense gave the offense a huge break when Preacher recovered a Notre Dame fumble on the Irish 13-yard line. Two plays later, Gunnar found the tight end in the back of the end zone. By the end of the third quarter, Alabama trailed by just a field goal, 17-14.

After three quarters of what was mostly a defensive struggle, both teams traded two touchdowns each to push the score to 31-28 for the Irish. With only 1:04 remaining in the game, Alabama's defense held, but Notre Dame's punt was downed at the Tide six-yard line. Gunnar had 64 seconds and 94 yards to go for the victory.

On first down, Gunnar handed off to Jamal, who went straight up the middle and busted a couple of tackles to the 17-yard line. Then Gunnar completed three consecutive short passes to march the Tide to midfield. Alabama called its second-to-last timeout with 22 ticks left on the clock.

Since the passing game was effective against Notre Dame's prevent defense, Coach Guthrie wanted Gunnar to keep throwing. Then disaster struck. As Gunnar stood in shotgun formation, the ball was snapped about five feet over his head. The pigskin skipped along the turf way back to the Alabama 34-yard line, where Gunnar dove on top of it before being snowed under by six Irish defenders. That play not only consumed 10 seconds, it lost the Tide 16 valuable yards. On second-and-26, Alabama was called for a false start, pushing the ball back to the 29. Gunnar's third-down pass was almost intercepted at the Notre Dame 45 with two seconds on the clock. It was fourth-down-and-31, but it might as well have been fourth-down-and-hopeless.

At that point, I'll admit it, I felt it was over for Alabama. So did everyone else—except for Gunnar. Everyone in the stadium and all the millions of television viewers knew what the Tide would try to do. The only thing they could do was heave a desperation pass into the end zone and pray for a miracle.

"Everyone get in the end zone," Gunnar said in the huddle, "and someone, please, catch the ball."

Alabama flooded the right side of the line of scrimmage with five receivers. As soon as he had the ball, they all ran toward the end zone like their pants were on fire. As Gunnar dropped back, I looked up at the scoreboard, which showed that time had expired, meaning this was it. After scrambling around in the pocket, he planted his foot, cocked his arm and let the ball fly. It seemed to hang up in the late afternoon sky for an eternity. I can still remember wondering if it would ever come down. The end zone was congested with navy and white jerseys. As the ball fell toward Earth, Alabama and Notre Dame players looked heavenward, spotted the ball and moved together toward the back corner of the end zone. A host of bodies leaped for the ball and I lost sight of it. All I saw was a bunch of bodies tumble in and out of the back of the end zone. Then the referee emerged from the pile with his hands raised in the air. Somehow, Ricky Fontaine came down with the ball. Touchdown. Alabama 34, Notre Dame 31.

I tried to be as professional as possible in my job, trying to do it in a dignified manner. But when Ricky pulled down that pass,

I instinctively leaped in the air and, as it turned out, pulled my hamstring. I didn't start feeling it until a half-hour later and Billy Ray had me go in for treatment with the players. Yeah, I took a lot of razzing.

As you probably know, that 71-yard TD pass was shown countless times on sports highlight shows the rest of the season. It was an instant classic. I never grew tired of seeing it.

After that play, the Fighting Irish faithful sat in stunned silence. Their players dropped to their knees and pounded the turf. The leprechaun mascot lay down at midfield, his arms and legs outstretched, apparently KO'd in disbelief.

When he saw that Ricky had caught the ball, Gunnar sprinted to the end zone and jumped into the mosh pit of Crimson Tide players celebrating. "I don't believe in your Church," Rayshard told Gunnar, "but I believe in you, man."

Even the usually unflappable Coach Guthrie was hugging players and pumping his fist.

While I was down on the field, after the crowd had dispersed, I was limping around and decided to pick a few blades of grass from the spot where Ricky had caught the ball—you know, for posterity's sake. No, I never planned on selling them on eBay or anything. I placed them in an aspirin bottle and closed the lid. I still have that aspirin bottle, though Kali thinks it's bizarre.

When I congratulated Gunnar afterward, he threw his arm around me and said, "I just wish my dad could have seen this." Then he paused. "Come to think of it, he probably did."

In the postgame press conference, Coach Guthrie was still shaking his head in disbelief. "I've heard of a Hail Mary pass," he said, "but that's the first 'Hail Mormon' I've witnessed. I just might convert to Mormonism."

The media asked about Gunnar. "It's good to see good things happen to him, because he's such a good kid. He's a guy who's got his priorities straight. He's a joy to coach."

The media asked Gunnar if he had prayed for a miracle before uncorking that pass.

"No," he said. "I've never prayed to win a game. Ricky made an amazing catch. I'm not going to say it was the result of divine intervention because I don't think that in the overall scheme of things, Heavenly Father cares which team wins or loses. We're all His children, so how can He play favorites? I'm sure he has far more important things to worry about, things with eternal significance than some football game. It was just a hard-fought, well-played battle between two great football teams. We're fortunate to come out on top. Our coaches and players worked hard and we were prepared for this game. The defense came up huge for us, especially Preacher."

Gunnar couldn't figure out why everyone was making such a big deal about his religious affiliation.

When Preacher was asked about The Play, he said, "I just want to thank the Lord. All praise be to Him. The Lord was with us. He carried us to victory. Man, I was praying there on the sidelines, callin' Jesus' name that someone would catch that ball. Like the Bible says, the Lord works in mysterious ways."

"Are you saying the Lord wasn't with Notre Dame?" the reporter asked.

"I don't know anything about that. I don't know what the Catholics believe. I don't know what their players were saying on the sidelines."

"And what about Hanshaw's performance today?" another reporter asked.

"It just goes to show you the Lord can work miracles."

If nothing else, it made for interesting copy. The next day, the headlines were filled with references to "Hail Mormon." The *Chicago Tribune* used "Heavenly Heave" above a photo of Gunnar throwing that pass.

On the flight back to Tuscaloosa, members of Alabama's media relations department made plans to launch a belated Heisman Trophy campaign. Usually, schools start hyping their top player during the summer, sending out little knick-knacks with catchy phrases. Alabama already had a name for its campaign: *The Mormon Gunslinger.* You can imagine how Preacher felt about that.

Hundreds of fans wearing crimson and holding signs were lined up around the tarmac at the airport. Gunnar signed dozens of autographs and posed for pictures. He and I would be talking and the photographers from the newspapers and media relations department would ask me to step out of the frame.

Monday afternoon before practice, they made Gunnar pose inside Bryant-Denney Stadium with his uniform on. The had him put his helmet in the crook of his left arm. In the other arm he clutched a football. There were a couple of rifles set up next to him. They applied a little makeup to his face and told him not to smile, which, for Gunnar, especially that week, was hard to do.

Within days, the media relations department printed thousands of postcards and posters with that picture on it with the words, "Alabama Football" superimposed on the top and "Gunnar Hanshaw—The Mormon Gunslinger—for Heisman" on the bottom.

At that point, no one could mention Gunnar Hanshaw without saying "Heisman Trophy candidate" in the same breath.

I don't know what Preacher disliked more—Gunnar receiving all that publicity or the Mormon Church receiving all that publicity. He wasn't alone. Most people, I believe, saw the word "Mormon" like they would a term of ethnicity or heritage, like "Californian" or "Irish" or "Chilean." Others, including some faculty members at the university, didn't like the use of Mormon at all. Some local religious leaders didn't like so much being made of a "non-Christian" denomination. They saw it as blatant proselytizing for the Mormon faith.

Gunnar stayed out of the fray. He was embarrassed by the publicity and stayed focused on football. When he was asked about it, he shrugged and replied, "Don't ask me. I'm just here to play football."

By Wednesday, "The Miracle In South Bend" T-shirts started appearing in area stores. They sold out in hours. After the Notre Dame game, Gunnar had taken off a sweatband from his right arm and had tossed it to a little kid wearing an Alabama shirt. Within days, that sweatband showed up on eBay. The bidding started at $100. A grandmother from Phenix City, Alabama, purchased it for $450.

After that game things changed with our early-morning seminary class. All sorts of kids turned out, just to see Gunnar. Attendance grew exponentially. We didn't have to bribe our students with donuts anymore. When non-LDS kids discovered that Gunnar was at the Mormon Church every weekday morning at 6 a.m., well, they just had to be there too. In fact, we had to move the class from a small Sunday School room to the chapel. Afterward, there were usually autograph requests—and Gunnar signed their complimentary copies of The Book of Mormon.

That same week, sports agents began schmoozing Gunnar. Somehow they got a hold of his phone number and they called him nonstop. It got so bad that Danielle stopped answering the phone. She eventually changed their number. It became such a circus-like atmosphere that the biggest fear for Gunnar—and Coach Guthrie—was that the team would lose focus, become distracted and be overconfident. By beating Notre Dame Alabama jumped from No. 25 to No. 11 in the national polls. Not only would Gunnar have to face a tough opponent every week, but also lofty expectations.

Everyone who had abandoned the Gunnar Hanshaw bandwagon a year earlier was on board once again. Even the curmudgeon sports writers like Chip Merriweather. A year earlier, Gunnar was widely criticized. They said he was unpolished, undisciplined and took too many chances. Suddenly, he was a great improviser. The year before, they had said he waited too long to get the ball off. Suddenly, he was gutsy and courageous in the way he stood in the pocket. The year before, they said he was too small too see over his towering line of scrimmage, too small to last an entire season. Suddenly, they said he made up for his lack in size with a huge heart.

Go figure.

Gunnar was embarrassed by all the fuss being made over him. He felt he was receiving too much attention and too much credit for Alabama's 3-0 start. Every chance he could he talked up his teammates and coaches. No one seemed to listen, though. Gunnar's time was being filled with interview requests and it got to the point where the university assigned two employees to deal just with Gunnar. One morning he appeared on the *Today Show* for a live interview.

"So," the host began, "what's a nice Mormon boy like you doing at *Alabama?*"

"Just playing football," Gunnar replied with a smile.

"A week ago nobody knew who you were. Now, you're a national celebrity. Talk about how you've reached this point."

"I don't know about that. Coach Guthrie has a great offensive scheme and we have all the talent in the world around me. My job is just to be calm and make sure we move the ball."

"You served a mission to a foreign country for two years, right?"

"That's right."

"How did that affect your life?"

"It was a great experience, one I wouldn't trade for anything. It was a turning point in my life. I saw change come to lives of people. I learned to care about others more than myself. I have a better understanding of who I am."

The words just spilled out naturally because he had answered the same questions so many times. But he always said them with conviction.

"According to the Alabama media guide, you're 25 years old. Is that correct?"

"Yes." It wasn't as if Gunnar had a receding hairline, a mortgage and five kids or anything.

"Does being five or six years older than some of your teammates and opponents give you an unfair advantage?"

Gunnar avoided controversy the way he avoided a rushing defensive end with anger management issues, but he had no choice but to answer the question as well as he could.

"Yeah, it is an unfair advantage," he said. "It's unfair that we as members of The Church of Jesus Christ of Latter-day Saints get to leave our families and other pursuits behind to go somewhere for two years and serve other people. Everybody should have that experience. It was the best thing I could have done with my life at that time. It has been a huge blessing to me."

"If you believe it is an unfair advantage, then, do you think there should be an age limitation imposed for college athletes as some are saying?"

"Absolutely not."

"Then how would you resolve this controversy?"

"I think every college in the country should have a missionary program."

"Do you believe you are a better football player because you served a mission?"

"Yes, just like I believe I'm a much better person because I served a mission. I suppose if a mission has helped me with football—it's helped me in the way I deal with adversity. A mission is all about overcoming adversity. So, when I'm in front of 80,000 screaming fans on a Saturday afternoon, it's not nearly as intimidating compared to some of the things I faced in the mission field. I've been in tough spots before, and that mission experience helps me put it all in perspective. I learned how to work hard, set goals and achieve them."

"Still, most guys your age have already graduated from college. You're older than many NFL players."

"That's true. That's why after games I enjoy a nice, refreshing glass of prune juice," Gunnar said, grinning.

The interviewer laughed and moved on.

"How much football did you play on your mission?"

"I threw the football with a companion only a handful of times. I did a lot of pushups and a lot of walking, but that was all the working out I did. There's no time in the mission field to worry about football. I came back skinnier and weaker physically than I was when I left. It took me a couple of years to get back that competitive edge."

"I guess what you're saying is, if it were really that much of an advantage, everybody would be going on missions."

"Yeah, you could say that."

Gunnar's teammates also had a hard time understanding how he could be 25 and still be in college. "Jamal never heard of a college player who's 25," Jamal would say, "except for my cousin Cletus. But he was held back from the fourth grade three times."

"You're more than halfway to 50, man!" E.J. Jefferson liked to say.

Yet the players respected him for his beliefs. They had a tough time understanding how he could live such lofty standards. His teammates marveled that he could be so busy with church responsibilities and being married, yet he could be a great student and the hardest working player on the team.

No matter how much Gunnar tried to disarm the age issue, it wouldn't die. It seemed like it was the biggest controversy in college football that season. I couldn't figure out why the media felt Gunnar had to defend himself. He certainly wasn't the first college football to play at the age of 25. The way people were talking, you would have thought he was almost eligible for Social Security benefits.

Several coaches in the Southeastern Conference weren't as understanding, of course. They said publicly that Gunnar was "a man among boys." They called into question the NCAA rule that allows student-athletes who serve religious missions or serve in the military to take time off, then resume their careers.

The way Gunnar saw things, all the controversy he caused was a blessing in disguise because every story written about him mentioned the Church. "I get to play football," he told me, "and do missionary work at the same time."

He was proving to be a perfect ambassador for the Church. Not only did he have to deal with the negative comments about his age, he had to deal with the Heisman hype. Oh yeah, and he still had to be a husband and a student and go to class and do interviews and sign autographs for adoring fans. Did you know that children all around Alabama sent him school reports they had written about him? Gunnar received e-mails from all over the country and all over the world. One missionary couple from Outer Mongolia even dropped a line to say how inspirational he was. Believe it or not, he was becoming an inter-national star.

CHAPTER TWENTY-SIX

Week by week, the scrutiny and attention intensified. The Saturday after the dramatic Notre Dame victory, some people wondered if there would be a letdown when Bama played host to Middle Tennessee State. A 52-9 victory pretty much answered that question.

It had become clear that Gunnar was becoming an icon of sorts in Tuscaloosa. At some places fans hold up signs referring to the Biblical reference, "John 3:16." During that Middle Tennessee State game, I noticed a couple of handmade signs in the crowd at Bryant-Denney Stadium created by some members of our Tuscaloosa ward during Family Home Evening. One read, "*And a Mormon shall lead them.*" The other said, "*Courage, brethren; and on, on to victory! D&C 128:22.*" Believe me, there were more than a few people scratching their heads about that Doctrine and Covenants reference.

A week later, 4-0 Alabama opened the conference schedule at home against Vanderbilt. The Commodores put up little resistance as Gunnar threw for 556 yards and the Tide rolled easily, 49-17. Gunnar remained No. 1 in the nation in passing and total offense. That's about the time the school introduced its line of "Mormon Gunslinger" bobblehead dolls (which, I might add, actually bore a striking resemblance to Gunnar) to mail out to media members and Heisman voters around the country and to sell to the general public.

Next up? Arkansas. The Tide traveled to Fayetteville to face the Razorbacks. Their defense was no match for Gunnar Hanshaw, however. Arkansas hung with Alabama for about a quarter. But before you could say "Whooooooo Pig Sooey!" Gunnar & Co. erupted for three second-quarter touchdowns en route to a 38-10 win. One of those touchdowns was the result of a fake field goal. Gunnar was in his customary holder's position, on a knee, and caught the snap and rolled out right. Then he turned and fired a TD pass to the kicker, John David Bender.

"I think maybe you were born to be a wide receiver," Gunnar told him afterward.

It was the middle of October by then and Alabama was 6-0 and ranked No. 7.

As you can imagine, Gunnar received a lot of mail that fall. He got a couple of letters, postmarked Provo, Utah, that asked why, since he was LDS, he didn't go to BYU instead of Alabama. "You could have done so much good for the Church at the Church school," they wrote.

"I didn't receive a scholarship offer there, or else I probably would have gone to BYU," Gunnar wrote back.

During his senior year Gunnar continued visiting hospitals, rest homes, and elementary schools, just like he did the year before. Only he couldn't do it anymore without being followed by reporters and cameras for feel-good footage for the 11 o'clock news across Alabama that night. Gunnar was embarrassed because it looked like a public relations stunt or something. When Gunnar made arrangements to make visits, he had to ask that it be kept out of the media. They obliged.

Meanwhile, Gunnar's Heisman's campaign continued to gain steam. Billboards with a picture of Gunnar, holding his crimson helmet in one hand and a ball in the other and flanked by firearms, were posted along roadsides throughout the state. Everyone talked about The Mormon Gunslinger. In fact, I bet a lot of people knew who the Mormon Gunslinger was but couldn't tell you who Gunnar Hanshaw was.

Many Heisman voters considered Gunnar among the top five favorites. Because of those firearms, I'm pretty sure the NRA would have voted for him, if they could have. The leading candidate, though, was a flashy running back named Darius Streeter, who played for the No. 1 ranked Miami Hurricanes. One week he ran for 278 yards and four touchdowns against Boston College and was considered the No. 1 pick in the upcoming NFL draft. As a sophomore the previous year, he had finished second in the Heisman Trophy balloting.

As if my time wasn't already spread too thin in the training room, in class and at practice—Kali was extremely patient and understanding that fall—I volunteered as Gunnar's unofficial personal assistant. I set up speaking schedules and other related commitments. He became inundated with requests to speak at firesides in Alabama. Bishops and stake presidents called asking if he could talk to their youth. Gunnar agreed to do it, of course. That's how he spent nearly every Sunday. He'd tell them to put the Lord first in their lives. He encouraged the young men to prepare to serve a mission.

Danielle, Kali and I would always go with him to these speaking engagements. Danielle was a pretty good sport about the whole thing, given she felt like she was sharing her husband with the entire nation. Later, requests came from cities like Baton Rouge and Knoxville, where Alabama had road games that season, to do firesides. Gunnar asked Coach Guthrie for permission, thinking he'd be turned down. To his surprise, Coach said yes, as long as it didn't interfere with team meetings and with curfew. Coach Guthrie completely trusted Gunnar and respected his Church commitments.

That fall the mission president in the Alabama Birmingham Mission wrote a touching letter to Gunnar. A couple of months before Gunnar and I arrived at Alabama, the mission area had been rededicated because things were not going well. In the dedicatory prayer, an Apostle of the Lord said that fortuitous events would unfold in the near future that would bring a positive image about the Church and open doors to missionary work. The mission president said it was his opinion that Gunnar was an answer to that prayer and many prayers offered previously and subsequently. Through his great example, not to mention great play on the field, the mission president said, Gunnar had singlehandedly helped soften many hearts and minds to the gospel.

Gunnar and I always felt like there was a purpose for going to Alabama, a purpose higher than just to play football. That letter confirmed those feelings. Knowing we had been called on another mission, a much different one from our first one, was humbling.

Some woman in Alabama was so smitten with Gunnar that she created a Web site in his honor—**mormongunslinger.com**. She said she created it because Gunnar had taken time after a game to sign autographs for her two young sons. Not only did he sign their game programs, he asked the kids their names and posed for a picture with them. Gunnar just had that kind of effect on people.

CHAPTER TWENTY-SEVEN

It was the same ole, same ole for Alabama against Ole Miss—another easy win, 45-13. It was almost becoming routine. Another blowout. Ho hum. This time, though, Jamal Page enjoyed a career day. The Rebel defense was so keyed on stopping Gunnar that it allowed Page to rush for 229 yards and four touchdowns. Gunnar even threw blocks for Page, who was well on his way to a 1,000-yard season. Because they played together in the backfield and were roommates on road trips, those two became good friends. Not once did Jamal have off-field problems that fall. He said it was the longest period he had gone in his life without getting into trouble.

"Jamal's the best running back in Alabama history," Jamal said, prancing around the locker room, wearing nothing but a towel and a broad grin. "Ain't nobody stoppin' Jamal. Jamal's got it all."

"Except maybe some humility," Beau Whittle replied.

"Man, whatchu talkin' 'bout?" Jamal said. "Humility is Jamal's best quality."

The Georgia Bulldogs posed a much stiffer challenge. Both teams were undefeated and the media viewed this matchup as a national championship elimination game, meaning the loser would fall from contention. Georgia had one of the toughest defenses in the country and the Bulldogs came into Bryant-Denney Stadium with a No. 8 ranking. With three minutes remaining, the score was tied at 14. Gunnar had his worst game of the year against Georgia—he was sacked four times and threw two interceptions. But, once again, he saved his best for last.

He drove the Tide to the 'Dawg 43-yard line after a couple of nifty runs and crisp passes. It was fourth-and-one with 32 seconds remaining. In a gutsy move, Coach Guthrie opted to go for it against the stingy Georgia defense. He risked giving the ball back to the Bulldogs with time to win the game. I remember some fans booing and saying it was not smart football. It was hard to argue with that.

Jamal Page lined up in the backfield and everyone figured he'd get the ball—it seemed to be the Tide's best shot at a first down. Georgia put eight defenders near the line of scrimmage, preparing to stuff him.

However, Coach Guthrie had other ideas. He had Gunnar fake the handoff then, hoist a pass into the end zone. As he threw it, my heart fell into my throat. An incompletion would give the Bulldogs great field position. But because Georgia, and the rest of the world, expected a run, the Bulldogs' defensive secondary was playing man-to-man coverage, leaving Ricky Fontaine open. He acted like he was a decoy, when in reality he was the target. He should have earned an Academy Award for that performance. He hauled in the pass in stride in the end zone. Bryant-Denney Stadium erupted. I swore I felt the stadium rock off of its foundation.

The Mormon Gunslinger had come through once again. After that play, some sportswriters labeled Coach Guthrie with a nickname of his own—the Riverboat Gambler.

Alabama's defense held on for the final few seconds to preserve the 21-14 win. Gunnar had engineered yet another fantastic finish. "With him at the controls," Jefferson told the media afterward, "we feel we can win a national championship."

That was the first time an Alabama player publicly talked about winning a national title. It wasn't the last, but there were still four regular season games left, including three straight on the road. Two of the opponents—Tennessee and Louisiana State—were in the Top 25. Yet the most difficult of all, I figured, would be the Iron Bowl against the dreaded Auburn Tigers.

Alabama was one of four undefeated teams left in the country, along with No. 1 Miami, No. 2 Florida and No. 3 Michigan. Two of those were from the Southeastern Conference.

A couple of days before the Mississippi State game, I received my MCAT scores back and learned I was right about my suspicions. I bombed. But after a lot of encouragement from Kali and Gunnar, I resolved to re-take the test in April.

It was a relatively short bus ride from Tuscaloosa to Starkville. Mississippi State was a mediocre team that season, but when

Alabama came to town, they filled the stadium with fans and with hopes of upsetting the mighty Crimson Tide, which jumped to No. 5 in the rankings. Though it was against Southeastern Conference rules, that didn't stop a large group of fans from smuggling cowbells into the stadium. It was a time-honored tradition in Starkville to ring those bells throughout the game. It was like being at a rodeo.

Alabama got off to a sluggish start and Mississippi State led at halftime, 14-10. In the second half, though, the Tide scored on each of their first four possessions to seize a commanding 38-10 advantage. Gunnar tossed three touchdown passes before sitting out the fourth quarter. Alabama won, 45-20.

That set up a showdown between Tennessee and Alabama in Knoxville. The Volunteers were ranked ahead of the Tide, even though they had lost one game, the season-opener against UCLA.

Tennessee's coach was always known for playing mind games in the press about opponents. Not that he came up with anything original the week of the Alabama game. He spent most of his time making a big deal about Gunnar's age. "He goes away for a couple of years supposedly teaching people about the Bible and comes back to play. He's what, 30 years old, playing among teenagers? Ther's just something un-Christian about that. The NCAA needs to do something about this issue."

Funny, I wanted to tell him, how it wasn't an issue the previous year when Gunnar was riding the bench. Of course, by then, Gunnar was used to those types of comments.

Let me tell you about Neyland Stadium, home of the Tennessee Volunteers, and a place where Alabama hadn't won in years. Some say it's the best place in the world to watch college football. On one side of the stadium you can see the Tennessee River, where fans arrive by boat. They tailgate for hours before kickoff and stay for hours after the game. On the other side there's The Hill, the historic center of the Tennessee campus. Rising above it all are the fabled Smoky Mountains.

Inside the stadium, there's Orange everywhere. It's like being on an island surrounded by a sea of Minute Maid. There were more than 104,000 fans in attendance that day, or about 100,000 more than the population of Ephraim, all decked out in Orange. The Vol players, wearing orange tops and white pants, ran through a big T formed by the Pride of the Southland Band, led by Smoky, the blue tick coon hound. I remember getting another major headache after hearing "Rocky Top" constantly sung by 100,000 fans. In fact, I heard it in my sleep for a whole week after leaving Knoxville.

The game was amazing—even the losing team had to agree. It had a little bit of everything, except defense. Both teams had solid defensive squads, but on that afternoon, the offenses were just too good. The Vols opened the game with an 80-yard drive for a touchdown and the Tide responded with an 80-yard drive of their own for a touchdown. Late in the second quarter, Tennessee led 20-17. Gunnar was marching the Tide downfield in hopes of tying the game, or taking the lead, by halftime. But as he scrambled out of the pocket, he planted his foot and braced for a bone-crushing hit by a Vol defensive tackle.

Coach Guthrie gasped and so did the rest of Crimson Tide Nation. Immediately, Billy Ray and I ran out onto the field to attend to Gunnar.

"It's my right ankle," he said, wincing. "I think it's just a sprain."

Turned out, it was a severe sprain. We were just relieved it wasn't his knee. We helped him off the field and into the locker room.

"When can I come back in?" he asked.

Billy Ray frowned. "You can play, but you'll risk doin' further damage if you do," he said. "If you call it a day, you can rest up and be close to 100 percent next week."

If we don't win," Gunnar shot back, "there *is* no next week."

The team doctor, Dr. Wayne Hickman, joined us and examined the ankle. He cleared Gunnar to play. He was a big Tide fan.

Meanwhile, with Gunnar in the locker room, Tennessee extended its lead to 27-17 at intermission.

"Are you sure you want to keep playing?" I asked him.

"As long as I can stand upright," he said, "I can play. They'd have to carry me out on an ambulance."

Billy Ray and I wrapped up his ankle so tight I wondered if he'd be able to even walk, let alone elude a pass rush. At the start of the second half, Gunnar hobbled back onto the field. Even some Tennessee fans cheered him out of respect.

Gunnar wasn't the same quarterback on one good leg, of course. His mobility was impaired and, because he planted his tender right foot to throw, his strength and accuracy were compromised, too. Yet watching him out there, he reminded me of a warrior, limping around, not giving up, wanting so badly to win. Every time he came off the field, he'd ask me to rewrap his ankle.

Somehow, he still managed to run the offense. Alabama matched Tennessee touchdown-for-touchdown. It was almost like a tennis match. Gunnar found other ways to move the ball, including handoffs to Jamal Page, who had another impressive game.

As the fourth quarter began, the score was 41-31. So much for a smashmouth Southeastern Conference defensive struggle. Like a couple of heavyweight fighters after ten rounds of absorbing punches, both teams looked physically spent, yet emotionally determined.

Alabama narrowed the deficit to 41-38 on Gunnar's touchdown pass to Rayshard Joyner, and, after a successful on-side kick, John David booted a field goal with 14 seconds left that tied the game at 41 and sent it into overtime. As per NCAA overtime rules, the offensive team gets the ball at their opponents' 25 yard line. First downs are allowed and the clock is turned off. If the first team scores a touchdown, the second team must equal that to keep the game going. They keep going until there's a winner or until someone drops from exhaustion.

Alabama and Tennessee traded touchdowns on their first two possessions to make it 55-55 going into the third OT. Tennessee got greedy, though, trying to strike quickly on first down with an ill-advised pass into the end zone. Beau Whittle intercepted the pass, giving the ball back to the Alabama offense again. All the Tide needed was a field goal to win. Gunnar completed a short pass on first down. Then he gave the ball to Jamal, who saw a wide open lane, and, like a runaway truck, he barreled into the orange-and-white-checkered end zone. The final score? 61-55. It looked more like a basketball score than a football score. When it was finally over, players collapsed on the turf. Even the Tide players were too tired to celebrate much. Alabama improved to 10-0 on the season.

That was the game that convinced the nation that Gunnar was no fluke and his upstart Heisman campaign was ratcheted up a couple of notches. A few websites listed him a solid No. 2 behind Miami's Darius Streeter. More importantly, Bama climbed to No. 3 in the polls.

Gunnar never lost touch with reality, or his responsibilities, despite the success he and his team were experiencing. The day after the Tennessee game, he quietly, without fanfare, did his duty. He and I went hometeaching and he gave a blessing to an elderly sister in the ward who was feeling ill. She thanked him profusely afterward. Gunnar later said that was the highlight of his week.

CHAPTER TWENTY-EIGHT

We had barely settled in after the trip to Tennessee when the team departed for Baton Rouge for a date in "Death Valley" against Louisiana State. If you're not familiar with college football, "Death Valley" is the nickname of LSU's stadium because, for visiting teams, it's a miserable place to play football. It's loud and crazy. As it turned out, most of the Alabama players felt like death warmed over during this trip to Baton Rouge.

The night before the game, while the players were with the coaches for meetings in the hotel, a couple of guys excused themselves to the bathroom. Then a few of more did. Before I knew it, Billy Ray summoned me. Players and coaches were throwing up, Gunnar included. I felt pretty queasy, myself. We administered nausea-relief medicine to everyone and they went to their rooms to bed. Most everyone was up throughout the night, though. To this day the exact cause of the ailment remains a mystery. Doctors say it was a case of food poisoning, perhaps a bad batch of chicken gumbo. Conspiracy theorists in Alabama believed it was deliberate.

Word got out about the Puke Festival we had in the hotel that night and that gave the Tigers great hope for an upset. The LSU student section unfurled a huge banner for the television cameras before the game, saying, "*Alabama's Season Going In The Toilet!*"

Those crazy Cajuns were plum hyped up for the game.

The television commentators wondered if "Death Valley" was where the Mormon Gunslinger's Heisman campaign would be buried.

The Bayou Bengals had a 7-3 record and one of the nation's top-rated defenses, but they had no answers for Gunnar—even though he was still just a week removed from a sprained ankle and even though his stomach had revolted against him. The Tigers tried everything to stop him. Sometimes, they blitzed seven players up the middle, but

Gunnar rolled out and found an open receiver. When the pressure came from the sides, he stayed in the pocket and found an open receiver. When they left seven or eight defenders in coverage, he tucked the ball under his arm and ran. Gunnar had become a guru at reading defenses. It was as if Gunnar could do anything he wanted on the field, even when his stomach was churning like a washing machine. At halftime, he lay prone on the hard tile in the bathroom for about five minutes before finally getting up and upchucking again.

In the third quarter, a beer bottle thrown from the stands thwacked Gunnar in the head, though, fortunately, he was wearing his helmet. In the end, he passed for more than 400 yards and three touchdowns in a 40-21 victory. The fact he did it while sick only impressed the fans and the media all the more.

Finally, the week Alabama fans had been waiting for all season had arrived—the regular-season finale against Auburn. The Tigers were only average, but, as was proven the previous year, records have little meaning when fierce rivals get together. It was the only topic the radio talk shows discussed for an entire week. World War III could have broken out that week and I'm convinced that the entire state of Alabama would have been oblivious to the whole thing.

There was a report out of Auburn that a group of students held a pep rally in a parking lot complete with a huge bonfire. News cameras showed Tiger fans hoisting a No. 22 Alabama jersey on a stick, being dragged on the blacktop, then having things thrown at it, then, finally, it was tossed into the fire as the throng cheered. Gunnar was burned in effigy. He thought it was hilarious.

Heading into the Auburn game, a reporter from *Sports Illustrated* came to Tuscaloosa to do a story on Gunnar. The Alabama media relations people informed him about the interview and he really didn't want to do it because he wanted to focus on the biggest game of the year. After all, he knew Alabama could win all of its games but the one against Auburn and that would be the one everyone in the state would remember.

Still, Gunnar realized that doing interviews like this was part of the responsibility of being a star quarterback. Besides, the Alabama media relations people were told it could be a cover story. Oh great, I thought. That's all he needed—an SI cover jinx.

To escape all the hype surrounding the game, Gunnar and I decided we'd fix a nice dinner for our wives at my apartment. We knew trying to go to a restaurant would have been impossible. So, on Wednesday night, we prepared an elegant meal with the help of the guy who was in charge of the team's training table. He made the food and we only had to heat it up. The girls were impressed, but not fooled. They knew the only items we knew how to make were *leche con platano* and avocado sandwiches.

After we washed the dishes, we played a game of Scrabble. We deliberately left the TV off, knowing it would have been impossible to not see or hear something about the game.

Before Gunnar and Danielle got up to leave, Danielle took Gunnar's hand and said, "Should we tell them?"

"Tell us what?" Kali said.

Gunnar nodded. Danielle smiled. "We're expecting!" she said.

Kali screamed so loudly that the neighbors called to ask if everything was all right.

"We just found out yesterday," Gunnar said.

I was so happy for them. I knew Gunnar would be a great dad.

Staring Gunnar in the face that week was a huge rivalry game, his final home game, a perfect record, a Heisman Trophy race, and a possible national championship. Only Auburn stood in his way. Still, I think knowing Danielle was pregnant served as the biggest motivator of all. What made it all that much sweeter was that his Mom flew out from California to be there.

Once again, he turned in an amazing performance. He completed his first 12 pass attempts, including three for touchdowns. At halftime, it was 28-3. The Tide crushed the Tigers, 44-16. When Gunnar came out of the game midway through the third quarter, he received a rousing standing ovation from the Alabama fans.

"They're the greatest fans in the world," Gunnar told the media afterward, "and it's been an honor to play here at Alabama. It's hard to believe this was my final home game, but there's still a lot of work yet to do."

Alabama had two weeks to get ready for the Southeastern Conference championship game at the Superdome in New Orleans. That first week, *Sports Illustrated's* cover story came out, with a picture of Gunnar throwing a pass against Auburn with the headline, "GUNNING FOR A TITLE." Under that it read, "Alabama quarterback Gunnar Hanshaw shoots down rival Auburn." I bought about 20 copies—for posterity's sake.

The article was very positive about Gunnar and about the Church. It said he had a decent shot at winning the Heisman Trophy. All season long I told him he'd win the Heisman, but he never brought it up and I don't think he ever thought about it. Reporters asked him about it all the time, about how it would feel to be the first returned missionary to win the coveted prize. Gunnar always downplayed such talk. He was always about the team, not himself. "If I were fortunate enough to win it, I'd have to take a saw and cut it into about 100 pieces to share it with all the people who helped us have such a good season," he said. Days later, he received his official invitation to attend the Heisman Trophy ceremony at the Downtown Athletic Club in New York City.

Coach Guthrie gave the players a couple of well-deserved days off after the Auburn victory. Then it was back to business. Florida, which won the Eastern Division of the SEC, was ranked No. 2 in the nation and the Gators were also undefeated. The only other unbeaten team, besides Florida and Alabama, was top-ranked Miami, which had already secured a spot in the national championship game—at the Orange Bowl in Miami—on New Year's Day. It was no secret that the winner of the Alabama-Florida game would meet the big, bad Hurricanes for the national crown.

But first things first. The Florida Gators were loaded with talent, including quarterback Jeb Zimmerman, who had an outstanding season, though he was overshadowed by Gunnar Hanshaw. There was an intriguing subplot, too. Coach Guthrie had been fired as an assistant coach by Florida's coach about eight years earlier. The media ate that up.

We got into New Orleans late Wednesday night and checked into our hotel. We stayed on Canal Street, which is a couple of blocks from Bourbon Street and the infamous French Quarter. You can believe that on this trip to Louisiana we were extremely careful about what we ate. We stayed as far away from the Cajun cuisine as possible.

The next day Alabama had its most rigorous practice session since two-a-days in August. Afterward, Coach Guthrie warned the players about distractions and to stay out of trouble. He set a curfew of 9 p.m. Several players grumbled when they heard that.

"I'm deadly serious about this, gentlemen," Coach Guthrie said. "If you violate curfew, you won't play Saturday. No excuses."

Bourbon Street might as well be called Temptation Street. It is a sultry, erotic place and I think it's the Devil's summer home when he's not in you-know-where. Gunnar and I walked around a bit, as long as we could stand without having to close our eyes—about 30 seconds. We saw prostitutes, half-naked people, X-rated theaters. We went back to Gunnar's hotel room and called our wives.

Some of the Alabama players should have cut their tours of Bourbon Street short, too, but they didn't.

The next morning I turned on the television to the sound of news reports about what had happened the night before on Bourbon Street. One group of Tide players got into an altercation with a group of Florida players at a bar. The Gators made disparaging comments about Gunnar, sparking an incident. However, later that evening, Alabama defensive backs Alonzo Passey and Jerome Lincoln were arrested at 1 a.m. for disorderly conduct after having a few too many beers.

Coach Guthrie was furious. At that day's news conference, he announced that the two players would miss the SEC championship game and possibly the bowl game. He sent them back home to Tuscaloosa in shame. Florida was already a three-point favorite before that incident. After that incident, the Gators immediately became a 10-point favorite. It was the worst possible time for a team to get itself embroiled in a controversy.

Preacher made matters worse when he predicted Alabama would "knock Florida on their (expletive-deleted). They're not even the best team in their own state! Bring on Miami!"

Coach Guthrie went ballistic when he read that in the papers that morning. He ordered Preacher to keep his mouth shut for once.

Morale was pretty low from what I could tell during that day's walk-through on the eve of the game. Coach Guthrie told the players they were not allowed out of the hotel, period, because of the actions of Passey and Lincoln. He nearly went hoarse from all of his yelling. The Tide sure looked uninspired. The walk-through ended when a disgusted Coach Guthrie stormed out of practice, angry because of his players' lack of focus. All the other coaches followed.

That's when Gunnar stepped forward.

"We're 12-0 and we've had a great year," he said. "But it's not just us. Our coaches have busted their tails to help us get to where we are. You can come party on Bourbon Street any time you'd like. But this is probably the only time you'll be in a position like this. Let's not muff it up now. Nobody believes we can beat Florida tomorrow night. Just like nobody thought we could beat Notre Dame or Tennessee. The difference this time, though, is that I get the feeling there are people on this team who don't believe we can beat Florida. We have a shot at a national championship! Last year at this time we were home sitting on our couches watching football. Tomorrow night the whole country will be watching us! The glory days of Alabama football are now!"

With that all the players began whooping it up. Then E.J. Jefferson quietly said, to everybody's surprise, "Hey, Gunslinger, why don't you lead us in one of your Mormon prayers."

No way was anybody going to challenge E.J., not even Preacher. Every player knelt down and removed their helmets. Gunnar prayed on behalf of the team.

The game was scheduled to kick off at 8 p.m. Eastern Time, thanks to television. It was torture waiting all day long in our hotel rooms. All we could really do was watch other games on TV. Every few minutes it seemed, the TV network was promoting the Alabama-Florida game. Gunnar kept busy reading scriptures, doing homework and running the hotel stairs.

Early that afternoon, Danielle and Kali arrived in New Orleans and they took a shuttle to our hotel. We met them in the lobby for lunch. Turned out that Kali slept overnight at the Hanshaws' apartment and she and Danielle stayed up talking until three in the morning. After lunch the girls left to join a group of boosters on a bus for the Superdome, where they attended a pre-game pep rally. Their seats were a couple of zip codes away from the field. When we arrived at the Superdome and gazed around the vacuous size of the place, we tried looking for our wives. We knew the general location of their seats, but we would have needed the Hubble Telescope to see them.

Alabama wore its road white uniforms while Florida was decked out in blue tops and orange pants. During warmups, Gator players and fans started making that annoying gesture with their arms like an alligator's jaw snapping up and down. I was surprised they didn't all come down with tennis elbow from that.

Coach Guthrie gathered the team together in the locker room and apologized for leaving practice. He said he had heard about the players-only meeting. "Gentlemen," he said, "you're the ones who play the games, not me and the other coaches. I've always believed that coaches get way too much blame for the losses and way too much credit for the wins. This week you've heard the media make a lot of the fact I was fired as an assistant coach at Florida. I downplayed it to the reporters, but just between us, I really want to beat these guys."

"Let's do it for Coach!" Jefferson shouted. "Go Bama!"

"Roll Tide!" shouted the rest of the team.

The first half was a defensive slugfest that ended in a 7-7 tie. Gunnar struggled a bit and between possessions he spent a lot of time on the headphones talking to the offensive coaches upstairs. With just a couple of minutes remaining, Florida led 24-20. Gunnar guided the Tide to the Gator 16-yard line, needing a touchdown to win.

He was sacked on first down, completed a short pass on second, and was tackled behind the line of scrimmage on third. That brought up fourth-and-15 with 19 seconds remaining. On the sideline, Coach Guthrie called for a four-receiver set with two crossing routes underneath, one fade pattern and one deep pattern. But when Gunnar saw Florida's defensive alignment, he decided to call an audible. He took the snap and executed a quarterback draw, dropping back a few steps and running up the middle. Gunnar exploded through the hole and juked a couple of linebackers out of their socks. No, he didn't get the first down. He did get a touchdown, though.

It was another Heisman Moment. Was there any doubt that Gunnar was the best college football player in the land? I didn't think so.

John David booted the extra point then kicked off to Florida. Time expired as the Gator return man was tackled. Alabama triumphed, 27-24. 'Bama fans poured out of the stands and Gunnar was hoisted up on the shoulders of his teammates. Members of the Alabama media relations staff handed out T-shirts and caps declaring Alabama the SEC champions. Afterward, in the team hotel, the players staged an impromptu party. Gunnar and I figured there would be cases and cases of beer, but we thought we had better show up, for a few minutes at least, to support the team. We walked into the room and saw everyone drinking a white-colored drink. Beau Whittle had called room service before the game and taught them how to make *leche con platano.*

CHAPTER TWENTY-NINE

Alabama was going to play for the national championship in less than a month, against top-ranked Miami, and in less than a week, Gunnar was going to go to New York City for the Heisman Trophy ceremony.

The media relations staff called to inform Gunnar that David Letterman wanted him to be a guest on his show in New York on Thursday, a couple of days before the Heisman Trophy presentation. *Letterman!* Can you believe that? Kali and I went with Gunnar and Danielle to New York for the taping of the show. He was even included in that night's Top 10 list (Top 10 Ways To Get Rid of Saddam Hussein: No. 8—"Send in the Mormon Gunslinger into downtown Baghdad with a truckload of footballs and tell him Saddam is an Auburn grad.")

Before he went on, Gunnar hung out in the green room with Harrison Ford and musical guest Bruce Springsteen. How cool was that?

Just before Gunnar's segment started, Dave introduced Gunnar while showing clips of Gunnar's pass against Notre Dame. After Ricky caught the ball, Dave said, "Eat your heart out, Regis Philbin!"

Then the band played Alabama's fight song as Gunnar took a seat next to Letterman. It was surreal to see him sitting there.

Dave asked Gunnar about the nickname and his mission, of course. I could tell Gunnar was nervous, but who wouldn't be? He did make Dave, and the studio audience laugh, though.

LETTERMAN: "Are you allowed to have any fun on these missions?"

GUNNAR: "Well, we get one day off a week."

LETTERMAN: "What kind of things would you do?"

GUNNAR: "We'd usually spend that day doing stupid human tricks."

When the interview ended, Letterman had Gunnar go down on

the street in front of the building where they tape the show and had him throw footballs through the open back windows of passing cabs.

We enjoyed our trip to New York, though we spent much of the time studying for final exams. On Saturday afternoon, we picked up Gunnar's mom at the airport and we all went to the Downtown Athletic Club in limousines. Once we arrived, Gunnar met Miami's Darius Streeter.

"Good luck tonight, and in the bowl game," Streeter said. "You're gonna need it."

Streeter was the favorite, but according to the media reports, it was expected to be one of the closest Heisman votes in history. Of course, there was a lot of pomp and circumstance associated with the program. The pre-Heisman show lasted about an hour. Finally, with Gunnar, Jackson, and three other candidates sitting on the front row, the president of the Downtown Athletic Club stood at the podium with an envelope. He opened it and declared, "The winner of this year's Heisman Trophy is . . . Darius Streeter of the University of Miami."

Everyone, including Gunnar, clapped. I clapped out of politeness. Turned out, I was more disappointed than Gunnar. Didn't those voters see what Gunnar's miracle finishes? His stats (4,109 yards of total offense and 34 touchdown passes)? The way he helped turn around Alabama football in one season? I thought it was one of the most remarkable stories in college football history.

"Sorry you didn't win," I said to Gunnar later as we went to dinner.

"Thanks, but it's no big deal," he said. "Who wants a 40-pound bronze doorstop, anyway?"

We returned to Tuscaloosa and, on Monday, the school president declared it "Gunnar Hanshaw Day" on campus. Who says there's no reward for second place?

Not that Gunnar went empty-handed in the awards department. He earned unanimous All-America honors and received the Davey O'Brien Award, emblematic of the nation's top quarterback.

It was hard to believe that he only had one more college game left in his career, but that game couldn't have been any bigger, a shot at the national championship. Miami was ranked No. 1 all season long, beginning with the first poll released in August. Alabama, on the other hand, began the season unranked and steadily climbed all the way to No. 2. The Hurricanes had the Heisman Trophy winner and the Tide had the runner-up. Some people were billing it the latest and greatest Game of the Century. So-called NFL draft experts were saying that though Gunnar was small for a quarterback on the next level, they still said he would be a first-round draft pick and an instant millionaire. Of course, Gunnar would shrug it off and say, "Oh, what do they know?" He was focused on the Orange Bowl and nothing else.

We had to leave for Miami two days before Christmas. Coach Guthrie allowed Gunnar and I to stay with our wives at the team hotel. Kali and I packed our gifts and we opened them in the hotel room on Christmas morning. After that we opened the blinds and had a great view of the beach. It was 70-something degrees and sunny. It was like Christmas in Chile. I was tempted to go down to the beach and see if anyone wanted to get baptized.

We gave Gunnar and Danielle a package of diapers, a Teddy Bear, some teething rings, and a little toy football. The football was my idea, of course. They didn't know if the baby was going to be a boy or girl, but I figured that with Gunnar being the father, it didn't matter.

It wasn't exactly a relaxing holiday season, though. In my spare time, Kali helped me study for the MCAT, though it was still four months away. After watching what Gunnar did in the face of adversity so many times, how could I not at least try again?

Football practices were long and hard. Not surprisingly, the Miami players started talking smack in the press. They gave Gunnar absolutely no respect, though the guy led the nation in passing and total offense.

"Gunnar who?" a Hurricane defensive back said when a reporter asked how Miami would defend Alabama's quarterback.

"All I can say," said a Hurricane linebacker, "is he better take his Geritol before the game. And he better strap on his helmet tight.

He's gonna want to go on another one of those missions to South Africa."

I suppose Miami had a reason—many reasons, actually—to be cocky. After all, the Hurricanes led the nation in total defense and had shut out five opponents that year. Plus, they had a clear home field advantage.

Even Miami's coach got into the act, saying on the local 11 o'clock news, "I don't think their quarterback has faced a defense like ours before." As if Gunnar had been playing all these weeks against St. Mary of the Poor, Blind, and Lame College.

To that, I said, "Yeah, well, you've never faced a quarterback like Gunnar before." I was so mad, I threw some French-milled soap at the TV screen.

Gunnar seemed oblivious to all of the talk. He continued to behave like a Boy Scout with the reporters. They tried to bait him and get him to respond to what the Miami players were saying. He wouldn't bite.

"It should be a heckuva game," he'd say with a smile.

Passey and Lincoln were reinstated to the team, though they had lost their starting jobs. Coach Guthrie tightened the reins on the players more than ever leading up to the game. Everyone knew what was at stake and they were on their best behavior. Even Preacher was quiet, at least for him.

The team held a low-key party at the hotel on New Year's Eve. Coach Guthrie told us we could watch Dick Clark's Rockin' New Year's Eve, but he wanted us to go to sleep right after that. We all slept relatively late on New Year's Day and, after breakfast and a stroll on the beach, Kali and I watched a couple of other bowl games. Gunnar and I said goodbye to our wives and we got on the team bus and headed over to the Orange Bowl four hours before that night's kickoff.

I went straight to work, taping ankles and making sure all the players were well hydrated. While I helped the guys with their stretching exercises, a bunch of Miami players took the field. Instead of stretching, they had a different manner of warming up. They strutted around the field, taunting the Alabama fans and players. They paraded around with their arms outstretched, nodding their heads and dancing to the rock'n'roll music that played over the loudspeakers. They were acting like the game was already over.

All Gunnar could do was smile while watching the scene unfold.

"Are you ready?" I asked him.

"Yeah, I'm ready," he said. "You know, I want to thank you for all you've done for me. If it weren't for you, I never would have had this opportunity. I'm just going to try to have a lot of fun today. It's the last football game of my life."

"Of your *life*?" I said.

Gunnar only smiled the smile of a man who knew something no one else did.

Late in the third quarter, he was still smiling as Alabama jumped on top, 33-14, after a 31-yard touchdown pass to Rayshard Joyner. It was Gunnar's fourth TD toss of the game. Alabama's defense shut down Darius Streeter every time he touched the ball. I wondered if the Downtown Athletic Club wanted a recount on that Heisman voting.

Couch potatoes across the country were looking for their remote controls. Miami, the team and the city, got awfully quiet. It was the first time in two seasons the 'Canes had given up that many points in a game. The Tide fans, on the other hand, began celebrating. It appeared Alabama had its national championship sewn up. But if anybody should have known that a game's not over until it's over, it was the Tide.

The Hurricanes exploded in the fourth quarter, beginning with an electrifying 100-yard touchdown return on a kickoff that brought the Miami fans back to life.

Meanwhile, Alabama's play-calling became conservative, just a steady diet of handoffs to Jamal Page in an attempt to milk time off the clock. Miami knew what was coming and shut down Bama's running game. When Coach Guthrie did decide to throw the ball again, Gunnar struggled.

Miami scored again on a 70-yard drive, highlighted by a 51-yard jaunt by Darius Streeter. The Hurricanes forced Gunnar to fumble on his own 11-yard line on the next play when he was blindsided by a merciless rush. He coughed up the ball and a Miami linebacker recovered in the end zone. Gunnar was slow to get up, but he hobbled off the field under his own power.

"Are you okay?" Billy Ray asked him.

"I'm fine," Gunnar replied. "My knee's a little sore. It's just an old dating injury."

The 'Canes tacked on the extra point, giving them their first lead of the game, 35-33 with 1:04 remaining. They were pulling a Gunnar-like comeback. Miami players started yapping again on the field while in the press box the sportswriters were typing the Tide's obituary. At that point, I have to admit, I lost faith.

Not Gunnar, of course. "We're going to win this thing!" he shouted to his teammates on the sidelines. "I don't know exactly how, but we're going to win!"

On the ensuring kickoff, Alabama fumbled the ball but recovered at the 15-yard line. It seemed like another nail in the Tide's coffin. I couldn't believe Alabama was so close to a national championship, only to see it slip away.

Gunnar limped onto the field. When Coach Guthrie saw him favoring his left leg, he nearly called timeout to put Dillon Redhage in the game. But I think Coach Guthrie realized that Gunnar had come this far and he was going to stick with him all the way, win or lose.

Standing in the shadow of their own goal line, Gunnar huddled up with his teammates. He glanced up at the scoreboard, which showed 51 ticks left on the clock. "We've got those guys right where we want 'em," Gunnar said with a smile.

Out of the shotgun formation, he took the snap and scanned downfield. There seemed to be 22 Miami defensive players on the field. It was easy to see Gunnar's knee was really bothering him. Unable to find any open receivers, he wisely threw the ball out of bounds. Second-and-ten, 42 seconds remaining, Gunnar underthrew his intended receiver. On third down, he drifted back to pass and he dodged a couple of Miami defenders, then took another ferocious shot in the back by the blitzing middle linebacker and went down head-first on the turf. How he held onto the ball that time, I don't know. Now it was fourth-and-16 from the nine. Twenty-nine seconds left.

Alabama called its second-to-last timeout while Billy Ray and I rushed onto the field to see if Gunnar had been knocked out or something. We peered into his facemask and I swear his eyes were spinning like a tilt-a-whirl. Billy Ray taught me what to do in case of a concussion. I even brought some smelling salts out to the field with me.

"Do you know where you are?" I asked.

"La Chispa," he said with a smile.

"Is it your knee?" Billy Ray asked.

"I feel fine," he said. I think he was functioning purely on adrenaline.

Gunnar grimaced as he stood up and tried to shift his weight to the left leg. Billy Ray told me he thought Gunnar had probably strained his anterior cruciate ligament and probably shouldn't be playing, but this was for the national championship.

While dropping back to pass, he saw Ricky Fontaine wide open over the middle. As he set up to throw in his own end zone, a couple of Hurricane defenders lunged toward him. Gunnar fired a dart downfield—into Ricky's arms—just as he was clobbered. Ricky was tackled at midfield. By getting the first down, the clocked stopped with 14 seconds remaining.

Hustling down to the new line of scrimmage, I noticed Gunnar was twirling his right arm around and around, as if it were bothering him. He was moving like Evel Knievel did after failing to jump the Snake River Canyon.

Armed with a fresh set of downs, Alabama had a chance. The Tide probably needed to get inside the Miami 25 to be in field goal range. Miami called timeout to set up its defense. Coach Guthrie called for Ricky to run a slant, Rayshard to go deep and Gunnar to find the open man. This time, the pocket collapsed and his only option was to run. He went left, he went right. Then he found a seam and hobbled through it. As he plowed ahead and picked up some great blocks—E.J. Jefferson pancaked a Miami defender on the play—to the 40, the 35, the 30, the 25. Then a Hurricane safety tackled him high, and a cornerback tackled him low. His right knee twisted in grotesque fashion and Gunnar lay motionless on the Orange Bowl turf at the 21-yard line. As the clocked stopped with one second remaining, the Tide players immediately surrounded him and Billy Ray and I ran out to the field to attend to him.

"Where does it hurt this time?" Billy Ray asked.

"Question is," Gunnar said, "where doesn't it hurt? I'll be okay. Now get me off the field so John David can win this thing." His knee was so swollen that he couldn't walk. That's when something unforgettable, and unforeseen, happened. Preacher jogged out to where we were and he and E.J. assisted him off the field. I nearly had to use smelling salts on myself.

With Gunnar out of the game, Dillon Redhage, the backup, would have to hold on the field goal. Fortunately, he had done it a few times during some of the blowouts that season when Gunnar had been pulled from the game. But this atmosphere was not like the one against North Texas back in September.

Gunnar hobbled down the sideline and found John David. "I'd feel a lot better about this if you were holding," the kicker said.

"You don't need me. This is your moment," Gunnar replied. John David trotted onto the field and both Miami and Alabama fans erupted for this classic finish of a national championship game. I sidled up to Gunnar. "He's going to make it," he assured me. "Guaranteed."

"Don't jinx him," I said.

"John David is going to split the uprights."

Predictably, Miami called a timeout in an attempt to ice him. Both teams huddled up on the sidelines, leaving John David all by himself. I felt sick for the kid. So much riding on a 36-yard field goal. If he made it, he would be cheered from one end of Alabama to the other. If he missed it, he would be reviled.

John David took a deep breath and lined up. He later told me he relaxed by humming "Come, Come Ye Saints" to himself. Redhage was on his knee, calling the signals. The snap was perfect and so was the hold. John David's kick was crisp and had the right height and distance. When the officials' arms went up in the air, Alabama fans went nuts, storming the field. It was Alabama 36, Miami 35. The Crimson Tide had completed an undefeated season and had captured the national championship.

John David was hoisted onto his teammates' shoulders. Gunnar was thrilled, though he showed it by simply smiling. Though he was in a tremendous amount of pain, there was no need for morphine for him. I don't think he felt any pain the rest of the night. We took him into the locker room, preparing to take him to the local hospital.

As it turned out, Gunnar had played the fourth quarter with a strained ACL in his knee, a concussion, and a separated shoulder. He basically played the final quarter with damp spaghetti noodles for ligaments.

Meanwhile, on the field, players celebrated, donning freshly minted national championship caps and T-shirts. Coach Guthrie accepted the Orange Bowl trophy on behalf of his team and the University of Alabama, then was interviewed on national TV as Gunnar and I sat in the locker room, aching to be a part of the celebration. When everyone convened in the locker room, Coach Guthrie quieted the players down and stood on top of a table.

"Gentlemen," he began, "this team has taken a few years off my life this season with all your close calls, but it was all worth it. This football team will go down as one of the best in school history and, as you know, that's saying a lot. Thank you for your hard work. Way back last January when we had our first team meeting of the year, I promised you that if you worked hard, you would be rewarded. I had no idea you'd be rewarded like this. The last thing I have to say is, 'Go Bama!'"

"Roll Tide!" the players shouted back.

E.J. Jefferson passed around victory cigars to his teammates— except for Gunnar, of course—as everyone did a lot of whooping and hollering and hugging.

While I was helping Gunnar change out of his uniform, Preacher, the man who, for two years, was Gunnar's nemesis, approached Gunnar and said, "We haven't always seen eye-to-eye. We have different beliefs, but I'm proud to be your teammate. You're an amazing football player. We couldn't have done this without you.

You deserve this." Then Preacher handed Gunnar the game ball.

"Thanks, Preacher," Gunnar said. One by one, every player on the team congratulated Gunnar and wished him well.

Later, E.J. and I lifted Gunnar into the ambulance and we accompanied him to the hospital. Billy Ray and the other assistant trainers stayed behind to prepare for the onslaught of players to treat typical bumps and bruises.

The team doctor made a couple of phone calls, and surgery on his knee and his shoulder was scheduled for the following morning. Danielle and Kali arrived at the hospital, and Danielle was upset to see her husband lying in the bed, barely able to move. Then Coach Guthrie arrived.

"Gunnar, I want to thank you for all you did for this program," he said. "It was a privilege being able to coach you. I'll tell you what I told the media after the game. I could coach a thousand more years and never have another one like you." Coach Guthrie was becoming misty-eyed, so he stopped right there.

"Thank you, Coach, for believing in me and giving me a shot to come to Alabama," Gunnar said. "Have I ever told you that you'd make a real fine bishop someday?"

"Huh?" Coach replied.

"Take that as a compliment," I told Coach.

Coach Guthrie also thanked Danielle for sharing her husband with the Alabama football program, and he thanked me and Kali for our service before departing.

A nurse dropped by to check on Gunnar and told us visiting hours were over. Danielle planned to stay in the room overnight and Kali and I were about to go so they could get some rest. Then Gunnar said, "Preston, would you mind giving me a blessing?"

I told him I'd be honored to do so. But I suddenly became very nervous. What would I say?

I placed my hands upon Gunnar's head and began the blessing. I felt prompted to say that his playing days were over, but I kept thinking to myself, "No, I shouldn't say that." Then I couldn't talk anymore. It was as if my tongue were stuck to the bottom of my mouth. That impression kept returning to me, so I uttered the words,

"Gunnar, your football career is over. It is time to move on to another phase in your life, in particularly as a father." Then I closed the prayer and opened my eyes.

"Thank you," he said quietly. "It's over. It was quite a ride, huh?"

I nodded. Then it hit me—when he told me just prior to the kickoff that night this would be his final game, he didn't just mean his final college game. He meant his final game, period.

"Isn't there a part of you that would like to see if you could play in the NFL?" I asked.

"When I was in high school, I wasn't planning on a mission," Gunnar said. "I was active and everything, but my life was consumed by football. I had my acronyms all wrong. I thought I was going to UCLA and then the NFL. But I belonged at the MTC. It took my injury to bring me to the place where I really belonged. I've never told anybody this, but when I decided to serve a mission, I promised the Lord that the gospel would come before everything, including football. To me, that means not playing on Sundays. After all the Lord has done for me, how could I go back on my promise?"

CHAPTER THIRTY

The team doctors allowed me to sit in and watch Gunnar's multiple surgeries. While I did, I realized more than ever that I *had* to go to medical school. I *had* to pass the MCAT. I wanted to be able to help people like that.

During that time, Danielle and Kali waited nervously in the hospital cafeteria. Gunnar made it through the surgeries in great shape and a couple of days later the four of us came home from Miami. Tuscaloosa was festooned with signs congratulating the team on its national championship. A parade was held and most of the players rode on floats, but Gunnar got to ride in a car. A crimson car, of course. He wore a cast on his leg and his arm was in a sling. He looked like he had been involved in a train wreck, not a football game. He threw his crutches in the back and spent the next hour smiling and waving with his left hand.

Doctors told Gunnar his knee rehabilitation would take about nine months. His shoulder, they said, would probably never be the same. Gunnar was inundated by interview requests from reporters wanting to know about his condition and his future plans. The school decided to hold a press conference for him, so he sat in front of a bank of microphones and made a brief statement before fielding questions.

"I wasn't expecting such a big crowd. Must be a slow news day," he began, drawing laughs from the assembled media. "Thanks for coming this afternoon. Many of you have wanted to know about my condition and my future. First, I would like to thank the doctors who operated on my knee and my shoulder. They have told me that I have a long road to recovery ahead just to be able to use my leg and arm normally again, let alone play football. That's why I have decided to hang up the cleats for good. I've had a great run here at Alabama, and it feels good to go out on top. I'd like to thank all my teammates, the coaches, the equipment managers and trainers, and everyone else involved with Alabama football. I'd also like to thank the

223

Crimson Tide fans for their support."

Chip Merriweather, looking quite natty in lime-green slacks and a plaid shirt that looked like a couch I had once owned, asked if there was any chance that, once healed, he would attempt to play in the NFL.

"No. My football career is over," Gunnar said. "There are other things I would like to do with my life."

"Like what?"

"Well, Chip, I want to graduate and my wife and I would like to focus on our family," Gunnar said. "My wife is expecting our first child in the summer. I want to be able to play catch with my kids and spend more time with my wife."

"Yeah, but what about the millions you could earn in the NFL?" a TV reporter asked.

"It's not meant to be," he said.

"That's got to be tough, considering all the money you could be making."

"There are other ways to make a living."

"What do you plan to do?" Chip asked.

"I'm a history major," he said. "I'd like to go to a high school and teach and coach football. I like working with kids."

Then Chip asked the $64,000 question. "Are your injuries the only thing keeping you from an NFL career?"

Gunnar hesitated for a moment, then smiled. "That's a good question and the answer is no. You know, my parents taught me that we should keep the Sabbath Day holy. I've always tried to observe that. If I hadn't been injured, I probably would have tried to play in a league that plays on Saturdays or Wednesdays or something, but even that isn't an option right now."

You could have heard a feather drop.

That press conference was the best thing that happened as far as ridding Gunnar of those annoying, money-grubbing agents who had been hounding him throughout the fall. After the press conference was over, Danielle kissed Gunnar and took his hand. As far as she was concerned, Gunnar was no longer on loan to the general public anymore. He was all hers.

For the most part, she was right. Aside from people who frequently wanted to talk football with him, Gunnar went back to being relatively anonymous. I helped him through his rehabilitation. I was sure that in the future, when his kids would ask about the gruesome scars on his knee and his shoulder he would tell them about his days playing football at the University of Alabama.

Gunnar and I graduated together that summer. My parents and Gunnar's mom attended the ceremonies. I'm sure there were times when Dad thought he'd never see the day that I would earn a degree. He probably felt like he didn't have to fret over me anymore. From then on, my relationship with my Dad became much more relaxed. I realized how much I loved him for all he did for me. I finally understood that all he ever wanted was for me to fulfill my potential and be happy.

Still, my work wasn't done. A week later, I took the MCAT again and I passed it. The day I received the results, Kali, Gunnar, and Danielle threw a big party for me. I was accepted to the University of Alabama's School of Medicine, where I started that fall.

Meanwhile, Gunnar was hired at Long Beach Poly High School in Long Beach, California, as a history teacher and assistant football coach. It was a chance to be near his mom again. It was a little ironic. Gunnar was the whole reason I went to Alabama, and now he was leaving, returning to his home state, and I was staying.

A week before they moved out West, Danielle gave birth to an eight-pound baby boy. He looked just like Gunnar. The night before the Hanshaws moved California, we all went out to dinner. It was a bittersweet evening. Both Gunnar and I were going on to new and exciting things in our lives. On the other hand, we wouldn't be together anymore, and I wondered if we ever would be again.

CHAPTER THIRTY-ONE

Before I entered medical school, I had no idea what I wanted to specialize in. Eventually, I decided to become a pediatrician. After two years with the Snow football team and two more at Alabama, I realized I'd had my fill of athletes. Actually, some of the athletes I dealt with acted a lot like little kids, so I guess I had some training in that area. Maybe my decision to be a pediatrician had to do with the birth of our two daughters, Summer and Amber. Kali was amazing. She not only helped me through med school, she was a wonderful mother. Gunnar wasn't around, but in some ways it felt like he was, thanks to the way he helped me learn how to study.

When he was three years old, Gunnar's oldest son, Michael (named after Gunnar's late father), started having trouble walking. He called me about it and I suggested he get him to a pediatrician in California as soon as possible. Not long after that, my worst fears were confirmed. Mikey was diagnosed with muscular dystrophy and by age four, he was confined to a wheelchair. There is no cure for the disease and the specialists told the Hanshaws that their boy would most likely die in his early 20s. Why, I wondered, did trials always seem to beset Gunnar?

After I finished med school, I embarked upon my three-year residency in Birmingham. In many respects that was perhaps the most demanding three years of my life. I tried to balance family life and church callings with 100-hour work weeks. When I completed my residency, it was time to start my own practice and try paying off my enormous student loans.

I kept in touch with Gunnar as much as I could, though we didn't talk all that often. A phone call here, an e-mail there. We were both so busy with our jobs and our families. Gunnar and Danielle had two more children after Mikey: daughters Ashley and Katie.

Gunnar loved teaching and coaching. After a few years, he was hired as Long Beach Poly's head football coach. His first season, his team won only three games. The next, in typical Gunnar fashion, the team reached the state championship game. He told me he enjoyed the kids he was working with, both on the field and in the classroom. Coach Guthrie called Gunnar and offered him a job as an Alabama assistant. Gunnar would have earned a lot more money, plus free cars and his own radio show, not to mention the glory and glamour of being back in the Southeastern Conference. He said he was flattered by the offer, but he graciously declined, explaining that he wanted to remain at the high school. He said he couldn't leave those kids. He came to work early to open the gym for kids who wanted to play. He stayed late some nights for those kids so they'd stay off the streets and out of trouble.

While I was trying to figure out how I was going to set up my practice, I worked long hours at the hospital in Birmingham. One night after a draining, 18-hour shift, I came home to find Kali and the kids asleep. There was a meal prepared for me, as usual, in the refrigerator. After I stuck the plate of roast beef and mashed potatoes in the microwave, I was clicking my way to ESPN when I stumbled upon CNN. What I saw flickering on the TV screen was a familiar sight that compelled me to stop and put down the remote control. Right there, on cable TV, were images of La Chispa. At first, I thought sleep deprivation had caught up with me.

The news commentator was talking about an earthquake that registered 7.5 on the Richter scale that rocked central Chile. According to the report, the epicenter was near La Chispa. In an instant, the names and faces of those people, people I hadn't seen or heard from in years, raced through my mind. I feared for their safety. I felt guilty that I hadn't kept in touch better with them. The damage and destruction I witnessed was something that I will never forget. Homes were flattened. Ferocious waves had swallowed up the businesses near the beach. It looked as though much of the town had been reduced to ruins. Rescue workers were laboring through the night, digging through the rubble, looking for survivors. A few dozen had died. I wondered if any of the victims were people I knew.

As I was about to pick up the phone to call Gunnar, to see if he had heard the news, the phone rang and I answered it quickly.

"Are you watching CNN?" Gunnar asked.

"Yes!" I said. "I was just going to call you!"

After talking about the disturbing pictures we were seeing, we decided we ought to go there. Of course, we had been married long enough to understand that our wives would have to grant us permission for this expensive spur-of-the-moment journey. They did. Then there was the little matter of asking our employers permission to leave suddenly. They okayed it. A couple of weeks later, after updating my passport, I found myself in the Miami Airport, waiting for Gunnar's flight from Los Angeles. We were Chile-bound again, 12 years after returning from our missions.

Our lives were so different at that point. Back then, the odds of Gunnar becoming an All-America quarterback at Alabama were slim. The odds of me becoming a doctor were even slimmer. Nonetheless, there we were, a couple of guys in our early 30s, with wives and kids, going back to the place that changed our lives forever.

We both wondered how much Chile, and particularly La Chispa, had changed. We didn't talk about it much, but we both wondered how many of those we had baptized were still active in the Church. We were almost afraid to find out.

"What do you think Carlos is doing these days?" I asked.

"He's probably the stake president, if he hasn't been translated already," Gunnar replied.

Still, our return to Chile wasn't so much about checking up on old friends. We just wanted to help those suffering people in La Chispa.

The red-eye flight from Miami to Santiago was just as long as I had remembered. Neither of us could sleep, so we talked about our church callings, our mortgages, and our kids.

Gunnar told me how little Mikey was happy almost all of the time, in spite of his physical ailments. He never complained. "One time, when he was about three years old, we were in sacrament meeting and I explained to him that we needed to be very, very quiet because this was Jesus' house. Then he looked me straight in the eyes and asked, 'Why? Is He sleeping?'"

Little Mikey would never be able to play competitive sports.

I know that must have been hard on Gunnar, but you never would have known it. They loved reading books together, playing checkers and watching games on TV. Mike was Gunnar's "assistant coach." During practices and games, he sat in his wheelchair, watching and offering suggestions.

"Dad," he'd say, "I think you need to throw to the tight end more."

We both brought our Spanish copies of the Book of Mormon to brush up on our language skills. Gunnar's Spanish was near-perfect because he used it so frequently at the high school. Mine had deteriorated dramatically. He had me read a scripture in Spanish. Gunnar started laughing.

"What's so funny?" I asked.

"It's the first time I've heard Spanish in a southern accent," he joked.

Eventually, we both fell asleep. We were awakened when other passengers opened their window shades and the sunlight poured into the cabin. The captain announced we were making our final descent into Santiago.

Other than the technological advances that occurred in those 12 years, like the proliferation of cell phones, I have to say Chile was pretty much the same. We bused from Santiago to Viña del Mar and gawked at the landscape we remembered so well.

We switched buses in Viña and headed for La Chispa. Very few people boarded that bus. The bus driver ended up stopping a couple of miles before reaching La Chispa. The driver explained that the road up ahead was closed. We would have to walk the rest of the way. Nothing new there.

We saw the destruction left in the wake of the earthquake. Palm trees snapped in half, debris scattered everywhere. At first we were a little disoriented because very few houses or buildings that we remembered were still standing. Then we looked in the distance, at the hill where Gunnar and I used to go to pray. We saw what appeared to be a building—with a steeple—still intact.

"You don't suppose ..." I said.

"Let's find out," Gunnar said.

Even though we were carrying a couple of suitcases filled with supplies for the people of La Chispa—food, soap, band aids, bottled water—stuff that Gunnar and I had gathered from our food storage collection at home, we walked as fast as we could. We didn't see any familiar faces, so we pressed forward toward the hill. As we got close to the top, a warm feeling filled my heart. Sure enough, the building had a sign that said, "La Iglesia of Jesucristo de Los Santos de los Ultimos Dias."

"Now that," Gunnar said, "is what I call a miracle."

Finally, La Chispa had its own church, with a gorgeous view of the ocean. It was practically the only building unaffected by the earthquake. There were dozens of Red Cross personnel swarming around. The Red Cross was using the church as a staging area and headquarters during the disaster relief effort.

Gunnar and I entered the church, which was filled with medical equipment and food. We noticed a man dressed in a white shirt with his back to us.

"Excuse us," Gunnar said. "We have a collection of supplies for the people of La Chispa. Could you please direct me to the person who is in charge here?"

The man slowly turned around and Gunnar and I nearly fainted right there on the spot.

"I am," he said. "I'm Bishop Diaz."

"*Bishop* Diaz?" I repeated.

He paused and looked into our faces. "Elder Brady! Elder Hanshaw!"

Bishop Diaz smiled and shook our hands vigorously. "Welcome to the La Chispa Ward," he said.

Those were the sweetest words I had ever heard.

"I've been praying for many days for help, but never imagined to see you two," he said. "There hasn't been a day that's gone by since you left your missions that my wife and I haven't thought of you and what you did for us. We were sealed in the Santiago Temple two years after I was baptized."

Certainly, he wasn't the same man who hadn't liked us and had hid out in the kitchen when we were trying to reactivate his wife.

"Where's President Ramos?" I asked.

"He's still a president. The stake president," Bishop Diaz said. "I can't wait for you to see my counselors." He led us to the cultural hall and there were first counselor Sixto and second counselor Maximo, loading supplies into boxes. Let's just say it was the kind of reunion in heaven I had always imagined. They had returned to La Chispa years earlier, then married and started families. Our hippie friends were family men with strong testimonies of the gospel.

"We never thought we'd see you again," Maximo said.

"Well, we've come back to help," Gunnar said. "Please, put us to work. By the way, Elder Brady is now Dr. Brady. Anything we can do, let us know."

"So, what's Carlos doing these days?" I said excitedly.

Bishop Diaz's smile melted away. "Elders, this is difficult to say, but Carlos has not been to church for many, many years," he said.

My smile melted away, too. "He and his wife started having marital problems," the bishop said, "and later they divorced. Carlos hasn't been the same since. He won't even talk to me or anyone in the ward anymore."

I was heartsick. Of all the people I had taught in Chile, I was certain that Carlos would be a stalwart member.

The bishop also told us that Hermana Raquel had died years earlier. Also, a few ward members had died in the earthquake, though nobody we knew. Some had been injured and were in the hospital about 20 miles away. Many more needed help. So we went to work. For the next two days, Gunnar and I did what we could cleaning up, rebuilding homes, tending to the sick and injured, giving blessings when asked. As we moved about the town, there were few familiar faces. So much of La Chispa had been destroyed, and many people had left. The Church, Bishop Diaz told us, was one of the few organizations still functioning in La Chispa.

On Saturday night we decided to visit the beach where we had baptized Sixto, Maximo, and others. After that, we passed by a tavern. We went inside, figuring Carlos might be there. Sure enough, he was sitting in a corner with his bottle of cheap Chilean beer. When Carlos saw us coming, he turned pale and pushed his bottle of beer away. We could tell he had already drunk a few bottles.

"Carlos, it's good to see you," Gunnar said.

"Leave me alone!" he shouted. "Can't you see I'm busy?"

"It's us, Elder Hanshaw and Elder Brady," I said.

"I know who you are. Now leave! You came here years ago and said you were my friends. Then you left me. What kind of friend does that? Go back to your country."

Then he took a big swig from his bottle. My heart felt like it was about to break. I wanted to remind him of what he had told me, that I had been sent to Chile to teach him the gospel. But I knew it would do no good. There wasn't much we could do for him.

"Carlos, we love you," Gunnar said. "Heavenly Father loves you. It's not too late to receive His help."

Gunnar and I turned and walked away, heading for the door. As I left the tavern, I cast one last glance back. To this day, that's the last image I have of Carlos—his head down on the table, surrounded by beer bottles. Unfortunately, it supplanted the image of him waving goodbye to us at the bus stop.

The next morning as we attended sacrament meeting in the church, we felt a great surge of joy for the dozens of souls who were serving in the La Chispa Ward. At the same time, we felt a deep sorrow for the one soul, Carlos, who was not.

The congregation was large and I couldn't help but think about the tiny house we had met in years earlier. Many of the members we knew, some we had baptized. One man sitting on the stand caught our eye, though. He looked familiar, but neither Gunnar or I could figure out who he was.

Then Bishop Diaz stood and announced that Hermano Cesar Sepulveda would be the first speaker. Gunnar and I wouldn't have been more shocked if the bishop said the first speaker would be Caesar Augustus.

The man's hair had turned from jet-black to silver. He had shaved off his mustache and beard. His countenance had changed as well. Hermano Cesar's talk was about his conversion to the Church. "In my younger days, I had an obsession with the Bible," he said. " But I was blinded by pride and greed. I did everything I could to destroy the

Mormon Church and run the missionaries out of town. When the two young Northamericans that are with us today came to one of my meetings, that all changed. In them I saw true disciples of Jesus Christ. In them I saw two young men who truly cared for the welfare of people's souls. That made me angry. I got angrier when they baptized a member of my congregation, Hermana Raquel. I continued speaking badly, and falsely, about the Mormons. I studied as much anti-Mormon literature as I could. One day, when Hermanos Sixto and Maximo were out helping the missionaries, I confronted them and said terrible things to them. Instead of lashing back at me, they simply told me they would like to be my friend. They invited me to their Church. Well, this made me even angrier. It wasn't until two years later that I decided I would go to the Mormon Church to see what would happen. They welcomed me warmly, like a brother. They accepted me and loved me. What happened to me I would compare to Saul's conversion in the New Testament. Hermano Sixto baptized me. I want to thank Elders Hanshaw and Brady for their examples to me. They didn't know it until now, years later, but they affected my life profoundly."

"I think that would qualify as another miracle, wouldn't you?" Gunnar whispered to me.

In the end, I guess Cesar Sepulveda figured if you can't exterminate 'em, join 'em.

Bishop Diaz asked Gunnar and me to share our testimonies, which we did. I'll admit that it was hard to look out into those faces, inside that beautiful building, and speak without bursting into tears.

After the meeting we spoke at length to Cesar. The Relief Society president stood up and introduced herself as Hermana Raquel's granddaughter. "She died firm in the faith," she reported, adding that four of Hermana Raquel's grandsons had served missions. Certainly, there was a group of people we had baptized who had fallen away from the Church, but we felt blessed that we had been part of the growth of the Church in La Chispa. That spark had turned into a blazing bonfire.

That night, Bishop Diaz held a special "Noche De Hogar" (Family Home Evening) at the church and it seemed like half the town of La Chispa turned out. During our time there we visited with old friends and made new ones. We realized, despite all the changes that had gone on there, La Chispa was still in good hands. The Lord's hands.

CHAPTER THIRTY-TWO

It was time to go back to our families and resume our lives. During our flight to Miami, we talked about how we wished we lived closer to each other. Our kids had never even met.

The night I returned to Alabama, Kali and I talked about moving to the West. We looked into it and within a few weeks, I received an opportunity to join a pediatrics practice in Long Beach, California. So we left Alabama—which was difficult to do because we had so many wonderful friends there. I had been at Alabama so long, I caught myself saying things like "y'all" and "you'uns" on a regular basis.

We bought a house in the same neighborhood, in the same LDS ward, as the Hanshaws. It was a brusque move for us. There happen to be plenty of differences between Southern California and the Southern United States, but we adapted quickly. Gunnar's kids and our kids became instant friends. It was great for Kali and Danielle, too, and they did almost everything together. Our two families spent weekends and Family Home Evenings together. We attended Dodger games and went to the beach as often as we could. My first patients were the Hanshaw kids. Gunnar even asked me to serve as a volunteer team doctor. It gave me an excuse to be on the sidelines with him again.

We had been in Southern California a few weeks when Kali asked me to drop off the kids at the elementary school and run a couple of errands. It was a Wednesday, my day off, so I didn't mind a bit. I remember driving by the high school that morning and seeing kids running outside, crying and shouting. It seemed too frantic to be a fire drill. I pulled over and got out of my car when I heard a teacher say, "Some guy's shooting a gun in there!"

Apparently it had just happened because the police and paramedics hadn't yet arrived, so I headed for the school entrance.

"Hey, you, don't go in there!" students and teachers yelled at me.

All I could say was, "It's okay. I'm a doctor."

Once inside, I witnessed total chaos. I weaved my way around the flood of screaming kids and teachers trying to exit the building, fleeing for safety. I knew Gunnar would be the last person out of there. I had to find him. I kept hearing shots fired, but I didn't know where they came from. Every once in a while I'd hear another gunshot and every time I rounded a corner, I didn't know if I'd come face-to-face with the gunman. If the gunfire seemed far away, I proceeded slowly and cautiously. Then I heard the sirens of police cars and ambulances. By that time, the hallways were deserted. I wondered if everyone else was out of the building but me.

I managed to look out a window and saw what appeared to be a couple of students being attended to by paramedics. I climbed the stairs and when I reached the top I saw, in the distance, what looked like a body sprawled on the floor. I sprinted over and was horrified to see Gunnar lying in a pool of his own blood. He was shaking. I took a deep breath and knelt down beside him, not knowing if the gunman would show up again. I felt myself go into a mild state of shock myself, but I knew I had to be calm.

"Gunnar," I said, "it's me, Preston. I'm going to help you."

Gunnar acknowledged me with a faint smile. "I knew you'd come," he gasped. "I'm sure glad I told you to be a doctor."

He was having difficulty breathing and was losing consciousness. I knew I had to act fast. I removed my jacket and shirt. I tore them into several pieces and applied them to his wounds as hard as I could with my hands to staunch the bleeding. It appeared he had been shot several times—once in the chest, once in the back and twice in the right arm. Bullets had ripped through his flesh and had done extensive damage.

Needless to say, I hadn't had much experience with these types of injuries. Being a pediatrician, I was more of an eyes, ears and throat guy. I handled a lot of colic, diaper rashes and ear infections. I'd never encountered a situation like this. Never mind the fact the victim was my best friend.

"Ironic, huh?" Gunnar whispered again.

"What?"

"The 'Mormon Gunslinger' getting shot."

I continued to hear sporadic gunfire. Not knowing the whereabouts of this madman on the loose, I carefully dragged Gunnar to an open janitorial closet. I remember thinking there was no way I was going to let his life end like this. I placed my hand upon his head and gave him a blessing. I begged the Lord to spare his life, if it were His will. Afterward, I tried to keep him from slipping into unconsciousness by talking to him about all he had to live for—Danielle and the kids. I recounted stories about the La Chispa Ward. I relived those fall days of college football, playing teams like Notre Dame, Tennessee, Florida. And, of course, the Orange Bowl against Miami.

I could tell his blood pressure was dropping fast and that if we didn't get him out of that school and to a hospital, Gunnar would be gone. I had been with Gunnar for nearly an hour at that time, though I kept hearing gunfire. I felt strongly that I needed to carry him out of the building, no matter the risks associated with that. Bending down, I summoned all the strength from my body and managed to lift Gunnar onto my back. I know there had to be a couple of angels bearing me up because I knew I couldn't have done that on my own. I moved through the eerily silent hallways until I met up with a couple of police officers who helped me carry Gunnar outside.

"It's safe now," they told me. "We got the guy."

Later, I found out that the one responsible for the mayhem was a forty-something man with a history of mental illness. He entered the school that morning apparently determined to kill as many people as he could. When he discovered that most had managed to get out of the building, he took a few hostages and demanded $2 million in cash and a private jet to take him to Mexico. That standoff lasted about 20 minutes. The man was standing near a classroom window and was shot dead by a member of the SWAT team.

Once we reached the exit, police, SWAT vehicles, and medical personnel had swarmed the place, as well as every news organization in Southern California. They lay Gunnar on a stretcher and placed him in the ambulance. I told the paramedics I was a doctor and that the victim was the football coach. They allowed me to ride with him to the hospital. They also told me six students had died that day and ten more were wounded.

On the way to the hospital, Gunnar's vital signs were fading. When we arrived at the hospital I called Kali and explained what had happened. She told me she had watched us exit the hospital on live television. I told her to watch Danielle's kids so she could come to the hospital as soon as possible.

"Is he going to live?" Kali asked, trying not to lose control of her emotions.

"He'll pull through," I said. But I wasn't sure.

The surgeons allowed me to watch the operation, which lasted several hours. Twice, his heart momentarily stopped beating. I saw them remove those metal slugs from his lifeless body and tried to fight back feelings of anger at the person who had done this to him. Most of the time I had my eyes closed, praying. For the next two weeks he was in intensive care, listed in critical condition. I fasted a lot, but even when I wasn't fasting, I spent most of my time at the hospital, praying for his recovery. Danielle was at the hospital almost non-stop. Late one night I encouraged her to go home, get a good night's sleep and be there for the kids. She agreed and kissed him gently on the cheek before leaving. Gunnar and Danielle had been preparing themselves for Mikey's death all those years, never dreaming that Gunnar would be the first one to go.

When we were alone, I sat next his bed and read Alma 26 aloud, hoping he could hear me. Gunnar was a fighter. I kept reminding myself that he was always at his best when it was fourth down. I remember Gunnar telling me a couple of times that he came to terms with his father's death by realizing that everyone has their time to go. We're all here on Earth on the Lord's timetable. If it were his time to go, what a life he had lived, I remember thinking.

Just then, his heart stopped beating again. Alarms went off and nurses and doctors burst into the room. I just sat there, helpless, praying for another miracle.

CHAPTER THIRTY-THREE

Five months later, I was standing on the sidelines, awaiting Long Beach Poly High's season-opener. The Jackrabbit players had just run out of the locker room in front of a capacity crowd. They wore a black patch on their jerseys to honor those who had died at the school the previous spring. A pre-game memorial was planned. I noticed students held up a large homemade banner that read, "We Miss You," with the names of the victims written below.

I scanned the sideline. Gunnar was conspicuously absent.

Between the national anthem and the kickoff, the public address announcer turned the time over to the school principal, Mr. Trimble, who stood at midfield with a microphone.

"Ladies and Gentlemen, on the morning of April 22, our school was devastated by a tragic event," he said. He then read the names of those who had lost their lives and asked the crowd to join him in a moment of silence.

Mr. Trimble continued: "While we are deeply saddened by that event, and we never want to forget those who lost their lives that terrible day, tonight we also want to recognize a hero among us. Without him, many more of us might have been killed. Ladies and gentlemen, please welcome Coach Gunnar Hanshaw."

Gunnar limped from the locker room and onto the field, carrying Mikey in his left arm. Danielle and the girls walked beside them. The spectators immediately rose to their feet and cheered. The principal invited them to join him at midfield. The ovation lasted three minutes. I know because I timed it.

"I am convinced Coach Hanshaw saved dozens of lives that morning," Mr. Trimble said. "He heard shots and he immediately thought of students and teachers. He had his class exit first, then, without regard to his own personal safety, he ran from classroom to classroom, warning students and teachers and helping them out of the school as quickly and safely as possible. He had ample opportunities to exit the building, but he wanted to make sure it was empty before he did. At one point, while making another sweep of the hallways, Coach Hanshaw confronted the gunman. He was shot multiple times in the arm, back and chest. Coach Hanshaw fell and the gunman ran to another area of the school, looking for more victims. If it hadn't been for the valiant effort of his longtime friend, Dr. Preston Brady, he might have died, too. Dr. Brady happened upon the scene and found Coach Hanshaw. Dr. Brady tended to Coach Hanshaw's injuries and carried him to safety. He did this believing the gunman was still at large. Dr. Brady, will you please join us at midfield?"

I did so, reluctantly, as the crowd applauded.

"I've been told that Coach Hanshaw nearly died a couple of times while in the hospital, but I suppose his will to live was too strong," Mr. Trimble said. "Initally, he was paralyzed from the waist down, but after extensive rehabilitation, Coach Hanshaw can walk, as you all just saw. He suffered severe nerve and muscle damage to his right arm. He still has trouble moving his fingers, and there's a constant numbness in his arm. However, he is back with us and we are lucky to be able to call him our coach, as well as our friend. During his long stay at the hospital, he was besieged by letters and cards from students. Students love him for coming early to open the gym to let them shoot baskets. They love him for his ability to speak Spanish. They love him for keeping the weight room open after school. As your principal, I love him for encouraging students and teachers to work hard and to make a difference."

Another long ovation.

"Tonight," Mr. Trimble continued, "we have a special surprise for Coach Hanshaw. Some friends of his contacted me months ago and told me they wanted to do something for him. We are pleased to have them with us here tonight. These gentlemen are former teammates of Coach Hanshaw's at the University of Alabama, where he was a star quarterback and led the Crimson Tide to a national championship."

Gunnar and I didn't see that coming. One by one, Mr. Trimble announced those men's names and they marched from the stands to where we stood at midfield.

"... Reginald 'Preacher' Stargell ..."

Preacher looked good in his lavender suit, though he had put on a lot of weight since his playing days. He spent five years in the NFL then launched his own ministry. He has his own weekly cable TV show.

". . . John David Bender . . ."

John David became a well-respected sports psychologist and motivational speaker in Alabama and throughout the Southeast. He joined the Church and is the Young Men's president in his ward.

". . . Ricky Fontaine . . ."

Ricky became a medical researcher, determined to find a cure for diabetes. He also joined the Church and serves in a bishopric.

". . . Beau Whittle . . ."

Beau became a successful owner of a chain of restaurants in Alabama. He even served a dish he called "The Mormon Gunslinger"— an avacado sandwich with *leche con platano.*

". . . Jamal Page . . ."

Jamal graduated from Alabama and was later hired on as a graduate assistant. Four years later, Coach Guthrie made him the running backs coach. Jamal still refers to himself in the third person. "Jamal's the best running backs coach in Alabama history," he likes to tell his players.

". . . E.J. Jefferson . . ."

E.J. was an NFL star and an eight-time Pro Bowl selection. Aside from a few wrinkles in the face, he looks exactly like he did when he was a player at Alabama. He still calls Gunnar "The Mormon Gunslinger."

". . . Rayshard Joyner . . ."

Rayshard also played for several years in the NFL, then, after an injury, went on play in to the Canadian Football League. While in Toronto, he met some LDS missionaries. He made peace with his understanding of the history of the Church and the priesthood ban issue. He never forgot feeling the Spirit when reading the Book of Mormon. He is a stake president in the Atlanta area.

After all of our old teammates were introduced, Gunnar and Danielle stood there, sobbing. I had already gone through a handkerchief and my shirt sleeve. Those players were like family to us.

"Dad," Mikey asked, "Why are you crying? Why are you sad?"

"It's okay, Mikey. I'm not sad. These are happy tears."

"Oh," Mikey said, kissing Gunnar's cheek.

Mr. Trimble handed over the microphone to Preacher and the place went silent.

"Gunnar, you had a profound influence on each of our lives," Preacher said. "On behalf of all of the coaches and players from our national championship team, it's my pleasure to announce that we have established an endowment for two scholarships in your name. One is for Long Beach Poly High School, set aside for an underprivileged student to attend the college of his or her choice. And in honor of the legacy you left us, we have endowed another scholarship in your name at the University of Alabama."

More cheers.

I don't remember much about that game, other than Long Beach Poly won. Still, everybody knew the game was anticlimactic. That pre-game ceremony more or less rendered the game meaningless in the scheme of things.

After the game, Gunnar and I met again with those former Alabama players to reminisce and catch up on their lives. They all had early flights the next morning, so once they left, Gunnar and I and our families were the only ones remaining.

Before we parted ways, Gunnar placed his left hand on my shoulder and squeezed it tight. "Thanks again," he said, "for saving my life."

I smiled and placed my hand on his shoulder. "Now we're even," I said.

That night after I tucked the kids in bed and kissed Kali goodnight, I poured myself a tall glass of *leche con platano* and sat down on the couch. My mind flooded with questions. What if I had decided not to go on a mission? What if Gunnar had decided not to go on a mission? What if we hadn't become companions and been sent to La Chispa? Had one of those things had not happened, where would I be today?

I'm glad I don't have to find out those answers. All I know is, without Gunnar, I'm sure I never would have met Kali, let alone married her. Without Gunnar, I never would have become a doctor. It's a hackneyed cliché, one that sportswriters and sportscasters use all the time, "So-and-so makes the players around him better." Well, Gunnar Hanshaw always makes everyone around him better, on and off the football field. If only those who know Gunnar solely as a football player, only as "The Mormon Gunslinger," could see him now. He can't throw picture-perfect spirals anymore (though he can still throw farther than me with his left hand), and he can barely run anymore, but he's still the same guy I've always admired. I don't think he ever harbored ill-will toward the man who shot him or questioned why he had to lose the use of his right arm. He never wasted his strength and energy on things like that. He's just happy to be alive.

People say a mission is a sacrifice, but I don't think that's true. You decide to serve the Lord because you love Him and feel indebted to Him. The Lord promises to pour out blessings upon those who serve Him. He does that and then you feel even more indebted than before. For me, the rewards from missionary service are far greater than anything I did during my two years in Chile. It's funny how I left my home and family with the desire to help strangers in a strange land. When it comes right down to it, I was the biggest beneficiary of all. I learned lessons I never could have learned anywhere else. A mission is a microcosm of life. There are ups and downs, like waves upon the ocean. No matter what the tide brings in, good or bad, you've just got to keep rolling forward. If you do that, and trust in God, things will turn out for the best.

Gunnar Hanshaw is living proof of that.

About the Author

Jeff Call lives in Cedar Hills, Utah, with his wife, CherRon, and their six sons. He served an LDS mission to Chile and later graduated with a bachelor's degree in journalism from BYU.

Jeff is a sports reporter for *The Deseret Morning News*, and is also a regular contributor to *BYU Magazine*. He is also the author of the best-selling novel *Mormonville*.